W9-BST-159

Praise for the Flower Shop Mysteries

Sleeping with Anemone

"Who knew a pretty flower shop called Bloomers could be fraught with so much danger and treachery? Kate Collins's Flower Shop Mysteries is one of my very favorite mystery series, featuring proprietor Abby Knight, an amateur sleuth who's spunky, courageous, and smart. Her family, friends, and neighbors are as quirky and delightful as a potful of pansies, and sexy hero Marco is worth his weight in sighs. Their latest adventure, *Sleeping with Anemone*, is a treat not to be missed, with some seriously creepy villains and an intricate plot that will keep you twisting and turning and guessing until the very end."
  —Kate Carlisle, author of the Bibliophile Mystery series

Evil in Carnations

"Collins isn't losing steam in her eighth foray into the world of florist and part-time accidental detective Abby Knight. The fun, family, and romance are still fresh, and the mystery is tidily wrapped up, with just enough suspense to keep readers flipping pages." —*Romantic Times*

"Ms. Collins's writing remains above par with quality and consistency: fun and breezy, intriguing and suspenseful, excitement and sizzle. She continues to get better and doesn't disappoint." —Once Upon a Romance Reviews

Shoots to Kill

"Colorful characters, a sharp and funny heroine, and a sexy hunk boyfriend . . . *Shoots to Kill* is a great mystery read!"
  —Maggie Sefton, author of the Knitting Mysteries

"Once again Kate Collins delivers an entertaining, amusing, and deliciously suspenseful mystery."
  —Cleo Coyle, author of the Coffeehouse Mysteries

A Rose from the Dead

"The tale is wrapped around the wonderful hallmarks of this series: a spirited heroine surrounded by zany characters, humor, and irreverence." —*Romantic Times*

continued . . .

"The latest Flower Shop Mystery is an amusing graveyard amateur sleuth that will have the audience laughing."
—The Best Reviews

Acts of Violets

"Abby's sharp observations bring laughs, while the intriguing, tightly plotted mystery keeps you guessing."
—Romantic Times

"A delightful, lighthearted cozy."   —The Best Reviews

Snipped in the Bud

"Lighthearted and fast-paced, Collins's new book is an entertaining read."   —Romantic Times

Dearly Depotted

"Abby is truly a hilarious heroine. . . . Don't miss this fresh-as-a-daisy read."   —Rendezvous

"Ms. Collins's writing style is crisp, her characters fun . . . and her stories are well thought out and engaging."
—Fresh Fiction

Slay It with Flowers

"Upbeat, jocular . . . an uplifting, amusing, and feel-good amateur sleuth tale."   —The Best Reviews

"What a delight! Ms. Collins has a flair for engaging characters and witty dialogue."   —Fresh Fiction

"You can't help but laugh. . . . An enormously entertaining read."   —Rendezvous

"Collins has created a delightful amateur sleuth."
—Romantic Times

Mum's the Word

"Kate Collins plants all the right seeds to grow a fertile garden of mystery. . . . Abby Knight is an Indiana florist who cannot keep her nose out of other people's business. She's rash, brash, and audacious. Move over, Stephanie Plum. Abby Knight has come to town."
—Denise Swanson, author of the Scumble River Mysteries

"An engaging debut planted with a spirited sleuth, quirky sidekicks, and page-turning action . . . delightfully addictive . . . a charming addition to the cozy subgenre. Here's hoping we see more of intrepid florist Abby Knight and sexy restaurateur Marco Salvare."
—Nancy J. Cohen, author of the Bad Hair Day Mysteries

"A bountiful bouquet of clues, colorful characters, and tantalizing twists . . . Kate Collins carefully cultivates clues, plants surprising suspects, and harvests a killer in this fresh and frolicsome new Flower Shop Mystery."
—Ellen Byerrum, author of
A Crime of Fashion Mystery series

"As fresh as a daisy, with a bouquet of irresistible characters."
—Elaine Viets, author of the Dead-End Job Mysteries

"This engaging read has a list of crazy characters that step off the pages to the delight of the reader. Don't miss this wannabe sleuth's adventures." —*Rendezvous*

"This story was cute and funny, had a good plotline [that] entwined a lot of interesting threads . . . an enjoyable read and a fine debut for this new mystery series."
—Dangerously Curvy Novels

"A charming debut." —The Best Reviews

"This amusing new author has devised an excellent cast of characters and thrown them into a cleverly tumultuous plot . . . a terrific debut!" —*Romantic Times*

Other Flower Shop Mysteries

Sleeping with Anemone

A Flower Shop Mystery

Kate Collins

AN OBSIDIAN MYSTERY

OBSIDIAN

Published by New American Library, a division of
Penguin Group (USA) Inc., 375 Hudson Street,
New York, New York 10014, USA
Penguin Group (Canada), 90 Eglinton Avenue East, Suite 700, Toronto,
Ontario M4P 2Y3, Canada (a division of Pearson Penguin Canada Inc.)
Penguin Books Ltd., 80 Strand, London WC2R 0RL, England
Penguin Ireland, 25 St. Stephen's Green, Dublin 2,
Ireland (a division of Penguin Books Ltd.)
Penguin Group (Australia), 250 Camberwell Road, Camberwell, Victoria 3124,
Australia (a division of Pearson Australia Group Pty. Ltd.)
Penguin Books India Pvt. Ltd., 11 Community Centre, Panchsheel Park,
New Delhi - 110 017, India
Penguin Group (NZ), 67 Apollo Drive, Rosedale, North Shore 0632,
New Zealand (a division of Pearson New Zealand Ltd.)
Penguin Books (South Africa) (Pty.) Ltd., 24 Sturdee Avenue,
Rosebank, Johannesburg 2196, South Africa

Penguin Books Ltd., Registered Offices:
80 Strand, London WC2R 0RL, England

First published by Obsidian, an imprint of New American Library,
a division of Penguin Group (USA) Inc.

First Printing, February 2010
10 9 8 7 6 5 4 3 2 1

Copyright © Linda Tsoutsouris, 2010
All rights reserved

OBSIDIAN and logo are trademarks of Penguin Group (USA) Inc.

Printed in the United States of America

Without limiting the rights under copyright reserved above, no part of this publication
may be reproduced, stored in or introduced into a retrieval system, or transmitted, in any
form, or by any means (electronic, mechanical, photocopying, recording, or otherwise),
without the prior written permission of both the copyright owner and the above publisher of this book.

PUBLISHER'S NOTE
This is a work of fiction. Names, characters, places, and incidents either are the product
of the author's imagination or are used fictitiously, and any resemblance to actual per-
sons, living or dead, business establishments, events, or locales is entirely coincidental.
    The publisher does not have any control over and does not assume any responsibil-
ity for author or third-party Web sites or their content.

If you purchased this book without a cover you should be aware that this book is stolen
property. It was reported as "unsold and destroyed" to the publisher and neither the
author nor the publisher has received any payment for this "stripped book."

The scanning, uploading, and distribution of this book via the Internet or via any other
means without the permission of the publisher is illegal and punishable by law. Please
purchase only authorized electronic editions, and do not participate in or encourage
electronic piracy of copyrighted materials. Your support of the author's rights is appreciated.

To my loved ones, who always give me purpose:
Julie, Jason, Natasha, and Jim.
To my support team: Nancy, Mary, Barb, Bonnie,
and Nanci S.
To Aunt Marian, whose courage, kindness, and gentle spirit
always inspired me.

ACKNOWLEDGMENTS

So many facts go into a book that it's impossible to remember where they all came from, but I sincerely hope to thank everyone who provided information.

Leon Dean, horticulturist, landscape designer, agriculturist, educator, and uncle, for his tremendous knowledge and support.

James V. Tsoutsouris, Esq., as always, for his legal expertise and delicious Greek salads.

Harry E. Ramsey, MD, for his medical counsel.

Aaron Rhame, for his assistance with police procedure in the K-9 division.

Diana Nielsen, florist, A.S.K. For Flowers, Plymouth, Indiana; and

Nulita, florist, Love In Bloom, Key West, Florida, for their knowledge and guidance.

Linci C., for a thirteen-year-old's point of view.

Barbara Ferrari, educator and friend, for her tireless and devoted promotional efforts.

Sergeant Lester O'Brien (1926–1987), police officer. Were he alive today, I imagine he would be the father Abby's dad is.

Writers spend hours researching information that may show up in only one sentence in the book—or be edited out entirely. Some information is made deliberately vague to fit the purpose of the plot. Nevertheless, I strive for accuracy and apologize for any errors I may have made.

PROLOGUE

A man stepped from the shadows into a circle of yellow light cast by a single bulb hanging from the high ceiling. He circled the rickety desk chair, the heels of his dress shoes striking the concrete floor, echoing in the chilly chamber. A predator circling his prey.

In the chair sat a large, bulky man, beads of sweat inching down his temples as he watched the other's every move. He jumped when the figure spoke.

"You ask me to believe this situation was caused by a florist?"

His manner was low-key, his voice smooth, almost amused. Still, the sweating man knew better than to trust outward appearances. Woe to the unwary who failed to sense the danger behind those hooded eyes and that deceptively calm demeanor. *"I know it sounds crazy, but you don't understand how persistent the woman is."*

"Perhaps not, but I'm beginning to understand how incompetent you are, my friend."

"Wait just a minute here," the sweating man said, twisting to keep him in sight. *"This isn't my fault."*

"Ah, but it is your fault," the predator hissed, serpentlike,

in his ear, sending a shudder down his spine. "I put the matter in your hands—did I not? You failed me, and now you want to blame this mess on a florist, as if that removes your culpability." Strong fingers gripped the large man's shoulders. "I don't believe you appreciate the ramifications of your actions, and to that I must take exception."

The big man swallowed hard, hoping his trembling couldn't be felt by the fingers digging into his flesh. How ironic that for once he was the one in the hot seat. "Let's not do anything hasty, okay? We both want to make money on this, so give me time to make it right. I promise you, I'll handle the problem."

The predator released him. "The problem*? Would that be the florist?"*

"See, that's the thing," the large man said, this time afraid to turn, unwilling to meet that cold gaze again. "It's not like she's just a florist. She studied law. She worked for a public defender. Now she believes she's some kind of crusader."

A long stretch of silence followed, broken only by a dripping faucet. Finally, from a distance, as though he'd receded back into the shadows, he said softly, "Her name?"

"Abby Knight."

Silence.

"Look, I swear I'll take care of her," the large man said, peering into the gloom. "Just give me a week. That's all I ask. One week."

Silence.

The man wiped sweat out of his eyes. Waiting.

"All right," came the reply at last. "But if you fail this time, you, my friend, are finished, and I shall put the problem *to rest myself. Permanently."*

CHAPTER ONE

"Free jelly beans!" I called to the people walking past my table. "Heart-shaped red jelly beans. Get them before they're gone!"

A pair of middle-aged women veered toward my table to dip their hands in the giant glass bowl, each taking a handful of the small cellophane-wrapped packages.

"Compliments of Bloomers Flower Shop," I said, "located on the New Chapel town square across the street from the courthouse. And if you'll sign my petition, you're eligible to win this beautiful arrangement of red callas, pink roses, blue delphiniums, and white carnations, one of Bloomers' many Valentine's Day selections." I pivoted the vase to display it from all sides.

"Lovely," one said.

"What's the petition for?" the other asked right on cue, bending down to see the names on the clipboard I pushed in front of her.

"You've heard that Uniworld Food Corporation is going to open a giant dairy farm on the outskirts of town, haven't you?" I asked.

"Sure," she replied, reaching for more candy.

Raising my voice to attract attention, I said, "Did you know that Uniworld's policy is to inject cows with bovine hormones to make the poor creatures lactate nine times more than normal, and that any Uniworld dairy product you consume will be loaded with those same hormones, which can disrupt your endocrine system and have all kinds of harmful effects on your body?"

"That's awful!" one of them declared.

I slid two glossy eight by tens toward them. "These are photos of hormone-injected cows. Take a look at those udders."

"Oh, my!" the other said as both women drew back in horror. "They're dragging on the ground!" Only a woman could begin to understand the cows' discomfort.

People were starting to gather behind the pair, so, holding up my clipboard with the yellow notebook paper on it, I continued. "This petition is to stop Uniworld from opening their dairy farm factory unless they guarantee, in writing, that they will not inject cows with hormones. Will you help by adding your names to this list?"

"We'll think about it," the first woman said with an apologetic smile, backing away, taking her candy and most of the crowd with her.

"What's there to think about except ending the poor animals' suffering?" I called.

Before they could escape completely, I added, "Remember Bloomers when you need flowers."

It was my first year exhibiting at New Chapel, Indiana's, Winter Home and Garden Show, and it couldn't have come at a better time. With the exposition center's cavernous hall filled with businesses from all over the county, where better to make people aware of the impending opening of the dairy farm, as well as to drum up business for my struggling flower shop? Where else would I be guaranteed masses of people desperate to escape the winter doldrums?

Rather than handing out free flowers to draw people in, I was giving away samples of my mother's jelly beans. Artisan candy was the latest in Mom's long list of creative endeavors, which included her infamous neon-hued Dancing Naked Monkey Table, her ginormous bowling pin–shaped hat rack, and her clothing and accessories line made out of one-inch wooden balls that gave a whole new meaning to the term *beaded jacket.* As with past projects, my mom, an excellent kindergarten teacher, expected me to sell her designer candy at Bloomers. Luckily she'd tested her initial batch on her family before offering it for sale; otherwise there would have been lawsuits involving blistered tongues and seared tonsils caused by her use of red pepper flakes for both flavor and color. She'd since switched to a recipe she promised was naturally sweet and mild.

Mom had sent her new batch with my thirteen-year-old niece, Tara, who promised I'd have amazing results. I hadn't had a chance to sample them myself, so I took Tara's word for it.

"We'll sign your petition," a young couple offered, stepping up to the table.

"It's like I said before, Aunt Abby," whispered Tara, sitting beside me, "aim for the young. The oldies just don't get it."

"Okay, first of all, I *have* been aiming young. I held two rallies on New Chapel U's campus, both of which were covered by the local newspaper." On page ten. Of the third section. Sadly, although my rallies brought out a lot of college kids who were more than willing to carry protest signs, the rallies weren't very effective because students didn't have a lot of buying power. I needed to reach serious shoppers.

"And second, don't let your grandparents hear you call them oldies." I glanced around to be sure my parents weren't heading toward us at that very moment.

"Don't worry. Grandma and Grandpa know they're cool. But you're gonna have to do better than that"—she pointed to my pathetically undersigned petition—"if you want to stop that farm factory from opening."

"I know that, thank you very much."

"You need more media attention, like a video on You-Tube. I can help you make one."

Tara was the only grandchild in our family, born when I was fourteen years old, which sometimes made her feel more like a kid sister than a niece. She had shown up at the center that morning allegedly to keep me company. While I appreciated her camaraderie, I was fully aware that Tara never volunteered for anything unless there was something in it for her. I had yet to learn what that something was.

Looking bored, Tara rocked her chair back on two legs. "So, when are you and Uncle Marco going to set a wedding date?"

Aha! There was her hidden agenda. "Grandma sent you here to bug me about that, didn't she?"

Tara looked offended. "Nuh-uh! It was totally my idea to help you."

Right. "Okay, fine. I'm going to say this once, so listen close. Marco and I are still in the discussion stage. And by the way, he's not your uncle. Have some jelly beans." I pushed the bowl toward her.

"Not now, thanks. And by the way, you're lucky you didn't have to try Grandma's first batch. I couldn't swallow for two days. If you ask me, she should stick to her clay sculptures, and you and Hot Pockets Salvare should set a date."

"How about just *Mr.* Salvare?"

Tara made a face. "He's way too cool for that. Hmm. Let's see. What should I call my aunt's boyfriend-and-possible-future-husband? Oh, I know. How about *uncle*?"

"How about no?"

Her chair came down on all four legs as she reached for the petition and added her name in balloon letters. "So, when is Mr. Not-My-Uncle Salvare going to show up?"

"You're just too cute for words, you know that? He said he'd come by in the afternoon. He's working on a private investigation this morning."

"My friends are jealous because you're dating him. How many boyfriends go from Army Ranger Special Ops to owner of a bar named Down the Hatch, *plus* being a private eye?"

"Your friends aren't jealous because I own Bloomers?"

"They'd be *totally* jealous if you owned Bloomers *and* were married to Mr. Army-Ranger-Bar-Owner-Private-Eye Salvare. How about Valentine's Day? It's the perfect day to get married *and* it's the day before my birthday. So, a year from next week on the fourteenth?"

"Tara, would you stop? We're already getting enough pressure from our families without you adding to it."

She grinned. "You are?"

"Your mother and your aunt Portia send me flyers from every bridal shop in the greater Chicago area, Grandma has caterers calling me once a week, and Marco's mom keeps tearing pages out of bridal magazines and mailing them to me. So trust me, when we make a decision, I'll let everyone know."

"Whatev." She rocked back on her chair. "So, going back to my birthday . . ."

Now we were getting to the real agenda.

"Want to know what I want for a present?"

"I'm dying to find out."

"You know the Barrow Boys are coming here to perform, right?"

"Who are the Barrow Boys?"

"OMG, Aunt Abby, I can't believe you haven't heard of the BBs. They're just the hottest new boy band to come across the ocean in, like, decades. My friend Sonya Hucks texted me last night that tickets are available right now because they added a show on Valentine's Day."

"So you want a ticket to the concert for your birthday?"

"Actually," she said, "I want you and Dreamy Eyes Salvare to *take* me to the concert."

The agenda unfolds. "You want us to escort you? Why?"

"Because Mom and Dad won't let me go unless I'm chaperoned, and you and Macho Marco are cool enough that I won't look like the biggest nimrod ever." Tara clasped her hands together. "Please, Aunt Abby? I can't tell you how much it would mean to me."

I studied her hopeful little face and felt a tug at my heartstrings. Tara was so much like me—blunt-cut, shoulder-length red hair, pert nose, freckles, short stature, and already showing signs of having curves—how could I resist her? In her acid-washed skinny jeans, banded-bottom flutter-sleeve plum top over a white turtleneck, and turquoise Blowfish ankle boots, she looked like a mini-model.

"I want written permission from your parents first."

"Awesome. I'll text Mom right now." Her thumbs worked her cell phone at warp speed.

Bored out of my mind, I glanced at my watch. It was ten thirty in the morning, an hour and a half into the show, and I'd gotten a meager fifteen signatures for my petition. Tara was absolutely right: I had to do better than that if I hoped to have any leverage at all when I went to court to ask for an injunction against Uniworld.

More people were coming up the aisle, so I rose to deliver my jelly bean pitch. As I stepped out from behind the booth, I caught sight of a lean, so-blond-he-was-almost-albino guy watching me from across the way. In his mid-thirties, he had a clean-cut Scandinavian look about him and was dressed as though he'd just stepped out of an IKEA ad. A decent-looking guy, I decided, until his hostile gaze met mine. Did he have a problem with me?

I smiled, hoping to disarm him, but it didn't work, so I turned my back on him and began coaxing people to sign the petition. After collecting a few more signatures, I returned to my seat beside Tara and tried to pretend I wasn't aware that the guy was still watching.

"Spook Face over there is weirding me out," Tara whispered.

"Ignore him. He'll go away sooner or later."

"Um, Aunt Abby?" She nodded in the man's direction.

Crap. He was heading toward us, sidestepping browsers with the easy stealth of a leopard.

"Call Special Ops Salvare," Tara whispered frantically. "We need backup."

I shushed her as the man approached. He picked up a cow photo for a closer look, put it down, then bent over the clipboard, running his finger down the list of names. Tara nudged me just as the man straightened, pinning me with his ice blue gaze.

"Good morning," he said in a smooth voice that registered a Germanic background. "I'm curious about this petition you have here."

My inner antennae quivered a warning. Something about

him set my teeth on edge. "I'm collecting signatures to halt Uniworld's—"

"Stop, please," he said at once. "You misunderstand. I'm curious as to what your petition is doing *here*, in this hall."

I decided to play it cool, find out whom I was dealing with before I went on the defensive. "Okay. First of all, let me introduce myself. I'm Abby—"

"Yes, I know who you are, Ms. Knight."

He knew who I was? My inner antennae were vibrating like crazy now. Trying not to appear nervous, I pasted a smile on my face. "How do you know me?"

"Your name is on the sign taped to your table."

Oh, right.

"I'm Nils Raand," he said curtly, "the local representative of Uniworld Food Corporation."

No wonder he was hostile. "Then I don't need to explain my petition, because you already know about your company's criminal treatment of their animals."

"Excuse me, Ms. Knight, but I must lodge a protest. We do nothing criminal to our animals. Everything is FDA approved. Check your facts before making false accusations."

I jabbed a finger at one of the photos. "So you're defending the practice of injecting cows with hormones to increase milk production, regardless of the cost to animal or human life?"

His gaze didn't move from my face, but I could see the tensing of his jaw, even though his tone remained eerily calm. "I did not come here to debate the issue with you. I came to ask you to put away the petition."

I folded my arms. "Well, I'm not going to do that."

Raand stared unblinking, as though he was trying to figure me out. "As you wish," he said at last, "but consider yourself warned."

"Warned? What is that supposed to mean?"

He shrugged, as though to say *figure it out*, while his chilly gaze flashed, *you don't want me to explain*. Then he turned and walked away.

"You can't sue me," I called. "What I'm doing is guaranteed by my First Amendment rights."

He didn't look back.

I pressed my lips together and glared a hole in the back of his crisply ironed shirt. I hated bullies, and Nils Raand was nothing more than a bully in chic clothing. Too bad for Nils, bullies didn't scare me.

CHAPTER TWO

With a huff, I turned toward my niece. "Do you believe that guy? What a jerk."

"Totally. But you were awesome, Aunt Abby. Way to tell him off."

"Thank you, Tara." At times like that, I was almost glad I'd suffered through nine hellish months of law school. If only it hadn't ended by my being booted out.

To show that Nils Raand's threats hadn't bothered me in the least, I picked up the clipboard and the candy bowl and went back to the aisle to round up more signers. A half hour later, I proudly displayed my petition to my niece. "Twenty-five new signatures. Not bad, huh?"

Tara glanced up from her cell phone and gave me an impish smile. "I'll bet I can get twenty-five more."

"You're on."

"Okay, and in return you'll buy me a Barrow Boys T-shirt before the concert?"

"You got it."

Tara grabbed the clipboard and stood in the center of the aisle, calling, "Heart-shaped red jelly beans! The best jelly beans in the world, right here at Bloomers—booth six, aisle one—and they're totally free. Sign the petition and get your . . . Uh-oh."

At the sight of a pair of stocky security guards striding toward us, Tara scooted around the table and got behind me. The guards wore black baseball caps, dark gray pants, thick black belts, and light gray shirts with patches on their shoulders that said SECURITY. They stood directly in front of me, shoulder to massive shoulder, looking as large and threatening as a pair of rabid rhinos. I was surprised they weren't smacking the palms of their hands with nightsticks.

More bullies. Great. My day was complete.

One guard placed his huge paws on the table and leaned toward me, nodding at my clipboard. "Looks like you got a petition there. That what it is? A petition?"

Stupid questions deserved smart-ass replies. "If it looks like a duck and walks like a duck, it's probably a duck."

"You want to hand it over?" He hitched his belt up over his belly and glanced around as though looking for an audience—or making sure there were no witnesses.

I pulled the clipboard toward me. "No."

"You tell them, Aunt Abby," Tara said, still crouching behind me.

"Know who sponsors this here Home and Garden Show?" the second guard asked, dipping a meaty fist into the candy bowl and fishing out a handful of packages.

"Yes," I said.

"Oh yeah? Who?" Clearly he thought he had the upper hand.

"Why? Don't you know?"

Behind me, Tara snickered.

The guard's chipmunk cheeks reddened with embarrassment. He straightened and looked around at the other booths, a thumb hooked in his belt about where a gun holster would rest. "Seems like this little lady don't want to cooperate."

The first guard, taking the same stance, also glanced around. "Seems like it to me, too. Seems like her lack of cooperation could cause a problem here."

"I was thinking that very thing myself," his partner answered, speaking to the ceiling.

Realizing their conversation wasn't going to get any deeper, I waited until their gazes drifted back in my direction, then said testily, "It's Uniworld, okay? I get it."

"What was that?" Guard Number One asked, cupping a hand around his ear. "Did I hear someone say Uniworld?"

His partner, watching people come up the aisle, began speaking out of the side of his mouth. "So tell me, little lady. You think it's polite to go around bad-mouthing the nice people letting you advertise your business here?"

Nice people?

"Give me a break," I said. "I'm paying Uniworld a hefty fee for this space. Do *you* think it's polite of them to sell dairy products loaded with hormones? Do you want your family drinking milk that could cause serious health issues down the road? How do you look in a bra? Because you'll need one when you start to grow breasts."

"Okay, here's how it is," Guard Number One said, leaning on his paws again, as the other guard discreetly felt his chest for signs of growth. "Stop with the petition and you get to stay at your booth. Otherwise, we show you the door. Got it?"

Hugging the clipboard against my chest, I scowled at him.

"I said"—he leaned closer, bathing me in onion breath—"do you *got* it?"

"Fascist bullies!" Tara shouted suddenly, jumping to her feet. "Stop harassing my aunt!"

"Hey," the guard said to her, holding up his palms, "calm down, there!"

Tara wasn't about to calm down. Now she had a cause, too. Climbing onto our table, she cried, "Hey, everyone! Look at the big apes Uniworld sent to harass my aunt! Harassment!"

"Get her down from there," the first guard said to me, looking ready to spit nails.

"Help!" Tara cried as the second guard reached for her. "Kidnappers! Call the FBI!"

"No one is kidnapping you," the guard said, trying to smile as a gathering crowd looked on. "You wanna come down off that table, please, little missy?"

"Make me!" Tara yelled, and began to chant, "Fascist bullies!"

The first guard snarled at me, "You stop her now or I'm gonna haul the both of you off to the security office while I call in the cops."

Yikes. That was publicity I didn't need. "Tara," I said, "stop. You're not helping."

"They wouldn't dare hurt us, Aunt Abby," she called. "We have witnesses. Hey, everyone! Come look—"

"Tara Kathleen Knight, come down at once!" a voice from the aisle called.

Tara froze as my mom elbowed her way to the front to give her granddaughter her most glacial glare. "Come down this instant, young lady."

Tara climbed down meekly. Maureen "Mad Mo" Knight was not to be disobeyed.

"Now, then," Mom said, using her steely teacher's glare

to gaze from me to the security guards, "what's going on here?"

"These men want me to hand over my petition," I said, showing her the clipboard.

Mom looked it over. "I see," she said thoughtfully, then turned toward the guards. "How did you hear about this petition? Did someone complain?"

"Yeah, we got complaints," the first guard said smugly.

"Complaints from whom?" Mom asked, looking quite smart in her tan wool coat trimmed in brown leather, brown slacks, and brown boots.

The guards exchanged glances, as though they couldn't decide whether they should be answering or asking the questions. "Our employer," one of them said.

"And your employer is . . . ?" Mom asked, continuing her interrogation.

"Uniworld," the first guard answered, raising his chin.

"I see," Mom said, standing with arms akimbo. "In other words, Uniworld is against the Constitution of the United States."

The two guards glanced at each other in bewilderment as a murmur of amusement went through the crowd. My mom hadn't spent six years teaching eighth grade civics for nothing.

"What's the Constitution got to do with this?" Guard Number Two asked, breaking open a package of jelly beans. His partner followed suit, making me wish I still had some of those hot beans in my possession so I could slip them into the bowl.

Mom gazed at both men in astonishment. "The right to free speech is guaranteed by the Constitution, gentlemen. Surely you know what the First Amendment says."

To show they didn't much care, both guards made a noisy show of chewing their candy.

Ignoring their rude behavior, Mom began to quote, "'Congress shall make no law respecting an establishment of religion, or prohibiting the free exercise thereof; or abridging the freedom of speech, or of the press—'"

I glanced at the men to see how they were taking Mom's impromptu lecture and spotted bright red dribble leaking from the corner of one guard's mouth.

Oh no. Not the jelly beans.

"'—or the right of the people peaceably to assemble—'" Mom paused, her eyes widening as she, too, caught sight of the red drool.

Then I noticed the other guard's lips had turned cherry red. Neither man had glanced at the other to realize what was happening, but Tara apparently knew, judging by the giggles she was trying to suppress.

Mom continued quickly. "'—and to petition the government for a redress of grievances.' Thank you."

The crowd burst into applause. The guards smacked their lips and reached for more candy. Tara clapped both hands over her mouth to stifle her laughter.

"Okay, I think my work here is done," Mom said hastily. "Tara, let's skedaddle."

She wasn't going to leave me holding the bag—or bowl, as it were. "Mom, may I speak to you for a moment?" I motioned for her to join me behind the table.

"I really need to go pick up your father at the dentist's office, Abigail."

I locked my arm through hers and took her with me, whispering frantically, "What did you put in the candy?"

"Nothing harmful. Just a little beet juice."

"Beet juice!" Tara snorted, doubling over with laughter.

"You told me I'd have amazing results with that candy," I whispered furiously to my niece.

She nodded in agreement, wiping tears from her eyes. Clearly, we had differing definitions of *amazing results*.

Suddenly, from another aisle we heard a scream, followed by "My teeth are bleeding!"

At that moment, the security guards caught sight of each other. "Hey, man, what's wrong with you?" the first one asked in an alarmed voice. "Your mouth is all bloody!"

"Yours is, too!" The second guard wiped his lips with the back of his hand, then stared at the scarlet stain. "What the hell is going on here?"

"I think I'm gonna puke," the first guard said, then loped off.

Tara held her ribs as she laughed harder.

His partner pointed at me. "You're in big trouble now." Then he ran off, too, holding a hand over his mouth.

When another horrified wail shattered the air, uneasy murmurs began to spread through the crowd. Hearing whispers of "poisoned candy," I called, "Everyone please calm down. The candy is colored with beet juice. Nothing to be nervous about."

Mom sank onto a chair, a look of extreme mortification on her face.

"Where is she?" a woman cried. Then the two older ladies who'd declined to sign the petition came hurrying up to the table. "Look what your candy did to us!"

They bared their teeth, revealing decent sets of chompers, except for their vivid crimson color. Others followed close behind the women, having also partaken of the sweets.

"It's nothing harmful," I assured them. "All natural, totally washable, beet juice."

After promising ten percent discounts at Bloomers to the irate bunch and sending them off at least partially soothed, I picked up the glass bowl and handed it to my chagrined mother. "We won't be needing this anymore."

"I feel just awful," Mom said. "I'm so sorry, Abigail."

"You were awesome the way you handled those big apes, Grandma," Tara said.

"Thanks, sweetie," Mom said. She sighed miserably as she set the candy bowl aside. "I don't think I'm cut out to be an artist."

I was so tempted to agree, but no way could I crush what was left of her spirit. "Are you kidding? Come on, Mom. You love creating art."

"That's true, but look what happened with my first batch of candy hearts. Really, whatever possessed me to use red pepper flakes? Do you know your dad thought my mistake was so funny that he put the candy hearts in a glass jar and set it on the coffee table as a display piece? And now"—she waved her arm in the air—"this fiasco. I just wanted to make the red brighter for your display. I guess I used too much beet juice."

"Okay, so you're not great with candy," I said. "Why not go back to your roots?"

She glanced at me as though I'd grown a horn. "Farming?"

"Your artistic roots, Mom. Your pottery wheel. You always enjoyed throwing clay. Am I right, Tara?"

"Totally. I love to watch you work on your wheel, Grandma."

Mom thought about it for a minute, then sighed. "Maybe you're right. Clay is a safe medium. I felt I'd exhausted the possibilities, but perhaps all I need is some inspiration to get me back in the groove."

Suddenly, Tara's eyes widened in alarm. "Uh-oh. Incoming at two o'clock."

I looked over to see two new guards approaching the table. "You!" one of them said to my mom. "Twenty minutes to pack up and get out."

"It's my booth," I said, rising, "and I didn't do anything illegal. Why do I have to leave?"

The guard laid a piece of paper on the table and tapped a thick fingertip on the lower edge. "That's your signature at the bottom, right?"

I glanced down and saw the rental agreement I'd signed when I paid my fee. "So?"

"So you disrupted the show and caused physical harm to the personnel. In other words, you broke the rules."

My mom's face turned white with shock. "Physical harm? But it was only beet juice."

"You didn't cause any harm, Mom," I assured her, "except maybe to a couple of egos."

The guard snatched up the paper. "We'll be back in thirty minutes to make sure you're gone."

"Fine," I shouted as they marched away. "Then I want my fee refunded."

"Fat chance," one of them called back.

As I stood there glaring at their double-wide backs, trying to decide if it was worth standing my ground, I noticed people watching us with grins and whispers, pointing to their teeth, no doubt spreading word of the jelly bean debacle. Would anyone take my petition seriously now? With a sigh, I pulled a cardboard box from beneath the table and began to stack my brochures inside.

"This is all my fault," Mom said in despair.

"No, it's not," I replied. "The petition was my idea. And I guess I did push the envelope a little by bringing it here."

"At least let us help you pack up," Mom said. "Tara, put your phone away, please, until we're finished."

"In a minute," Tara muttered.

"Would you write my name on your petition, Abigail?" Mom asked. "And let me know if you're going to hold another rally? I want to be there."

I paused to gaze at her in astonishment. "Really?"

"I did grow up on a farm, you know. Milking cows was one of my daily chores, and I certainly recall how the poor beasts would bellow in pain if I was late getting to them. I can't imagine the kind of suffering they'd have every single moment of their lives with their udders swollen so full they look like gigantic watermelons. What Uniworld is doing is unconscionable, and I'm proud of you for taking a stand."

"Thank you." It wasn't often she encouraged me to be a dissenter. Make that ever.

Tara showed me her cell phone. "Look! Mom says it's okay."

"What's okay?" my mother asked.

"I'm taking Tara to a concert for her birthday," I said.

"Correction," Tara said. "You and Sal are taking me—*if* you hurry up and buy those tickets."

"Who's Sal?" Mom asked.

I gave Tara a fierce scowl. "You are *not* going to call Marco *Sal* . . . or Dreamy Eyes, or Hot Pockets, or any other silly name."

"So . . ." She gave my mom a sly smile. "Uncle Marco, then?"

* * *

With my materials boxed, I slipped on my navy peacoat, wrapped a green and blue plaid scarf around my neck, and put on my Kelly green wool beret, which Marco said brought out the Irish in my eyes. "Okay, I'm ready. Who wants to carry the flower arrangement?"

My mom was standing across the aisle with Tara, completely absorbed in a display of garden decorations.

"Hello. We need to get out of here," I called, glancing at my watch.

"How about a birdbath for the backyard?" Tara asked, pointing to one of the items.

Mom shook her head. "Too common."

I picked up the vase of flowers. "Let's get going before the guards come back."

"I like bright and cheerful and fun," Mom continued, oblivious to my warning.

"Tara, will you grab my book bag?" I asked.

My niece turned around. "What?"

"The canvas book bag with the petition inside. Isn't anyone listening?"

"Sorry," Tara said, springing into action. She came to a sudden stop and pointed at my beret. "What is that—*thing*—on your hat?"

"A brooch," I said, trying to juggle the vase and the box.

"A *brooch*?" she chortled. "You're wearing a *brooch* on your hat? Are you, like, the Queen of England or something?"

"May I slip in a reminder here?" I said. "I haven't bought those concert tickets yet."

"Seriously, Aunt Abby, promise me you won't wear that nasty thing to the concert. I'd die of embarrassment."

"Wear what nasty thing?" Mom asked, turning at last.

"Uh-oh," Tara said with an intake of breath. "Darth Vader approaching, stage right, and he's brought the storm troopers."

I glanced up the aisle and saw Nils Raand, accompanied by a half dozen security guards, bearing down on us.

"Let's move it, people," I called. "Time to blow this planet."

CHAPTER THREE

We didn't stop running until we reached my bright yellow car, where we paused to catch our breath, making white plumes in the frosty air.

"That was cool," Tara said. "We escaped just in the nick of time, like in the movies."

"They wouldn't have dared to touch us," I assured her. "It was all for show."

"I'm not so sure about that," Mom said as we stowed the supplies in my tiny trunk.

"Trust me, Mom, this isn't the first time Uniworld has tried to unnerve me."

"You never told me they tried to unnerve you," Mom said, a frown creasing her brow.

"Because I knew you'd worry."

"Thank you. Now I'm worried."

"Nothing bad's going to happen. PAR is behind me—Protectors of Animal Rights. Remember when I protested Dermacol Laboratory's use of animals to test their cosmetics last summer? I did that with PAR's help. We closed down a puppy mill last winter. And other PAR groups prevented two Uniworld farm factories from opening last year by rallying local citizens. No one got hurt either time."

"Is PAR organizing the protests here in New Chapel?"

"That's my responsibility."

"But they're here in town working with you?"

"No, but a very competent PAR representative is advising me. Naturally, Uniworld wants to stop the protests, but I refuse to let a few threatening letters scare me off."

Mom gasped. "They've actually threatened you?"

Why didn't I learn to keep my mouth shut? "In a polite way, like, 'please cease and desist.' I'm not dealing with gangsters, you know."

"Can we go now?" Tara asked. "It's, like, zero degrees out here."

"In a minute, Tara," Mom said. "Abigail, I've changed my mind. Let someone else try to stop that farm from opening. You have your whole life ahead of you. I don't want to read in the newspaper one morning that your car was pushed into a ditch."

No matter what the threat was, in her imagination, I always ended up in a ditch.

"That's the problem with our society, Mom. 'Let someone else do it. I'm too busy. I don't want to be bothered.' If everyone said that, we'd have huge, horrible problems, like drugs in our water supply, poisons in our plastic bottles, pesticides in our vegetables—"

"But we do have those problems," she said.

"Exactly. Look, if it helps you worry less, all I'm planning to do for the moment is collect more signatures so I can take my petition to court and ask for an injunction. And what is Uniworld going to do about that? Shoot me?"

"I'm freezing here," Tara called, rubbing her arms.

"What does Marco say about your protesting?" Mom asked.

"He's behind me one hundred percent." Although that figure might be subject to change when I finally got around to telling him about the threats. I gave Mom a hug. "Don't worry about me. I know what I'm doing. I'll see you soon, okay?"

"Can't. Move," Tara said through tightly squeezed lips. "Frozen. Solid."

"You should have said something earlier," Mom said, and pushed the button on her remote. Across the lot, her headlights flashed. "Go sit in the van. I'll be right there."

Tara still pretended to be frozen into a Popsicle. Mom turned to give me a hug, then held me at arm's distance. "Be careful."

I held up my hand. "Promise."

"You promised to get engaged, but that hasn't happened yet, has it?"

"It won't happen any sooner because you keep asking, either."

We locked gazes, glaring stubbornly. Then her gaze moved upward, landing on my beret. "Is that what Tara was talking about earlier?"

"Mm-hmm," Tara managed.

"How pretty," Mom said, our dispute put aside. "Is it an antique?"

"I don't know," I said, fingering the brooch. "I found it in a shipment of flowers from Hawaii. I called the supplier, but he had no idea how it got in the box, so he said to keep it unless someone contacts him about it."

"May I see it?" As I removed my hat, Mom took her reading glasses out of her purse for a closer look at the brooch. "Is it a lily?"

"Anthurium," I said. "You can tell by the heart-shaped leaf and the long yellow spadix."

"Spadix?" Tara repeated with a snicker, her lips apparently thawed. "Is that another name for a guy's—?"

"Tara!" my mom said.

"Well, that's what it looks like!" she cried.

Mom tapped the back with her fingernail. "It could be made out of wood, or some type of pottery. I'll bet it wouldn't be hard to copy."

As I put my beret back on, I caught a familiar gleam in her eye. I had a feeling she'd found her inspiration.

"Hey, Buttercup, you're back early. How was the show?" Marco asked, getting up from his desk to come around and greet me. He was in his office catching up on paperwork, and as usual, looking so yummy it was all I could do to not devour him then and there. Fortunately, I can suppress my appetite.

Marco had on a black T-shirt with a Down the Hatch logo on the front, close-fitting blue jeans, and scuffed black boots. There wasn't anything extraordinary about the outfit, but the male inside it was a different story. How lucky was I to have found a guy who was not only brave, educated, *and* street-smart, but also honest, and with a dry wit that never failed to amuse me? Throw in a hard-bellied body, sexy voice, thick, wavy dark hair, and dark eyebrows over soulful, deep brown eyes, and he was one heck of a man.

He also had a firm, expressive mouth that was a genuine pleasure to kiss. Such as now. "You taste like peanut butter," I told him, nibbling his lips. "Mmm. Makes me hungry."

"You're making me hungry, too," he growled. We kissed again; then my stomach decided to join in the chorus, growling loud and long and not at all provocatively, definitely spoiling the romantic flavor of the moment.

"Sorry. I haven't had lunch. I guess I should eat something."

He turned and stretched across his desk for an open bag of nuts, affording me a great view of his backside. Hmm. Hot Pockets wasn't such a bad nickname after all.

He held out the bag. "I'll share these with you. So, what happened? I thought the Home and Garden Show ran until five o'clock."

I grabbed a handful of peanuts and took a seat in one of the sleek black leather chairs in front of his desk as he relaxed in the matching chair beside me. "There was a slight hitch."

Marco's eyebrows rose. Such an endearing expression. So I gave him the whole story, from my petition failure through the candy disaster, omitting only my promise to Tara. When I stopped talking and reached for more nuts, I noticed Marco's mouth quirking up at the corners, as it usually does when he's amused.

"So, other than causing a minor panic with bleeding hearts, ticking off Nils Raand and two security guards with your petition, and getting your mom, Tara, and yourself booted out of the exposition center, how was the show?"

With a sigh, I leaned my head against the back of the chair. "Forty-three signatures. It's disheartening, Marco. People simply don't want to take a stand against injustice. I mean, everyone is busy, but how can they close their eyes to what's happening?"

He drew my hand to his lips and pressed a sensual kiss in my palm. Tingles ran up my arm and landed in my pleasure zone, bringing a blissful sigh to my lips that made me forget my frustrations.

He kissed the inside of my wrist. "I'm sorry you're having a bad day. Did anything good happen?"

"I promised Tara I'd take her to a Barrow Boys concert on February fourteenth for her birthday gift. Have you heard of the Barrow Boys?"

"Sure. I spend long hours on stakeouts, don't forget, so I listen to lots of radio. The Barrow Boys are a good group. I like their music."

Good thing, since that was how he'd be spending part of Valentine's Day.

"That reminds me"—he pulled me onto his lap—"I finished my investigation this morning and got a nice fat check from it. So what do you say I take you to dinner somewhere pricey?"

"You are so on."

"How about Adagio's? I'll pick you up at six."

A. Mazing. I was thinking the same thing! Putting my arms around his neck, I said, "How about I wear my green silk dress?"

His pupils darkened as though he was already imagining me in that dress; then he kissed me, a deep, slow, intimate kiss that made me thirst for more. He was such a sucker for green.

"I've got to call for those concert tickets before they're all gone," I told him, reluctantly ending our kiss. "Tara would be crushed if she didn't get to go."

I reached for my coat and he stood to help me put it on. How many guys did *that*? "Oh. One more thing. Tara wants us both to take her. She needs two chaperones, and we were selected as the cool ones. Is that okay with you? It *is* on Valentine's Day." I held my breath.

"Sure."

Was Marco not the best? I didn't call him my hero for

nothing. "Great! Thanks. She'll be delighted." I put on my beret, then paused. "I have to warn you, Tara has joined the campaign to get us to set a wedding date. I told her we were still discussing it."

"Are we?"

"Discussing it?"

"We haven't been."

"We haven't?"

"Maybe we should."

"Wait. Are we talking about *discussing* setting a date or *actually* setting a date?"

"Discussing."

"At dinner?"

"Yep."

I gave him a light kiss and headed for the door. "See you at six."

That was another great quality about Marco. He was always open for discussion.

I left Down the Hatch through the back exit and headed up the alley to my flower shop two stores away. Wow. Hard to believe we were seriously going to discuss setting a date for our wedding. After we'd promised our families we'd think about it, Marco hadn't said anything further on the subject. I thought he'd been avoiding it. Maybe he thought I'd been avoiding it, too.

Okay, I *had* been avoiding it. The last time I'd made that big decision, my fiancé, Pryce Osborne II, dumped me two months before we were scheduled to walk down the aisle. So, sure, I was a little shy about taking that step again.

Still, I knew I shouldn't compare Pryce to Marco. Pryce was a spoiled, self-centered mama's boy who was used to getting his way, whereas Marco was considerate, helpful, family oriented, and had a strong work ethic—everything a husband should be. He had so many pluses, I doubted I could list them all, although, come to think of it, I probably should. Just for, you know, peace of mind. In fact, as soon as I had a few free minutes, I'd write them down.

So tonight we'd lay it all out on the table. I was actually getting excited.

I reached the back entrance to Bloomers and tugged on the heavy, fireproof door, cringing at the loud noise made by ancient, rusty hinges as I inched it open. But at the one-foot mark it stopped, refusing to budge until I wedged myself halfway inside and leaned my shoulder into it. Once in the building, I had to grab on to the handle and pull back as hard as I could until it slammed shut. Darned old door! It seemed to get worse by the season.

I'd gone before the city building commission in September to ask permission to put in a wider door, along with a small loading ramp, because as it was now, deliveries were a hassle. But so far, my request had been ignored. To see if there was a problem with my request, I had sent a letter to Peter Chinn, the assistant city attorney, who oversaw the building commission. When that didn't garner any reply, I sent more letters, then called *and* e-mailed his office repeatedly, but he was ignoring me, too, and I *really* hated to be ignored. I wanted a new door!

Despite its flaws, I dearly loved the narrow, three-story redbrick building that housed Bloomers. Built around 1900, it had original wood floors, tin ceilings, and brick walls, giving the shop a cozy feeling modern structures simply couldn't duplicate.

I took off my coat and hat and hung them on hooks along the wall behind the door. To my right was a small kitchen. Straight ahead, down the steep stairs, was a basement where we stored big pots, bags of potting medium, tall floral stands, and anything too large to fit in the workroom. Beyond the kitchen and tiny bathroom was the workroom, my favorite place in the whole world. And beyond that was the sales floor, also known as the shop, with a Victorian-inspired coffee-and-tea parlor in an adjacent room.

For a moment, I stood just inside the workroom doorway, breathing in the sweet floral aromas and basking in the coziness of the space. It was jam-packed with dried flowers, silk flowers, baskets, vases, and two huge, walk-in coolers filled with fresh flowers. It also held a desk with my computer equipment on it, a large worktable in the center, and rows of shelving on two walls. As my assistant, Lottie Dombowski, always said, "A place for everything and everything in its place."

Before I forgot, I called the Hot Tix hotline and ordered three tickets for the Barrow Boys concert. I ended the call just as Lottie came through the purple curtain. She had on her usual pink sweatshirt, white jeans, and pink sneakers, and today her short, brassy curls sported silver barrettes.

Lottie owned Bloomers before I did. In fact, I worked for her during summers home from college, making deliveries and assisting in the workroom. She was a big woman with a big heart and a bigger family—four boys, quadruplets, who were about to turn eighteen.

Her husband, Herman, the love of her life, had developed a critical heart problem that racked up tens of thousands of dollars of medical bills. As a result, Lottie was forced to sell Bloomers to pay down the debt, so I decided to buy it, with the bank's help, of course. Having just flunked out of law school and been jettisoned by Pryce, I needed a reason to get up in the morning, other than to stick pins in a rag doll with Pryce's name on it. Now I had that reason—a mortgage the size of Texas.

"What are you doing back so early?" Lottie asked. "Did something happen?"

"You could say that."

"Is that why you're grinning from ear to ear?"

"No," I said, and giggled. Giggled? Was I actually giddy at the thought of getting engaged? Was I twelve?

"You want to tell me about it? I'll bet you didn't have lunch yet, did you? Come on back to the kitchen and I'll heat up some of the stew I brought in this morning. Grace can handle the front. The shop's been quiet all morning."

"Would you like coffee with your stew?" Grace asked, breezing into the workroom. I could always count on Grace to know exactly what was going on, mostly because she loved to eavesdrop. "I've got a fresh pot on. It's got a touch of vanilla and a pinch of cinnamon in it today. And I made a batch of blueberry scones that will knock your socks off."

Coffee and scones were two of Grace's many specialties, along with her incredible instincts and her ability to keep our coffee-and-tea parlor humming along.

"I'd love both. Thanks."

Grace Bingham was a sixtysomething Brit whom destiny kept throwing in my path. I'd first encountered her when she was the nurse at my elementary school. Later, she'd worked with one of my brothers as a surgical nurse at the hospital, and then as Dave Hammond's secretary when I clerked for him. She finally retired last year, for about ten minutes, then grew bored and jumped at the chance to work at Bloomers.

I'd added the coffee-and-tea parlor as a way to draw in more customers, locating it in an unused storage room off the main shop, but Grace was the one who had created the

Victorian theme that had become a hit on the town square. She brewed the best tea in town, had a secret recipe for coffee, and made fresh scones daily, the flavor depending on her mood.

We removed ourselves to the parlor so both women could hear about the Home and Garden Show mishap while I tucked into the steaming stew. I decided to save my news about our engagement discussion. They could process only so much information at a time.

"What a shame your mum's red candy spoiled your stand against tyranny," Grace said. She assumed her lecturer stance, holding the edges of her cardigan as though they were lapels. "As Thomas Jefferson said, 'Enlighten the people, generally, and tyranny and oppressions of body and mind will vanish like spirits at the dawn of day.'"

"That's what I'm trying to do," I said with a sigh, "enlighten the people."

"Sweetie, are you sure you want to go up against a giant food corporation?" Lottie asked. "You're just one little gal."

"PAR is behind me, Lottie. They've stopped Uniworld before."

"But just how aggressive did Uniworld get those other times?"

"Why?"

Lottie left the room and returned with a letter-sized white envelope. "This was pushed under the door this morning."

"Not another one!" As with the previous letters, my name was typed on the front in bold caps, with no stamp or return address. Inside would probably be the same demand for me to stop harassing the "poor farmer" so he could get on with the opening of his new dairy farm, which was how Uniworld was portraying their new operation. Except that this so-called poor farmer was actually a skilled manager who would be overseeing a large operation that in no way resembled a small dairy farm.

I tore open the envelope and unfolded a piece of plain white paper. Unlike the others, this missive had only one line on it: *PLAY WITH FIRE, EXPECT TO BE BURNED.*

Well, *that* was different.

CHAPTER FOUR

Both women, reading the letter over my shoulder, gasped. I wasn't exactly delighted myself, but because of my brave speech, I made a show of marching over to the waste can and letting it fall inside.

"Um, sweetie, you might want to let the cops see that one," Lottie said. "You know, in case someone tries to burn down the building."

"I agree with Lottie, dear," Grace said. "Not to alarm you unduly, but the tone of this communiqué is rather dire, isn't it? It sounds as though they're growing exasperated with you. I wouldn't casually dismiss it."

"With no identifying marks of any kind, how would it help the cops?"

"Fingerprints. DNA. Matching the printer ink and font," Lottie listed. She watched way too much *CSI*. Our police force didn't even have a unified computer system, let alone the technology to match printer ink. And DNA? Forget it. The state lab was usually backed up two months or more on serious criminal investigations. An anonymous letter would rank somewhere around zero on their to-do list.

They gazed at me, waiting expectantly.

Fine. If it made them happy. I retrieved the letter and put it in my purse. "I'll give it to Sergeant Reilly next time I see him."

A knock on the front door made us all jump. It was the FedEx driver, signaling he had a delivery. I waved at him, mouthing, *Meet you at the back door.*

"I'll go let him in," Lottie said, and headed for the curtain that separated the display area from the workshop. "I know you have trouble with that door."

"That reminds me," I said. "I've got to find out why my door request is being ignored."

"Which reminds me," Grace said. "I've got to get a new key made. Mine is bent."

Not to be outdone, Lottie paused to say, "And that reminds *me.* I forgot to tell you about the UPS guy that showed up this morning."

I picked up the phone at my desk in the workroom and dialed the city attorney's office. I'd punched in those numbers so often I had memorized. "Peter Chinn, please," I said to the woman who answered.

"He's not in right now. May I take a message?"

This was the game we played every time I phoned. "When will he be in?"

"Your name, please?"

"Abby Knight, and don't pretend you don't recognize my voice. You've got a stack of messages with my name on them and I have yet to receive a return call from your boss."

"All I can do is leave a message for Mr. Chinn."

"Will it do any good? Does he ever read them? Does he actually work there?"

"Will there be anything else?"

"Don't you feel bad taking messages, knowing Mr. Chinn will ignore them?"

"He doesn't ignore every message."

"Oh, I see. Just mine. Wonderful. You know, all I want to do is replace a back door and put down a ramp. Is that such an unreasonable request?"

"I wouldn't know."

Why would she? She only worked there. "Would you give Mr. Chinn one more message from me, then? Tell him I'm tired of being ignored, so I'm going to talk to a reporter with the *New Chapel News*."

"I believe he's in now. Hold, please." All of a sudden I was listening to a Billy Joel song. Amazing what a hint of bad publicity would do.

When she came back on the line she said, "You'll need to resubmit your request."

"Wait. What? Resubmit it? Why?"

"We have no such request on file."

"Yes, you do."

"We don't."

"You have to have it. I delivered it myself."

"We don't."

"You just now discovered that? You didn't notice all my letters, e-mails, and voice messages asking about the status of my request and wonder what they were all about? How is that possible?"

"I don't know."

She didn't know much, did she? "Fine. I'll resubmit it, and I'm still going to call my friend at the *News*."

I slammed down the phone, then took a deep breath to cool my temper. When the phone rang a minute later, I thought, *Aha! My ploy worked!* But it was just a pushy salesman trying to get me to carry his company's line of candles. I told him no thanks, then plucked a slip from the spindle and studied it, forcing myself to focus on the words in front of me. Arranging flowers always calmed me down.

Okay. This order was for an anniversary bouquet, and the client wanted red and pink roses in it. Hmm. How about a few stems of red spiral ginger and blush pink callas to liven it up, along with gorgeous hanging amaranthus to give it softness? Perfecto.

"Damn dumb door," Lottie muttered as she came back to the workroom carrying two long boxes of flowers. "I'm sorely tempted to get my boys to take it off."

"Can we do that?" I asked as she laid one of the boxes on the table.

"It'd be just our luck someone would rat us out." She grabbed a towel from under the worktable. "We'd better wait for a permit."

"We've been waiting, Lottie. Since September. Now I'm told I have to resubmit my request because somehow the first one is missing."

"You're pulling my leg."

"I wish."

As Lottie prepped the roses so she could place them in buckets with floral solution, I worked on the anniversary arrangement, still mulling over the door situation. Was my request really missing or was I being ignored? Maybe that kind of screwup happened routinely, and I just wasn't aware of it because I'd never submitted a request before. Maybe I should give the planning commission the benefit of the doubt and try once more before talking to a reporter.

Bang!

I jumped off the stool as the noise was followed by shattering glass. I dropped my floral knife and dashed through the curtain one step ahead of Lottie, just as Grace hurried out of the parlor. On the floor inside the shop, a few feet from my yellow frame door, was what appeared to be a brick wrapped in burning newspaper. It was lying in the midst of shards of beveled glass, the newspaper edges curling as they turned to black ash.

"Good heavens!" Grace cried. "I'll get water." She hurried back to the parlor as Lottie grabbed the towel she'd slung over her shoulder and dropped it over the brick.

I jumped over the glass, opened the door, and ran outside, but other than two women coming out of the realty agency next door, and a few others across the street who were heading my way to see what had happened, I didn't spot any likely culprits.

As I stepped back inside and saw Lottie's expression, I knew she was thinking about that anonymous letter. I certainly was. "Maybe you should call Sergeant Reilly now," she said.

By the time the squad car pulled up, a crowd had gathered in front of Bloomers, its numbers growing larger by the minute. I was betting that by suppertime, the whole town would know about the burning brick, including my parents.

"Nothing to see here, folks," Reilly said as he strode toward the shop. "Move it along."

He was pretty much ignored.

Sergeant Sean Reilly was a good-looking forty-year-old, a fourteen-year veteran of the New Chapel Police Department. As a rookie, he'd worked with my dad, then later with Marco during his short stint as a cop. As a result, Reilly and I had become friends, which had come in handy considering how many times I'd gotten myself in a bind.

Now he stood inside the shop taking notes while Lottie told him about the brick and the previous letters, Grace taped cardboard over the broken door to keep out the cold wind, and I phoned the glass company to have the beveled pane replaced ASAP. *That* would cost me a bundle. When I hung up, Reilly was gazing at me in that know-it-all way of his. Considering the morning I'd had, I really wasn't in the mood for one of his upbraidings, so I grabbed a broom to finish sweeping the floor.

"Don't you think you should have called us after you received the *first* letter?" he said.

"The other letters said that I should stop harassing the poor farmer so he could open his dairy farm. Why would I call the police for that? And if I had, what would you have done about it? Order DNA tests and put your best men on the case, or file it away under crank mail?"

He knew I had a point but wouldn't admit it. "So who have you ticked off this time?"

"You say that like I regularly tick people off."

He gave me a level gaze, his pencil ready to write.

"Uniworld," I muttered, sweeping harder.

"Uniworld Food Corporation? You ticked off the whole company?"

"Abby's trying to keep their new dairy farm operation from opening here," Lottie answered, trying to be helpful. "They do very bad things to their cows."

Reilly wrote it down, shaking his head. "I should have guessed who was behind those campus protest rallies."

"Abby got a nice write-up in the *News*," Grace said proudly.

Reilly crouched for a look at the brick, using his pen to lift away burned twine and peel off layers of charred newspaper at one end. He rose to his feet. "I'll take it with me. I doubt we'll find anything, but you never know. I think I'll also pay a visit to the Uniworld Distribution Center and see what they can tell me about the incident."

I scoffed. "Like they'd admit to anything."

"Maybe not," he said, "but at least they'll know the cops are watching."

The bell over the door jingled, and Marco stepped inside, inspecting the brown paper covering the gaping center as he shut the door. He acknowledged Reilly with a nod, then immediately spotted the brick. "What the hell? Someone tossed that through the door?"

"After setting it on fire," Lottie added, in case he'd missed the charred newspaper.

"What kind of idiot would pull a stunt like that?" Marco asked.

Reilly whispered, "He doesn't know about the you-know-whats?"

Oh, very professional, Reilly.

Marco glanced at me. "What you-know-whats?"

"Someone shoved a letter under the door today," I explained as Reilly pulled it out of the back of his notebook and let Marco read it. "I didn't think anything of it until the brick hit."

"Wasn't her first letter, either," Reilly the instigator added.

Marco glanced at me in concern.

"It's Uniworld," I assured him. "They're using scare tactics to get me to back off. I didn't mention the letters before because I didn't think they were anything to worry about."

"What do you think now?" Marco asked.

That I didn't care for his pompous tone, but then I reminded myself that he was just showing his protective side, and since that was a plus, I held my tongue.

"I'm going to take a ride out to Uniworld," Reilly told him, "have a talk with people there, see if I can rattle some cages."

Marco put an arm around my shoulders and said to him, "Thanks, man. I appreciate it."

"Me, too, Reilly," I said. "And make sure you ask for Nils Raand, the guy in charge."

"Just so you know," Marco added, "Abby's going to tone down her protests. Maybe that'll put an end to the threats."

I was? Irked, I pulled away from him. "If I tone *down* my protests, how will I keep Uniworld from opening their milk factory? By writing them poems?"

At Marco's raised eyebrows, I said contritely, "Sorry. I didn't mean to snap at you, but I can't let Nils Raand, or anyone else at Uniworld, believe I can be frightened off."

"You can't let them burn down your flower shop, either," he countered.

"They won't burn it down," I said. "This is about intimidation. Bullying. If they'd wanted to burn down Bloomers, they'd do it when no one was here."

"Maybe there's something you can do besides holding those protest rallies," Lottie said. "Something a little quieter and less risky."

"That's why I'm collecting signatures for a petition, so I can ask for an injunction," I explained to Reilly, "but I've got only forty-three. I need five hundred to be effective."

"How about meeting with a Uniworld rep to discuss your concerns?" Reilly asked.

"That's a lovely idea," Grace said hopefully.

"No risk there," Lottie chimed in.

"It's something to consider, Abby," Marco said.

I was on the verge of explaining how Uniworld had operated in other cities, pretending to be sympathetic to concerns about the milk production, then proceeding as planned, and how the only things that had stopped them were citizen rallies and marches. But I knew I'd be wasting my breath on this gang. All they wanted was for me to be safe.

"Fine."

Everyone smiled.

"How about if I see what I can set up with Raand for Monday?" Reilly offered.

What the heck. It was Saturday. If he set up a meeting, maybe I wouldn't have to worry about any more bricks being heaved through my door. Maybe a day to let recent events settle in would be a good thing. I could regroup, decide what my next move would be. "Okay."

At that, Reilly left; Lottie went back to unloading flowers; Grace returned to the parlor to make tea; and Marco gazed at me thoughtfully. "So, no more protests, right?"

"I didn't agree to that."

"You agreed to a meeting."

"I agreed to *try* a meeting. That doesn't mean I've given up the idea of protests if the meeting doesn't get results."

He lifted my chin and gazed into my eyes. "Repeat after me: no more protests. You can't afford to have your business go up in flames."

"Marco—"

"No. More. Protests."

Bossiness. Definitely had to have a minus column.

He gave me a kiss on the cheek, then headed for the door. "Six o'clock in your green silk dress?"

I gave him a sharp salute. "Yes, sir. Will that be all, sir?"

He rolled his eyes, then opened the door and found an even larger crowd standing outside. "You'd better stay out of sight," he warned, then disappeared into their midst.

When the onlookers saw me in the doorway, a ripple of excitement went through them like a wave, and suddenly a reporter with a mic hurried toward me, followed by a cameraman and two reporters carrying mini–tape recorders.

"Miss Knight!" they called over each other. "Can you tell us what happened?"

"Has your life been threatened?"

"Will you give a statement?"

I stood on tiptoes to see over the crowd. No sign of Marco. "Okay if I get my coat first?"

Yanking my wool peacoat and beret from the hook by the back door, and yelling for Lottie to bring my clipboard and a pen, I donned the garments during the seconds it took me to get back to the sidewalk, arriving breathlessly just in time for a photographer to shoot his first photo of me. Then, with the camera rolling, and the photographers clicking away, I answered the reporters' questions and told my story. And during it all, Lottie was handing out business cards and collecting the signatures of outraged citizens—finally—who were actually booing Uniworld by the time I finished.

"Do you think that was wise?" Grace asked, when Lottie and I came back inside. "Painting Uniworld as—what were your words—pigheaded money-grubbers? Should you have waited until after your meeting with Mr. Raand to talk to the press?"

"Too late now," Lottie said, counting the names. She showed me the petition.

"One hundred seven! We're one-fifth of the way there." I high-fived her, then glanced at Grace. "Don't frown. This is way better than meeting with Raand. He'd just blow me off."

Grace sighed. "I only hope you haven't made a worse enemy of Uniworld."

"I'm not afraid of them, Grace."

"I'm reminded of a quote by Sir Isaac Newton," Grace said.

Of course she was. Everything reminded Grace of a quote.

"'Tact is the knack of making a point without making an enemy.'"

Huh. She had me there.

When I arrived home at my apartment at five fifteen that evening, my best friend and roommate, Nikki Hiduke, was in the bathroom preparing for a dinner date with her new beau, Deputy Prosecutor Gregory Morgan, or, as I thought of him, Deputy Damn-I'm-Handsome!

"Hey, what's up?" I called as I shuffled through the mail left on the table.

"Abby," Nikki cried, hurrying out with a tube of lipstick in her hand, her blond hair starched into stiff spikes like a very tall, slender Lisa Simpson's. She gave me a hug. "I saw the news. I'm so glad you're okay. I can't believe those bastards tried to burn down your store."

"They weren't trying to burn it down, Nik, just to frighten me. Remember the woman from PAR telling us about Uniworld's scare tactics?"

"Sure, stuff like hate mail and smear campaigns. She didn't say anything about burning bricks." Nikki glanced at the clock. "Quick! Turn on the TV. They should be doing a recap of the local news now, and you're the lead story!"

Sweet. I dropped the envelopes and dove for the remote on the coffee table, startling Simon, Nikki's white cat, who had curled on the sofa for his predinner nap. He arched his back and hissed, then realized it was me and came to climb on my knees and rub his cold nose against my chin as the television flickered.

"Yes, Simon. I see you. Love you, too, Simon. Have you gained weight? Get *off*, Simon. My knee is numb!" I placed him beside me so I could watch the reporter's interview. "Do I look pale?" I asked Nikki.

"You look fine. By the way, I didn't know you were going to be at the Home and Garden Show collecting signatures this morning or I would have volunteered to help."

"You did know. I told you yesterday."

"Seriously?"

Lately, Nikki was so wrapped up in Morgan that she couldn't even remember what she had for breakfast. To think Morgan once annoyed her as much as he did me. But those good times were over.

"Wow. You sure let Uniworld have it," Nikki said.

"Look at that crowd, Nik. They were totally with me."

Nikki got up close to the screen. "Is that a flower pin on your beret?"

"It's a brooch I found in a shipment of flowers, and please don't say it's nasty."

"Are you kidding? It's retro. Look how fashionable you are. Jillian will be so jealous."

That would be a first. My über-fashionista cousin strove to possess whatever the latest trend dictated. If I were to best her, well, things could get ugly.

The report ended, so I clicked off the TV and headed for my bedroom to dress for dinner. "Maybe all this bad press will do the trick, and I won't have to go to court to ask for an injunction."

"Let's hope that's all the bad press does," Nikki called from the bathroom. "After that flaming brick incident, I'd be a little nervous."

"Do you sincerely think anyone from Uniworld would do anything to me now? I mean, who'd be the first on the suspect list? Anyway, Reilly was going to talk to Nils Raand, the head honcho at the distribution center, about meeting with me to discuss the situation, so hopefully we can come to a peaceable agreement."

I paused, catching sight of a magazine lying on my bed. "*Today's Bride*? Did you buy this for me?"

"It came in the mail. No note with it. Hey, are you going out tonight?"

I pulled my green dress on over my head, fuming. I'd bet anything Marco's mom sent that magazine. "Marco is taking me to Adagio's. Why?"

"Greg just got a dining membership at the country club, and his Lexus is in the shop, and I hate to take my old beater, so . . . can I borrow your car?"

Borrow my Vette? My pride and joy? Okay, yes, I was a tad particular about whom I let use my carefully repaired and repainted 1960 Corvette but, truthfully, Nikki wasn't the most mindful driver in the world. "I guess so. But be really, really careful, okay?"

"It's just a car, Abby. Besides, nothing bad happened last time I used it."

Unless you counted those two scratches on the bumper and the odor of greasy onion rings that clung to the interior for *weeks*. But hey, she was my best friend. How could I refuse her?

Seriously, I wanted to know. How could I refuse her?

* * *

Marco lifted his wineglass and waited until I did the same. We were in the elegant Adagio's, New Chapel's one and only cosmopolitan restaurant, at a cozy corner table for two, set with real china, white linen tablecloth and napkins, and a votive candle in a crystal goblet. Marco had worn a black and gray tweed jacket over a black shirt, with gray pants, and looked so sexy it was hard for me to stay in my chair.

Gazing at me over the flickering candlelight at our table, he said, "You in that green dress?" He dropped his voice to a throaty growl. "Dangerous."

"Thank you. And you in, well, in anything? Totally dangerous."

He touched the rim of his glass to mine, suddenly serious. "To us."

"Yes, to us." He wasn't going to choose now to have our discussion, was he? I mean, we'd barely sat down.

His dark eyes held my own. "To our future."

My cell phone rang. Marco waited, glass in the air.

"Sorry. I'll just turn that off." I set down my wine and pulled my phone out of my purse. "Um, maybe I should take this. It's Nikki. I told you she's using my car, right?"

"Twice. That's okay. I know you're worried. Go ahead."

I smiled at him. What an understanding guy. "Nikki? What's up?"

"Abby, I think someone's following me," she whispered tensely. "What should I do?"

"Where are you? Isn't Morgan with you?" I glanced over at Marco, and he raised his eyebrows questioningly.

"I dropped Greg off and went to find a parking space, but the lot was jammed, so I was looking for off-street parking when this white van— Omigod, Abby, he's right on my bumper!"

Make that *my* bumper. "Step on the gas, Nikki! Get out of there."

"What's happening?" Marco asked, leaning toward me.

"A van is following Nikki," I whispered. "She dropped Morgan off, then–"

"I floored it, Abby. The van's still right behind me," Nikki cried, in a panic.

"Honk the horn and keep driving, Nik. Try to attract attention."

"There's no one on the road," she cried, "and where's the damn horn button?"

"It's not a button! It's—"

"Let me talk to her." Marco took my mobile and handed me his. "Call 911."

While I called the police, he pressed my phone to his ear. "Nikki, where are you? Heading toward Concord Avenue? Good. Keep going. Forget the horn. No, do *not* let the van pass. Drive down the middle of the road if you have to. He might be trying to run you off. When you get to Concord, cross the intersection and pull into the gas station on the corner."

I gave the dispatch operator Nikki's location and ended the call, my stomach in fist-sized knots. What if the van ran Nikki off the road? What if she ended up in a ditch? My mom's worst nightmare had just become my own.

"Okay, Nikki," Marco said, "as soon as you pull up in front of the door, put the car in park, kill the engine, grab the keys . . . Hello?" He looked at the screen, then, with a muttered curse, started punching buttons.

"What happened?"

"Dropped call." He held my phone to his ear, listened, then cursed again. "Nothing."

"I'll try your phone. We've got different phone companies." Quickly, I entered Nikki's number in Marco's phone, tapping my fingers on the tabletop as I counted the rings. "Four, five, six—either she should have answered or the call should have gone to voice mail—eight, nine, ten." I clapped his phone shut. "She's not answering."

Marco tossed down a twenty-dollar bill for the wine and ushered me toward the coat-check closet. I thrust my arms into the sleeves as he held open my navy coat, then clung to his arm so I wouldn't slip in my heels as we hurried to his car.

He drove as fast as he could, but it still took more than ten minutes to reach the north side of town. When he screeched into the gas station, two cop cars were there, lights flashing, and my yellow Corvette was parked in front of the gas station/convenience store's door. As we hurried toward the entrance, I took a hasty glance at my car, and everything looked fine, luckily.

When we stepped inside, Reilly and another cop were with Nikki, who was seated on a folding chair with a bottle of water in her hand. When she saw me, she started to cry.

Marco, Reilly, and the other cop formed a huddle to discuss the situation, while I went straight to Nikki to hug her. "Are you okay? Did you get hurt?"

She took a deep breath and blew it out, wiping tears off her cheeks. "I'm okay, other than wanting to vomit."

"Did you see the guy who was following you?"

"There were two people, Abby. I didn't see their faces, but I noticed their van when I circled through the parking lot. I thought they were looking for a space, not for a car to steal."

And then my bright yellow Vette went sailing past their thieving little eyeballs.

Nikki took a sip of water. "Remind me to never borrow your car again."

No problemo.

Within minutes, an APB went out for a white van with no markings and two people inside. Unfortunately, since Nikki hadn't seen their faces, the search was going to be difficult. Reilly took her back to the country club to meet up with Morgan, who'd been frantically phoning her, not realizing Nikki had hit a dead zone. Since she'd lost her appetite for a heavy meal, she and Morgan planned to hail a cab back to our apartment for a light supper of toast and eggs.

"Take my car," Marco told me, as we left the gas station. "I'll follow you in the Vette, just in case anyone tries anything."

Still my hero. "Thanks, Marco." I gave his arm an affectionate squeeze. "Are we going back to Adagio's or do you want to call it a night?"

"Your choice."

Hmm. If we went to the restaurant, I'd have to leave my car parked on a main street, and after what had just happened, that wasn't something I was ready to do. But Marco lived on a quiet block with little traffic. "How about we pick up a pizza and go back to your place?"

"Okay, but Rafe will be there. We'll have to get two pizzas."

Darn. I'd forgotten about Marco's younger brother, a supposedly temporary houseguest who'd now been there a month. After Rafe had dropped out of college one semester shy of graduation, Marco's mom had asked him to take Rafe under his wing to get him back on track. I was still waiting for that to happen.

"How about your place?" Marco asked.

"Two words. Nikki. Morgan."

"Right. Let's just grab a sandwich at Down the Hatch."

In my green silk dress? At least we'd be fed quickly, and since my stomach was starting to eat itself, it worked for me. "Let's go."

But once back at Marco's bar on a crowded Saturday night, we found nowhere to sit but in his office, so we pulled chairs up to his desk and gobbled our sandwiches as though we hadn't eaten in weeks. Quite romantic.

"I almost forgot," Marco said, swallowing a mouthful of barbecued beef. "Reilly said to tell you Nils Raand agreed to meet Monday afternoon at two o'clock. If that time doesn't work, you should call the distribution center and leave a message."

"I wonder why Reilly didn't tell me."

"You were busy. I told Reilly no problem. Grace and Lottie will cover." He gave me his sexy little grin. "Right?"

"Yes." Still, he could have asked. Making assumptions was not a positive attribute.

"It'll be quiet here at the bar, so I'll be able to make it, too."

Wow. With no invitation or anything—not that I minded his company. "So you're going with me, then."

"Damn straight. Raand's not going to intimidate you while I'm around."

I put down my sandwich and wiped my fingers on a napkin. At least that was how it looked to Marco. Actually I was counting to ten. "That's sweet, Marco, and I appreciate your support, but Raand's not going to intimidate me."

"You got that right."

"But not because you'll be there, Marco. Because I won't let him. It's all about mental attitude."

"Trust me, Sunshine. It won't come to that."

Arrogance. Straight into the minus column.

MARCO

Pluses	Minuses
Protective	Bossy
Confident	Arrogant
Open-minded	Stubborn
Sexy	
Hardworking	
Brave	
Trusting	
Family oriented	
Generous	
Kind	
Understanding	
Supportive	
Great with children	
Strong	
Soulful	
Considerate	
Devoted	
Calm	
Levelheaded	
Sensitive	
Helpful	
Earns a good living	

CHAPTER FIVE

Even though I had to park my Corvette in the city parking garage and tip the attendant extra to make sure no one touched my car, I was really glad to see Monday come, because Sunday was a serious bummer. After church, I was swarmed by concerned family and friends who'd seen the cable news report about the brick and had all kinds of warnings for me; after lunch, Marco and I saw a boring war movie—his choice, since I picked last time—and after supper, I had to do laundry that had piled up all week, while he watched a football game.

All of which made Monday a real treat, especially since the sun was out, the snow had melted, and Valentine's Day was rapidly approaching, which meant an increase in profits for my struggling flower shop. Another bonus: The window repairman arrived promptly at eight thirty a.m., so that when Grace opened the shop at nine, a brand-new beveled glass pane greeted the customers. And there were lots of them, some making straight for the parlor to get their morning java, some browsing the arrangements and gift items on display, and others placing orders for the holiday.

I saw many of our regular customers and met new ones.

Some who I thought were new seemed to know me, so I pretended to remember them when they stopped to say how terrible it was that a person couldn't feel safe on her own town square. One woman in particular looked familiar—how do you forget hair that big?—and I nearly said something chatty to her, but then someone asked me a question about flowers, and I lost track of her.

Although we barely had a moment to breathe, it was a great morning, profit-wise. Amazing what the threat of a store burning to the ground could do to motivate shoppers.

Suddenly it was almost two o'clock and Marco was there to escort me to Nils Raand's office.

"We had the most amazing day," I told Marco as we pulled into the huge parking lot in front of the Uniworld Distribution Center. "I am so psyched. Mark my words. Before we leave Raand's office, I'll have a signed agreement in my hand."

"I think you're being a little naive, Sunshine. You're talking about a huge conglomerate here. Nothing happens swiftly in that environment."

We dodged a semitrailer truck leaving one of the dozen loading docks that ran across the front of the warehouse, then walked up to a small, steel door on the end of the building nearest to us. Marco held it open and I stepped inside, gazing around in wonder at the rows of two-story-high shelving stocked with boxes of goods. Small cherry pickers were at work loading and unloading more boxes, their beeps echoing through the enormous space.

Marco pointed toward the ceiling, where we could see an office with a big window that overlooked the operation. We headed toward a staircase that would take us to it, but before we were halfway up, a woman in a neat navy suit appeared at the top. She ushered us into a reception area and offered us a selection of beverages. Marco took a glass of water but I declined. I didn't want to have to balance anything on my knee, especially if things got heated. I might end up dousing Raand with it.

When we stepped inside Raand's office, he came around his desk, his gaze flickering over Marco, coolly assessing him, before lighting on me and turning downright icy. "Miss Knight."

"Mr. Raand, this is Marco Salvare, my, er"—what should I call him? A boyfriend? It sounded so twelfth grade—"partner."

Raand shook Marco's hand, each man taking the other's measure, while I glanced around. His office appeared to have come straight from an IKEA showroom—light wood, simple lines, and no personal touches at all. Not one photo, award, coffee mug, or pencil cup. The top of his desk, a long, straight-legged table, was bare, save for an intercom/telephone and a silver laptop. The entire room seemed sterile and off-putting, just like Nils Raand.

"Please. Sit." Raand indicated a tan leather sofa against the wall. I put my purse on the floor by my feet, as Marco settled beside me. Raand looked comfortably relaxed in an adjacent brown chair, his hands resting on the chair arms. "So. What can I do for you?"

"Give me an assurance that no hormones will be used on your cows," I stated.

"Cows must have the lactation hormone in order to produce milk," he replied.

"Their own natural hormones, not a synthetic version cooked up in a laboratory," I countered. "I'm sure you've seen studies on the effects of syn—"

"Studies, Miss Knight," he cut in sharply, "can be manipulated."

"Your studies, perhaps," I shot back, as his expression stiffened. "You saw the photos of those poor cows. Did they look natural to you? How would you like it if your mother—"

Marco put his hand on my arm to stop me. "Look, Mr. Raand, you know what Uniworld is doing isn't right. And you know these protests aren't going to go away, not here in New Chapel or anywhere else in the country, especially with PAR working so hard to get the word out. All this negative publicity can't be good for Uniworld's bottom line. So go back to whoever makes decisions on the health and safety of your product and tell them it's time to change their policy. Then we'll get the media in to take photos of you signing an agreement to stop using synthetic hormones, the protests will go away, and everyone will be satisfied."

Raand tapped his fingers on the arm of his chair, studying Marco as though he were plotting how to dissect him. "Interesting idea." He got up from his chair. "You will hear from me." Then, giving us a slight nod, he strode out of the office.

Wait. What just happened?

"That was easy," Marco said, standing.

"Are you serious? We didn't accomplish squat."

"He got the message, Abby. You'll see."

I rolled my eyes. "You thought *I* was naive."

"Give me a little credit, Sunshine. I excelled in hostage negotiations. I know how to reason with difficult people. It's all about hitting them where they're vulnerable, and for a big company, that means their bottom line. Profits. Keeping shareholders happy. You watch. Within the week, things will start happening."

I went to the doorway and glanced out into the hall, but

Raand was nowhere to be seen. Instantly, his secretary rose from her desk. "Is there anything I can do for you?"

"Yes. Get Mr. Raand back here for a real discussion."

"Mr. Raand is in a meeting."

"You mean he *was* in a meeting. He walked out before it was over."

"We'll schedule this for another time," Marco said to me, trying to lead me out

I wasn't about to let Raand control the situation. I sat on a chair in the waiting area. "I'm not leaving until he comes back."

We were escorted out by the same beefy security guards who'd eaten Mom's candy. Marco said it was my fault. Wasn't he supposed to support me?

At four o'clock that afternoon, my mom breezed in and motioned for Grace, Lottie, and me to follow her. Then, away from curious customers, she opened a small gift box to show us her latest work of art, something that vaguely resembled my brooch, except that the elegant anthurium of the original was nowhere to be seen.

"That's so—retro," I said, trying to pump enthusiasm into my voice.

So intently were Lottie and Grace studying Mom's copy that neither spoke for a full thirty seconds. Then Grace exclaimed, "Oh, it's a flower!"

"An orchid," Lottie chirped. "No, Dutch iris. A bright red lily."

"Anthurium," I said quietly.

"My next choice," Lottie said, smiling broadly at my mother. "Very nice, Maureen."

"Lovely," Grace said.

Mom heaved a sigh. "Thank you for being kind, but I know it's awful. I couldn't seem to get it to come out right."

Lottie put a hefty arm around my mom's shoulders. "It is not awful, Maureen. It's simply more of a modern style than we're used to, like art psycho."

"Deco," I murmured.

"Art deco," Lottie said quickly, her plump cheeks staining scarlet.

Psycho fit better.

"Thank you, Lottie," Mom said dispiritedly, "but I think I'd better go back to my studio and try again. Abigail, may I borrow the brooch this time?"

"Absolutely." I darted around a pair of shoppers and through the curtain.

"Shall we try to sell this copy anyway?" I heard Grace ask her. "I've just the spot for it, here, on the middle shelf of the armoire. See? It's visible from all parts of the room."

I'd get Grace for that. "Here you go, Mom." I presented her with the brooch from my beret, which she set carefully inside the box.

She kissed me on the cheek. "Thank you, honey. I'll bring it back in a few days. And remember your promise."

"How could I forget?" I called as she hurried out.

"What promise is that, love?" Grace asked. "Your engagement?"

"Yes. And did you really need to tell Mom you'd place her brooch on the middle shelf where it's visible from all parts of the room?"

"Your poor mum," Grace said quietly. "One has to feel sorry for her, poor dear. She never gets it quite right, does she?"

"At least she left smiling," Lottie said, passing behind us. "Crisis averted."

The bell jingled and my cousin Jillian sashayed in.

"Forget I said that," Lottie muttered, and hurried into the workroom, while Grace slipped into the parlor to refill coffee mugs and teacups.

"Abs, there you are," Jillian called breathlessly. "I need help."

She was twenty-six. She'd just figured that out?

Jillian Ophelia Knight-Osborne, my only female cousin, was the daughter of Aunt Corrine and Uncle Doug, and the wife of Claymore Osborne, brother to the swine who jilted me. Jillian was a year younger than me, which should have given me an advantage, except that she was a head taller, a hundred times richer, and a heck of a lot thinner. Which was to say that I was short, poor, and busty.

What we had in common were genes. We both had shoulder-length red hair—hers was a shimmering copper waterfall of silk; mine was more of a rust-colored twine— and freckles—hers a soft sprinkle of cocoa powder across her dainty nose; mine a shower of cinnamon. We also had the Irish stubbornness gene, which had resulted in many disagreements as kids and even more as adults. We functioned like sisters, basically, always battling for the seat by the window.

"I need a gift for a bridal shower," she said, her gaze scanning the room for possibilities. "But it has to be *trés* chic. Extraordinaire. Fantastique! And I need it today."

Jillian also had the show-off gene, which, luckily, had missed me. Today she was wearing a short black cashmere swing coat, black fishnet tights, ankle-high black patent spike-heeled boots, and a black leather beret. Clearly, we'd both read the same article in *Lucky* saying berets were hot this season. . . . On second thought, Jillian would have seen it in *Vogue*.

"How about crystal candlesticks?" I asked, ringing up my customer's purchase.

"Are they Tiffany's?"

I thanked the customer, then turned to my hapless cousin. "Tiffany's!"

She flapped her arms. "The shower is tonight, Abby. Help me!"

"In case you hadn't noticed," I hissed, "we're a little busy at the moment."

"You're right! I've never seen so many people in here. You should have someone throw a burning brick through your door more often."

Another difference between us: the common sense gene.

While I took another payment, Jillian roamed the displays, examining, weighing, pondering, and rejecting everything. She ended up in the parlor sipping cups of espresso until we closed up shop at five o'clock.

"Okay," she said, returning from the bathroom, "what am I going to take to the shower?"

"How about a gift certificate?" I asked. "The bride-to-be can pick out something for herself later or apply it toward wedding flowers, which would give me her wedding business."

Jillian put her hands on my shoulders and bent at the knees so she could look me straight in the eye. "Do you recall me using the word *extraordinaire?* Is there anything *extraordinaire* about a gift certificate?"

"Perhaps an original piece of art deco jewelry?" Grace suggested as she passed by.

Jillian's eyes widened with enthusiasm—or maybe from too many espressos. "Art deco?"

Grace had cleverly redeemed herself. I led Jillian to the armoire. Obviously she'd overlooked my mom's brooch during her initial search, because it was right—nowhere. "Grace, did you move it?"

"No, dear. Look on the middle shelf."

"I don't see it."

Grace came over to join the hunt. Then Lottie came to help. Then the four of us did a search of the entire room, but the brooch was gone.

"Great," Jillian said, slipping on her coat. "I'll have to hope Claymore can come up with an idea." With her cell phone to her ear, she gave me a quick wave and hurried out.

Grace flicked off the overhead lights, turned the sign to CLOSED, and locked the door. "It's a puzzle about that brooch, isn't it? Could someone have nicked it, then?"

"What else could it be?" I asked as we headed for the workroom to clean up.

"Will you tell your mum, do you think?" Grace asked.

"She'd probably feel honored," Lottie said, "creating something worth stealing."

As I swept trimmings off the floor, I considered what to do. If I told Mom her piece was stolen, she might think it was worth duplicating. If I told her someone had purchased it, I'd have to make up a price that wouldn't hurt her feelings—and then pay her. Or maybe I just wouldn't say anything at all and hope she didn't notice it was missing.

My cell phone rang. Marco's name appeared on the screen and I answered it.

"Hey, Sunshine, are you coming down to the bar for dinner?"

"Um, was I supposed to?"

"We never did get to have that discussion."

Oh, right. The discussion. In the background, I heard guys shouting and laughing, glasses clinking, and the noisy whir of a blender crushing ice. Ugh. "You know, Marco, after the busy day I've had, what I really need is to go home and unwind."

At a sudden furious pounding on the front door, I said, "Hold on," and followed Lottie through the curtain.

"Oh, dear Lord!" Lottie cried, then opened the door, letting in a blast of cold air. There stood Jillian, beret gone, hair awry, purse strap broken, and designer coat torn at the shoulder. She fell into Lottie's arms, sobbing hysterically. "I was kidnapped!"

Wow. Marco was right. Things were happening.

CHAPTER SIX

"Marco, someone tried to kidnap Jillian. I have to call the police."

Quickly, I ended the call, dialed 911, spoke to the emergency operator, then hung up and hurried over to my cousin to hear her story.

"I was talking to Claymore on the phone when I left here." *Sniffle.* "I put my phone in my purse, turned the corner, and *bam*! Someone snatched my beret. When I went to see who it was, some thug twisted my arm behind my back and pushed me toward the street. I struggled and tried to get away, but he shoved me into this dirty old van, then climbed in with me and shut the door. Then the van pulled away." *Sniffle.* "I thought for sure I was going to die."

"Good heavens!" Grace exclaimed. "Did you get a look at his face?"

"He was wearing a ski mask." Jillian wept, abandoning Lottie to switch to Grace's shoulder. "He snarled something about giving it up, and I said, 'Give up what? I don't know what you're talking about,' and then he grabbed me by the arms and shook me. Then he said in this whispery, scary voice, 'Don't play games with me, Abby Knight,' just like that. So I said, 'I'm not Abby.' And he said, 'Right.' And I said, 'No, seriously. I'm her cousin.' And he said, 'No way.' And I said, 'Surely you've heard of me. I'm Jillian Knight-Osborne, the well-known wardrobe consultant.'"

Dear God. She gave the kidnapper her name.

Marco rapped on the front door, and Lottie let him in. At the same moment, a squad car pulled up, lights flashing, and two cops got out, one of them Reilly.

Jillian blew her nose on a tissue Lottie offered. "Then the guy said in this hoarse voice, 'You swear you're not Abby Knight?' And I said, 'I told you I'm her *cousin.* Would you like to see my ID?' Then he banged on the roof, the van stopped, he opened the door, and shoved me out! Look at my purse! It's ruined." With an angry sniff, Jillian brushed her hair away from her face, then patted the top of her head. "And he still has my beret!"

With Marco and the cops there, Jillian repeated her tale. She'd gathered her wits sufficiently to embellish it, so I knew she was going to be okay. Unfortunately, I wasn't feeling so hot. Cold, actually. Shivering, teeth-chattering cold.

I hugged myself for warmth as the cops began questioning her. Was she sure the man had called her Abby Knight? She was. What had he said to her exactly? She couldn't remember. It was all a bit fuzzy. What color was the van? Dirty. Okay, white. How old was the man who grabbed her? She couldn't tell by his voice because he whispered, but his arms were thin, so probably a teen. Could she give a description to their sketch artist? Only if they wanted a drawing of a guy wearing a ski mask. Did she see a license plate number? Puh-leez! She was facedown on the street.

"Sweetie, you look as white as a sheet," Lottie said to me, while the cops finished up. "Come on. Let's get you a glass of water."

Lottie escorted me into the parlor with Grace hurrying ahead of us. "A nice bracing cup of tea is what she needs."

I sank down on a chair at one of the ice cream tables and rested my forehead in my hands. Moments later, Marco pulled up a chair and put his arms around me. "You okay?"

I nodded, turning against his chest. It felt safe there. Warm and safe, melting the cold.

"Reilly wants to talk to you," Marco said quietly, rubbing my back.

"Here's a glass of water, sweetie," Lottie said.

"And a cup of herb tea," Grace said, setting a cup and saucer next to the glass.

I reached for the water as Reilly sat down at the table and got out his notebook. His partner stood behind him, keeping an eye on the front door. In the other room, Jillian was retelling her story to someone on her cell phone.

"Have you noticed anyone following you lately?" Reilly asked. "Any suspicious vehicles, or this white van your cousin described, parked outside the shop or your apartment?"

I shook my head.

"From what your cousin said," Reilly began, "it seems likely that the perps are the same two who went after Nikki."

Stating the obvious. I took a sip of water. It didn't want to go down. I switched to tea.

"It also seems likely that they were, in actuality, after you both times."

Hence the chattering teeth.

Reilly glanced at me to see if I was paying attention. "Plus, we have the threatening letters and the burning brick."

Why was he drawing this out?

"Naturally, we'll be actively looking for these people," Reilly said, "but until we figure out who's behind this, it's best if you're escorted to and from work."

"I'll handle that task," Marco said.

Great. Now I was a task.

"Also," Reilly continued, "don't leave the shop or your apartment to run errands unless someone is with you."

"We'll see to that on our end," Grace said. I smiled my thanks, but there was no way we could manage the shop with two of us gone at the same time.

"And last"—Reilly glanced at Marco, then cleared his throat—"you need to keep a low profile. That means stopping your campaign against Uniworld."

"No!" I put down the cup, sloshing tea. "That's what they want me to do!"

"Abby, whoever is behind this kidnapping attempt isn't fooling around," Reilly argued. "Confinement is a class-A felony, punishable by thirty years in prison."

"You know very well who's behind it. Nils Raand. Go tell him about the thirty years in prison, because Marco's little pep talk obviously didn't do the trick." I glanced at my hero and rubbed his arm. "Sorry."

"No, you're right," Marco said. "I didn't give Raand enough credit for his cunning. That's my fault, but I sure as hell won't make the same mistake twice." He gazed earnestly into my eyes, making me go all gooey inside. "Look, baby, I know you're upset and scared, but you don't have to worry. I won't let anything happen to you. I'm here for you."

Aw. How could I argue with that? I laid my head on his shoulder, nestling in the crook of his neck. Besides, if Marco was going to play bodyguard, I really wouldn't have to give up my campaign.

As Grace brought a pot of tea to the table, Reilly slipped his notebook in his pocket and stood up. "I'll pay another call on Raand first thing in the morning."

"Helloooooo," Jillian called, coming into the parlor. "I was the victim, remember? Don't I get any tea?"

"I'll take you home in my car," Marco said as we got ready to lock up the shop. "I'm going to leave the Prius at your place. In case of an emergency, I don't want you to be without transportation. Rafe will bring me back here to get your car."

"Then are you going to keep the Vette at your apartment?"

"Unless you object."

"Oh no. That's very thoughtful of you." Always looking out for my safety—another of those pluses that made him so great.

He kissed me on the forehead, so I refrained from reminding him to be really, really careful with my car. Of course he'd be careful. If I couldn't trust the man I was thinking about becoming engaged to, I shouldn't think about becoming engaged to him.

"So . . . you won't let Rafe drive it, will you?"

He chuckled.

Was that a no?

Marco insisted on walking me up to the second floor of my apartment building, and waited while I opened the door, to be sure Nikki was home. "Nikki?" I called.

"I'm in the living room," she called back.

"All clear," I said to Marco.

He gave me a long, hot good-night kiss that made me wish he weren't leaving. "I'll be here at seven forty-five in the morning," he promised.

Awesome. My very own limo service. I locked the door

behind him and removed my coat and hat, calling to Nikki, "You'll never believe what happened today."

"Hold on," she called. "I have to pause the movie. We're watching *Titanic*."

I stepped into the living room and found Nikki and Morgan sitting on the sofa, wrapped in a comforter.

"Come join us." Nikki held out a bowl. "Greg made cheese popcorn."

"One of my many hidden talents," he said.

Nikki ruffled his hair. "You're so cute. You remind me of Leo DiCaprio."

If only Morgan would float out to sea.

Deputy Prosecutor Greg Morgan had the blue eyes, perfect teeth, and golden brown hair of a choirboy, looks that had opened many doors for him, some into bedrooms, but the most important one straight into the prosecutor's office. Everyone at the courthouse adored him. Indeed, it was almost impossible not to like him—unless you'd had a huge crush on him in high school and he'd totally ignored you until you came home from college with breasts.

I tolerated him because of Nikki and because his position on the prosecutor's staff gave him access to information that was helpful in solving murder cases, when I was able to pry it out of him, not that he could ever admit to helping me and still keep his job.

"Tell us what happened," Nikki prompted.

"Jillian was kidnapped," I said, "but the kidnappers meant to get me."

Nikki gasped. Morgan sat forward. "Is Jillian okay?" Nikki asked.

"Shaken, mostly," I said.

Morgan began firing questions at me. "Were there any

witnesses? Were statements taken? Who are the officers involved? Any suspects?"

"Slow down, Greg. I'll tell you what happened." I dipped my hand in the popcorn bowl and perched on the side chair to tell the whole story, except halfway through, my stomach got queasy, so I pushed the bowl aside.

When I finished, Nikki said, "Listen to Reilly, Abby. You absolutely have to call PAR to tell them to find someone else to fight Uniworld. You can't risk your life for those cows."

"Come on, Nikki. Not you, too."

"Seriously, Abby," Morgan said. "Pull back and let the police do their job. I'll do everything I can to see that those jerks are brought to justice, whoever they are. We can't have this sort of thing happening in our town. And forget about going after Uniworld. This issue with their milk has to be resolved in a court of law. And just so you know, they've hired local lawyers to represent them, and they have unlimited funds at their disposal."

That was news to me. "Who?"

"Chinn, Knowles, and Brown," Morgan said.

"Wait a minute. Peter Chinn is the assistant city attorney. That's a conflict of interest."

"You'd think so," Morgan said, "but it happens all the time. When that much money is involved, there are no conflicts. It's all about influence, Abby."

"Then why were other towns able to stop Uniworld?" I asked.

"My guess is that Uniworld was unprepared for attacks by interest groups. They probably thought they'd kept information about their hormone supplementation quiet, not realizing the information got out anyway. But that made Uniworld's legal team shrewder. As a result, anyone who tries to stop them now is in a no-win situation."

"Maybe you can help our cause, Greg," Nikki suggested, entwining her arm with his.

He gazed at her fondly. "I wish I could, but I'm a law enforcement officer, and it's not a criminal matter. I don't have any expertise in civil law. The kidnapping, well, that's a different story. Bringing these kidnappers to justice is what I do. And a word to the wise, Abby. If you keep fighting Uniworld, you can bet they'll turn up the heat until you have no choice but to give up or risk losing everything. Are you willing to make that sacrifice for those cows?"

I sank into the chair in a fit of gloom. There had to be some way to fight back.

I was not in the best of moods the next morning as I slid into the passenger side of my car. Although I had the sexiest escort in town, I missed driving my Vette. I missed the feel of the steering wheel in my hands, the surge of its mighty engine under my feet. I also missed feeling safe in my own hometown. It made me all the more irate about Uniworld's seemingly unlimited power and influence.

As I buckled myself in, my cell phone rang. At the same time, Marco's began to chirp. He flipped his phone open and glanced at the screen. "It's Reilly."

My screen had Grace's name on it. I glanced at Marco. "This isn't good."

"Abby, dear, there's been a break-in," Grace said. "I wanted to prepare you before you saw the police car out front. They've just now arrived, so I must go."

"What did they take?" I asked, but she'd already ended the call.

Marco shut his phone and glanced my way. "Did you hear?"

Frowning, I leaned back against the headrest. "Grace told me there was a break-in."

Marco reached over and gently squeezed my hand. I couldn't even begin to voice my dismay, so I said nothing, only squeezed back. I feared Morgan's prediction that Uniworld would turn up the heat had just begun to come true.

Marco pulled up behind the squad car and let me out. While he went to park the Vette, I hurried toward the yellow door, my stomach churning in dread. Through the sparkling new glass pane I could see Reilly talking to Grace and Lottie, and behind them, a cop taking photographs. With my heart in my throat, I stepped inside and gazed around in disbelief.

This wasn't just a break-in. My beloved Bloomers had been thoroughly trashed. Fresh flowers lay broken and trampled amidst pieces of pottery, glass, and wax candles. Shelves were swept bare. Display cabinets were upended. My beautiful dieffenbachia were uprooted. Potting soil clumped messily all over the wood floor. Everything in the glass-fronted cooler was destroyed. Uniworld had turned up the heat all right.

The women had attempted to sweep up the mess, but must have stopped when the police arrived. Grace still had a dustpan in one hand and a broom in the other. Lottie clutched a paper bag full of broken merchandise. Feeling sick, I leaned against the door.

"Oh, sweetie," Lottie said, and dropped her bag to come hug me. Grace headed for the parlor, no doubt to get me a cup of tea.

"Take a few deep breaths," Lottie instructed. "It'll clear your head."

The bell jingled and Marco stepped inside, his jaw dropping as he glanced around.

"Did they wreck the other rooms?" I asked.

"The workroom," Lottie said sadly.

My haven! Marco put his arms around me, holding me close as I fought back tears. "Want me to check out the damage?" he asked.

"Please," I said. I waited until he'd gone through the curtain; then I turned to Reilly. "This is Uniworld's doing, Reilly, and it has to stop!"

"Abby, I talked to Raand a half hour ago," Reilly said. "He stated that Uniworld had nothing to do with the letters, the brick incident, the attempted carjacking, or the kidnapping."

"And you believed him?"

"Raand is squeaky clean, Abby. No record whatsoever. More important, he threatened to sue the department and the town if we continue to harass him or Uniworld. So we'll take fingerprints and see what other evidence we can find, but in the absence of any solid proof, I don't know what more we can do."

"Well, there's something more I can do," I said. "I'll hold a press conference to let the public know what Uniworld has been doing to harass and intimidate me."

"Abby," Reilly said, "before you take that step—"

"Do *not* try to talk me out of it, Reilly. They can't be allowed to pull this crap."

"Sweetie," Lottie said, "can I make a comment here? What if Uniworld isn't behind the break-in? What if it was a plain ol' robbery?"

"After everything else that's happened?" I asked. "Isn't that a little too coincidental?"

"Lottie," Reilly said, "why did you mention robbery? Are you missing any cash?"

"No, thank the Lord, they didn't find our cash," she said. "I mentioned it because of what happened while Abby was at the Home and Garden Show Saturday morning. A UPS man came by asking for a package he claimed was delivered here by mistake. Thing was, he wasn't our usual UPS man, and we haven't had anybody else's package delivered here. Plus he was looking around, nosy as all get-out.

"So I started asking questions, like how long he'd worked for UPS and where our regular guy was, making him as twitchy as a cat's tail. When I asked where he left his van—you know how our guy leaves it at the mouth of the alley—he said he must have the wrong business, and took off. So now I'm wondering if he was casing the shop."

Reilly looked pensive. "How old was he?"

"Maybe twenty, twenty-one," Lottie said.

"There haven't been any other robberies on the square recently," Reilly said as Marco emerged from the workroom, "but businesses on the north side of town have had a string of break-ins, mostly smash-and-grabs for whatever cash they can find. We think it's a gang of teenagers looking for drug money. Maybe the gang is changing locations."

"Would they really target a small flower shop?" I asked.

"Why not?" Reilly said. "They're not bank robbers. They're looking for easy access. Maybe they got frustrated when they couldn't find any cash and decided to tear up the shop."

"Was the alarm tripped?" Marco asked.

"No," Lottie said. "I found the door open and walked in to this mess."

"How would teens know how to bypass our alarm system?" I asked Reilly.

"It's not easy," Reilly admitted, "but it can be done. Kids today are techno-geeks. The more robberies this gang commits, the better they get. We can't rule them out."

I still wasn't convinced, but how could I prove it was Uniworld?

Marco's gaze met mine and I knew what he was going to say. I just didn't want to hear it. "If I give up now," I told him, "Uniworld wins."

"I think they've already won, Sunshine."

At lunchtime, we took a short break from cleaning to get a bite to eat. Lottie headed out to pick up a sandwich from the deli, and Grace went home, wanting to change into something more suitable. Marco brought me a bowl of chili, but couldn't stay. Rafe needed a ride to a job interview, so Marco promised he'd be back later to help with the cleanup.

While Lottie ate her sandwich in the kitchen, I sat by myself in the parlor at a table in front of the bay window, taking comfort in the hot, spicy stew of ground beef, tomatoes, onions, chili peppers, cinnamon, and black beans. I turned my chair so I couldn't see the mess in the shop and gazed outside instead. There sat the stately limestone courthouse, the symbol of justice. It almost seemed to mock me. Was there justice when big money was involved?

I sighed, feeling blue. I couldn't continue to suffer Uniworld's backlash and hope to keep my business running. I couldn't subject Lottie and Grace to possible danger, either, and I couldn't ask Marco to babysit me forever. So did I even have a choice?

I spotted Peter Chinn ambling across the courthouse lawn, heading toward Franklin Street, turning up the collar of his black wool topcoat. There was no mistaking New Chapel's assistant city attorney. In his late thirties, Chinn was half Asian, half Caucasian, and quite obese. He had short, black hair, small eyes, an upturned nose, a small mouth, and a chin buried in rolls of flesh. I watched as he stopped at the realty next door, then came toward Bloomers, a stack of pamphlets in his hand. I went to the door and unlocked it, opening it a few inches.

"I'm handing out schedules of town meetings," he said, offering me one. "We're giving them to all local business owners."

I took one and looked it over. "I'm surprised a busy man like you would have time for this, when you don't seem to have a moment to answer even one quick e-mail."

He glanced over his shoulder. "Can I come in for a minute? We need to talk."

So now he wanted to chat? I opened the door wide. "Sure. Come see what your pals at Uniworld did."

He stepped inside and gazed around, his face going slack as he took in the extent of the damage. "When did this happen?"

"Last night. Looks like I should install stronger locks. Or do I need to submit a request for that so you and the committee can ignore it, too?"

He pulled out a handkerchief and mopped his forehead, which was beaded with sweat despite the cold temp. "I'm taking a risk coming here, so cut the sarcasm. I had nothing to do with this, nor do I know who did. And just to make this clear, I don't handle the Uniworld account. I don't even know which attorney in our firm does. But I can tell you that if you want that new door and ramp installed, you need to stop your campaign against the dairy farm."

"So you don't handle the Uniworld account; you just deliver their threats?"

"This is merely a friendly tip from me to you. Give me your word that you and your supporters won't oppose the farm opening, and you can start looking for a contractor."

One word. It was that simple. Lottie and Grace would

certainly be relieved, as would Marco, Nikki, and my parents. Plus, I could stop worrying about losing Bloomers; I wouldn't need an escort; and I could get my car back. But could I live with my conscience?

"Explain something to me, please, Mr. Chinn. How does my stand against the dairy farm affect my request for a new door and ramp?"

"Just tell me yes or no," he snapped.

Before Chinn's arrival I probably would have jumped at the chance to make the trouble go away. But his thinly veiled threat made me angry all over again. Still, could I afford to turn down his offer? "I'll have to think about it."

"Don't take too long, Ms. Knight. You have no idea what you're up against." He opened the door, pausing to say, "And if you tell anyone about this conversation, I'll deny it."

Lottie came through the curtain just as Chinn left. "What the heck did he want?"

If I told her, I knew she'd be upset that I didn't accept his offer. I handed her the brochure. "He left this for us."

CHAPTER SEVEN

It took the rest of the week to get Bloomers back up to speed. We had to scrub and polish the wood floors, restock flowers, repair cabinets, and replace vases, candlesticks, bric-a-brac, and all the other gift items that had been broken, plus keep the coffee-and-tea parlor open to generate some income. And although our insurance policy covered most of the damage, I could still feel the swoosh of air through my wallet as money drained out.

Adding to my anxiety, I hadn't made a decision about my position on the dairy farm, and the opening date was less than a month away. Before Peter Chinn's visit, I'd managed to send e-mail alerts to people who'd volunteered to help, encouraging them to collect signatures for the petition and get them back to me, but none had come in yet. Frankly, I was almost relieved. Repairing my flower shop had to come first. At least Uniworld seemed to have halted its attacks, perhaps waiting to see what I would do.

My parents were appalled by the break-in, but Mom wasn't all that upset about her art deco brooch having gone missing. She assumed it had been trashed along with everything else, and we didn't see the need to tell her otherwise. I also didn't voice my suspicions about who was behind it, and as it turned out, I didn't need to. They'd already concluded it was Uniworld and were adamant that I not do anything to put myself in further danger. Luckily, I could tell them with a clear conscience that I hadn't scheduled any more protests. Yet.

By the end of the week, Dad had seen to the installation of a stronger dead bolt and a better alarm system, and had sat down with Marco for a face-to-face on how Marco was going to keep me safe, as if a former Army Ranger wouldn't know. Marco was a good sport about it, though, which went straight into his plus column.

Mom did her part by delivering a new brooch, a copy so good I had no problem putting it out on the middle shelf of the armoire. Unfortunately, with the brooch came the name of another wedding caterer Mom felt sure I'd want to interview, just so I'd be ahead of the game when the time came to get married. I tucked it in a file marked *Someday*.

Finally, we were ready to announce our grand reopening to take place the following week on Valentine's Day. So, on Friday morning, we strung a banner across the bay windows outside, and crossed our fingers. Fortunately, it worked. From the moment we opened our doors on Valentine's Day, customers flocked in, and the ring of the cash register had Grace, Lottie, and me smiling for the first time in a long while. At that moment I truly believed I'd faced down the worst that could happen.

Tara phoned in the middle of the Valentine's Day rush to complain that her parents were rethinking the idea of letting her attend the concert. Apparently, my cousin Jillian's attempted kidnapping, along with the break-in and threatening letters, had rattled Tara's parents enough that they didn't want their only child exposed to potential harm.

"Please, Aunt Abby!" she cried. "You have to talk to them. I'll die if I miss the BBs."

"I'll figure out something," I assured her, then placed a call to my brother. After I'd spent fifteen minutes arguing Tara's case, it came down to Tara staying home or my brother and Kathy attending the concert with us, only sitting discreetly in the back.

"You won't get tickets at this late date," I argued.

"You're forgetting the scalpers," Jordan said. "I know a guy who can get two tickets for me, no problem."

"Bragger! It'll cost you plenty, and you'll probably have to stand."

"I don't think so. But hey, my daughter is worth it."

Knowing Tara would paint herself chartreuse before being seen with her mom and dad, I made Jordan promise to let Tara ride with us. Then I called Tara with the good news.

"Awesome! Thank you *sooooo* much for everything, Aunt Abby," she cried. "Don't forget I want to get there early to buy a Barrow Boys T-shirt. So I'll see you and Uncle Marco at six, okay? Bye."

"Hey, what did I tell you about calling him—" Too late. She'd hung up.

It wasn't until five o'clock, when we turned our sign to CLOSED, that we were able to sit down and take stock. Grace, efficient as always, had tea and scones waiting, so the three of us took a welcome break at a table in the parlor.

"How much do you think we made today?" I asked Lottie.

"Enough to keep us afloat for a few more months," she said.

"And it won't be long until Easter," Grace reminded us. "Another big cash holiday."

My cell phone rang, Marco checking in. "We had our busiest day of the year," I told him.

"Good for you, Sunshine. Hey, do you need to go home to change for the concert?"

The concert! I glanced down at my outfit—turtleneck sweater, brown pants, brown boots—then hopped up and started for the back. "Nope. I just need to clean up here first."

"Don't worry about that, sweetie," Lottie called. "We'll cover. Just go have fun."

Marco took Tara and me in the Prius, with Tara's parents following at a safe distance in their car. Although we arrived early, the Expo Center parking lot was nearly full, so we had to park in an out-lot bordering the two-lane state highway and hike a half mile over frozen ground. When at last the glass double doors of the Expo Center were within sight, so was a long line of fans waiting to get into the main lobby.

Once we finally made it inside, Tara shuffled Marco and me past the food stands lining the inside wall of the lobby, straight over to the souvenir booth, where she selected a lime green hoodie for herself, then decided I should have one, too. On the front was the Barrow Boys' logo in shiny black surrounded by hot pink and lemon yellow hearts, a perfect match for her glossy pink clutch purse and the skinny, colored plastic headbands in her hair.

Since it was her birthday, I obliged her by tugging the hoodie over my turtleneck sweater—not a look I particularly liked. Tara, beside me, said, "Aren't we awesome?"

"Practically twins," Marco said, with a wink to me.

"Wait!" Tara said, and removed two of her headbands to put in my hair.

I hated headbands. They made my ears stick out. But it was Tara's birthday . . . and how long was that excuse going to hold up?

"I want to get a photo of the two of you," Kathy whispered in my ear, then tiptoed off before Tara could see her.

I put an arm around Tara so Kathy could snap a picture. Then Marco, Tara, and I presented our tickets and headed into the main hall, while my brother and sister-in-law squeezed into the back to stand and watch the show. So much for Jordan's scalper friend.

The Expo Center had been transformed from exhibit hall to concert hall, with a stage lit by enormous spotlights, a backdrop of flashing colored lights, gleaming instruments on black metal stands, and giant speakers blasting Barrow Boys songs.

"I'm so excited," Tara said, bouncing on the wooden folding chair. "I can't believe I'm going to see the BBs in person! Thank you so, so, so much, Aunt Abby and Uncle Marco."

She shifted away before I could elbow her.

"Thanks for inviting me," Marco said.

Like he had a choice. A week into being my escort, he had yet to complain about being there early to take me to Bloomers, or leaving the bar at a busy time to bring me home, or running my Vette through the car wash because he always chose routes with slushy puddles even though I suggested better ways to get there. What a sport!

At seven thirty, the show kicked off with a warm-up band; then, at eight thirty, amidst earsplitting screams, the Barrow Boys swaggered onstage, took up their instruments, and began to play their new hit song, something about never-ending love, although I barely heard any of it. Marco seemed to be enjoying the music, yet I could see he was also keeping an eye out for trouble. Ever the vigilant guardian.

At the intermission, with Tara declaring the need for a bathroom break, Marco surveyed the huge number of teens flocking out the exit and decided it would be best to meet Kathy in front of the ladies' room and have Kathy accompany Tara inside, while Jordan stayed with me.

"I have to go with my mom?" Tara cried as Marco used his cell phone to call Jordan.

He held his hand over the phone to whisper, "You can pretend you don't know her."

At Tara's pleading look, I waited until Marco had finished his call, then said, "I can take her to the ladies' room."

"You'll be more secure staying here in plain view of the off-duty cops posted around the room," Marco replied, donning his Army Ranger persona. "We could be separated in the lobby. My cell phone is on vibrate and ring so you can reach me no matter what, but if anyone seems the least bit suspicious, yell for help first. The security cops will be here in seconds. Let's go, Tara, or you'll miss the BB's first number."

With one backward scowl at me, Tara hurried after him. As soon as she had cleared the aisle, my brother scooted in from the other side and sat down.

"Feet hurt?" I asked with a snicker.

"My daughter is worth every penny."

"How many pennies would that be?"

"Shut up."

For the next ten minutes, my brother and I chatted—actually, he bragged about how many operations he had performed in the past week and I scanned for Uniworld terrorists. When people began to stream back to their seats, Jordan left, and I turned to watch for Marco and Tara until I got a crick in my neck. After another ten minutes, my cell phone vibrated. I saw Jordan's name on the screen. "Where are they?" I whispered into the phone. "The show's about to start."

"Don't know. I'm going to the lobby to see what the holdup is."

I slumped down in my seat, feeling suddenly vulnerable, as the BBs resumed their places onstage. They began to play, and still there was no sign of Marco and Tara. And now my brother was gone, as well.

When the band went into their second song, I started to panic. Surely the line for the ladies' room wasn't that long. I tried to call Marco, but it went to voice mail, so I texted: *WHERE R U?* I texted Tara next, then tried to phone my brother, and when I couldn't reach him, either, I grabbed our coats and began to make my way up the row past dozens of knees.

My cell phone vibrated just as I reached the heavy exit doors. Marco's name was on the screen but I couldn't hear what he was saying because of the loud music. "Hold on," I called.

I pushed open the door, hurried up the hallway into the lobby, and saw cops everywhere—not the familiar New Chapel blue-shirted variety, but the brown-and-tan-uniformed sheriff's police. They were corralling employees and the few concert attendees who'd stayed in the lobby, and as soon as they spotted me, one of them commanded, "Hold it right there."

I came to a stop. "Marco?" I called into my phone. "Are you there?"

"I'm here, Abby. Where are you?"

"In the lobby. What's going on?"

"Wait. I'll hold up my hand."

In the midst of all the confusion, I finally saw Marco gesturing for me to come toward him as he talked with one of the cops. I caught sight of my brother's red hair and saw him beside Marco, speaking to another cop. Then my gaze was drawn down to the floor, where Kathy was kneeling, clutching Tara's shiny pink purse and crying.

Something happened to Tara.

My heart began to hammer so hard I couldn't breathe. I was so paralyzed, Marco came to get me. I clutched his arms for support. "What happened?"

"Tara is missing."

I heard the words but couldn't wrap my mind around them. "Missing?"

"She was kidnapped from the ladies' room."

Oh, God! My head swam. "Wasn't Kathy with her?"

"The ladies' room was jammed," Marco explained, "so Kathy told Tara she'd meet her outside when she was finished. I was waiting for them a few feet from the door. When intermission was over and Tara still hadn't joined us, Kathy went back inside to see what was taking so long, but Tara wasn't there. An attendant was cleaning, so Kathy showed her the photo she took of the two of you. The attendant hadn't seen her but recognized Tara's purse. Apparently, she found it on the floor behind the trash can and was going to turn it over to the lost-and-found department."

"Someone kidnapped Tara from the washroom right under your noses?"

Marco pointed to people standing near the souvenir booth. "See those girls talking with the cops? They're Tara's school friends. They reported seeing a blond woman with a spider tattoo on her neck in the washroom, smoking a cigarette. Before the girls went back to their seats, they noticed the same blonde assisting an old lady in a long, baggy coat and knit hat toward the door, where a man was waiting. They said they noticed her because it was weird for someone to bring an old woman to a Barrow Boys concert.

"They didn't get a look at the man's face because he had a hood pulled up over his head, but they were able to give a good description of the woman—long, white blond hair with black tips, tattoo, heavy black eye shadow, black clothing. The cops are guessing the old lady was Tara in a disguise. She must have been Tasered or given an injection of some kind, because she was leaning heavily on the blonde, as though she didn't have the strength to walk. The police are corroborating the girls' story now with other witnesses."

I didn't know what to say. I felt sick inside. I couldn't begin to imagine the terror my brother and sister-in-law were feeling. I had chided Jordan for coming along to protect Tara, and none of us had been able to do it.

"The police have issued an Amber Alert and sealed the exits," Marco continued, "in case the girls are wrong and Tara's still in the building. They've brought in a search dog, and a helicopter will be here soon for an aerial search, in case she's on foot. They'll find her, Abby."

I could hear Kathy keening in grief, and my eyes welled with tears. I pushed through the people around her and knelt at her side, wrapping my arms around her shoulders. "Kathy, I'm so sorry," I said, the words catching in my throat.

She lifted her head, her eyes sad and frightened. "We have to find her, Abby," she whispered, clutching one of my hands. "We have to find my baby."

"We will, I promise."

One of the cops came to talk to her, so I stepped away.

"Marco, I have this horrible feeling that the kidnappers were after me and got Tara by mistake."

Marco wrapped his arms around me and pulled me close. "I didn't want to frighten you, Sunshine, but I was thinking the same thing. Still, we can't rule out that someone had a grudge against your brother. He's a doctor, and rightly or wrongly, people sometimes take revenge against a doctor when something goes wrong."

"They sue, Marco. They don't kidnap the doctor's kid. Jordan didn't even decide to come with us until today, so how could a kidnapper have planned it? I must have been their target. Nothing else makes sense except that Tara has the misfortune of looking like me."

"Okay, if that's true, think about what happened when they realized their mistake with Jillian. They dropped her off. So they'll probably do the same with Tara."

"What if they gave Tara some kind of drug that paralyzed her? She could by lying along the side of the road somewhere, freezing to death." I handed him his coat and Tara's jacket so I could put my coat on. "I'm going outside to look for her."

"Abby, it's twenty degrees out there. Stay in here where it's warm. I'll look."

"No, Marco. I'm going. If I have to wait around in here, I'll lose my mind."

"You won't get out the door without an okay from the sergeant."

Crap. Marco was right. I didn't know the sheriff's chief officer at all. Why couldn't the Expo Center be in city jurisdiction instead of county? Reilly hated it when I got involved in police business, but he usually capitulated.

I glanced at the stern face of the sergeant, who had set up a command station on one side of the doors. There was no way he was going to give me the okay to help. But damn it, there was no way he was going to stop me, either. "Create a diversion, Marco. I'm going out."

"Past that big cop at the door? I don't think so." Marco took Tara's coat from me. "I'll be back in a moment. The canine handler will need this to establish a scent pad for his dog."

As Marco strode off with the coat, I wound my scarf around my neck and headed for the exit. Permission or not, I was going to look for my niece.

"Excuse me, I need to leave," I said to the tall cop guarding the glass doors.

He gazed down at me over the bridge of his nose. "No one leaves."

"I know those are your orders, but I'm the victim's aunt and I really need to help search for her. Here. Do you want to see my ID?"

"No one leaves."

"Look, it's my fault she was kidnapped, okay? I have to get out there and find her. Wouldn't you do the same for your niece? Don't look away. You know you would. Tell you what, just keep looking the other way and I'll dart out."

"One more time. No. One. Leaves."

I huffed in frustration. "Ever?"

"No one leaves."

"Is that all you're programmed to say?"

He scowled at me.

I saw Marco heading toward me, so I said to the cop, "See that former New Chapel police officer coming over here? He just got the okay to leave. If you don't believe me, ask him."

As Marco strode up, I used the distraction to slip past the cop and out the door, where the flashing red and blue lights of a half dozen cop cars illuminated the light snow covering that had fallen earlier, giving the scene a surreal, almost festive appearance. I pulled the scarf tighter around my neck and charged across the icy parking lot, afraid to look back for fear the cop was on my heels.

"You didn't have to do that," Marco called. "I got the okay."

I glanced back at him in surprise. "It's okay for me to help search?"

"No, it's okay for me to take you home. The sergeant wants you out of his hair. Seems he's heard about some of your exploits."

Whatever. We headed for Marco's Prius so he could retrieve his flashlight, gloves, and a wool hat, and then, as we walked away from his car, I heard something snap beneath my boot. I glanced down and saw a thin, glossy, curved object sticking out of the snow. "Marco, shine the flashlight down here."

He illuminated the ground while I plucked half of a skinny pink headband out of the snow. "This is Tara's. She was here, Marco! Look. Here's the other half."

"Don't touch it. Leave it there for evidence."

I quickly backed away, still holding the other piece.

"Abby, are you positive Tara was wearing that headband during the concert?"

"Yes. She gave me the yellow and orange ones and kept the pink, green, and black."

Marco pointed to the ground. "These shoe prints are recent. We need to move away."

"Do you see Tara's? Small, with a pointed toe and narrow heel?"

He stepped back a few feet, then crouched down and

shined his light on the area. "There's a set with a pointed toe. And there's a set with a one-piece sole and a deep tread pattern. I'd guess a fairly new woman's running shoe."

I showed him the bottom of my boot. "They're not mine, and Kathy had on boots, too."

"Here's a larger print with deep, wide treads, a man's hiking boot possibly. But if they belong to the kidnappers, why would they have brought Tara here?"

I bent to take a closer look. "Do you think Tara got away from them and came here—maybe hoping to hide in one of our cars?"

Marco rose and began to search beyond the car. "If they used a Taser on her instead of a drug, she could have recovered quickly enough to escape. Maybe they caught up with her here. I see more of the same three sets of prints heading off toward the highway."

"You'd think if they realized they nabbed the wrong person, they'd have let her go."

"Either they haven't discovered their mistake or it wasn't a mistake."

"Or maybe Tara saw their faces. . . ."

I stopped. Marco didn't say anything, but I knew he was thinking the same thing: If the kidnappers were afraid of being identified, they'd probably kill her.

A helicopter flew overhead, its powerful searchlight aimed at the ground, allowing us to see three police officers, one with a dog on a leash, heading in our direction. Marco walked out to talk to them while the big German shepherd led his handler straight to the half headband in my hand, and then barked to alert the officer.

I turned over the piece of headband as Marco explained why we were there. The K-9 handler introduced himself as

Officer Ray Aaron of the Sheriff's Police, then asked us to step away so the other cops could take photos and collect evidence. With the wind blowing the snow around, I feared Tara's trail would be lost, but Officer Aaron assured me that the cold air would actually help preserve her essence.

"A search dog's goal is to locate the source of the scent," Aaron explained. "His ability to track isn't affected by cold weather, only by heat, which can dissipate DNA."

When Eros, the German shepherd, was given the command to search, he put his nose down and headed toward the highway. But at the edge of the road, he began circling.

"He's lost the scent," Aaron explained. "We'll continue across the road to see if he can pick it up, but my guess is that the kidnappers had a vehicle waiting here."

My heart sank as I stared up the dark, windswept road. A half mile ahead was a junction, with on-ramps that led to an interstate highway. Tara could be headed anywhere in the country.

I turned to study Uniworld's Distribution Center on the other side of the road, where at least two dozen semitrailers were parked in rows between the road and the loading docks, and even at night, trucks were loading and unloading. I watched as a semi backed up to one of the bays, where an overhead door was raised to move the cargo inside.

"Can you search for my niece over there?" I asked Officer Aaron, pointing toward the warehouse.

"If Eros picks up the scent," he said, "you bet we will."

We crossed the highway and Eros was again given the command to search. The dog sniffed the air for a moment, put his nose to the ground, and headed into the parking lot, weaving in and out of the big rigs. Alongside one trailer, he stopped and barked.

Officer Aaron crouched down to shine his flashlight underneath, then called back to us, "Looks like the same kind of headband, but in green."

It had to be Tara's. I clasped my gloved hands together and whispered a quick prayer. It seemed as though Tara had ducked under the truck to hide and lost her headband there. But where was she now? Surely if she could see us or the cops, she'd come out of hiding.

And how had she managed to lose two headbands? Mine were on so tight they pinched my scalp. She would have had to take them off. But why now?

"Marco," I cried, "I think Tara's leaving a trail."

"That's why it's so vital to have a search dog," he replied.

The wind had grown fierce, blowing the snow into spirals. I pulled my scarf up to cover my nose and mouth and watched anxiously as Eros worked his way down the trucks parked at the loading docks. All at once he began to strain at his leash, leading his handler into an empty bay, where they disappeared from sight. Moments later, I heard a bark.

"Eros found something!" I called to Marco. "Maybe it's the third headband. Come on!"

As we approached the empty bay, I heard the squawk of the police radio, followed by Aaron's response: "County eight-one. I have a ten-zero and need a supervisor."

A ten-zero? I glanced at Marco for an explanation.

He sighed heavily. "A dead body."

CHAPTER EIGHT

A *search dog's goal is to locate the source of the scent.*
I leaned against Marco, so light-headed I thought the ground was going to swallow me.

Please, God, not Tara. I'd never forgive myself if I brought this tragedy upon her—indeed, upon our whole family. I couldn't begin to imagine the heartbreak of losing her.

"Take a deep breath," Marco said. "Do you want to sit down?"

I shook my head. "Marco, please, would you go see? I need to know how—what happened."

He gazed at me for a moment, as though unsure. "Stay here, then."

I paced back and forth, trembling in fear, counting the minutes until Marco returned. When at last he came around the corner, I held my breath.

"It's okay, Sunshine. It's not Tara."

I burst into tears of relief, burying my face in his coat. Marco held me. "It's a blond woman. She matches the description Tara's friends gave."

"How did she die?"

"It looks like she was run over."

I shuddered, trying not to picture it, and wiped icy tear-drops off my eyelashes. "But why did Eros bark?"

"He found Tara's black headband in front of the loading dock door. Aaron called for backup so they can search the warehouse."

"Marco, if Tara comes through this, I won't get involved in any protests ever again."

"Can I get that in writing?"

After four squad cars unloaded more cops, Aaron briefed his sergeant, who immediately had all employees vacated from the warehouse. Within ten minutes, grumbling workers shuffled outside to wait while Eros tracked inside off-leash. I huddled against Marco, waiting, worrying, praying, until finally we heard the squawk of the sergeant's radio as Aaron reported in. The sergeant turned to give his men a thumbs-up. "He found her."

I stared at Marco in astonishment. "They found Tara! Oh, my God, they found her!"

Marco put his arms around me and nearly lifted me off the ground in an exuberant hug. As we waited near the doorway, I heard the sergeant contact his men at the Expo Center so they could tell Kathy and Jordan the joyous news. The sergeant spotted me standing with Marco and came toward us.

"I thought you were on your way home," he said to me.

"This seemed more important."

Officer Aaron appeared at the door and motioned for me to come forward. "Your niece wants to talk to you."

I stepped inside the big warehouse to find one of the sheriff's deputies with Tara, whose petite body was enveloped in an oversized black wool coat. Tara held out her arms to me, as she used to when she was little and wanted to be picked up. I ran to her and hugged her against me. "I'm so glad you're safe. Are you okay? Did they hurt you?"

Tara's face was pale but her eyes blazed with anger. "I was Tasered, Aunt Abby! It hurt, and I couldn't move."

"I'm so sorry." I hugged her again. Tara couldn't begin to understand how sorry I was.

Breathlessly, Tara began to relate her escape. "A creepy woman in a bad blond wig Tasered me in the bathroom, then wrapped this smelly coat around me, dragged me through the lobby and outside where her scuzzball boyfriend was waiting. The Taser had worn off when they shoved me into a junky old van sitting in the parking lot, but I pretended like it hadn't so she wouldn't use it on me again. I waited until she was climbing into the passenger seat; then I jumped out and ran to hide among the cars.

"I thought maybe Dad had forgotten to lock his car—he does that a lot—so I ran there, but I couldn't get in. That's when I dropped one of my headbands, to let you know I'd gotten away. Did you find my headband trail? Is that how you knew to come here?"

"Yes! The search dog followed your trail straight here. That was fast thinking, Tara."

"I knew I had to do something. But the creeps caught me again and tied my hands together. Then they put tape over my mouth and drove me over here. They parked the van behind a big semitruck, then started arguing, so I managed to get out again."

"I can't believe you got away twice."

"It wasn't that hard. They tied my hands in front, so it was easy to get the tape off my mouth. And they forgot to tie my feet. They weren't very smart, as far as kidnappers go."

I wanted to laugh, but the seriousness of the situation kept me from it. "Do you know what the kidnappers were arguing about?"

Tara rubbed her eyes. I could tell she was exhausted. "The scuzzball wanted to take me inside the warehouse, but Blondie said that was a stupid idea. She wanted to go where no one would hear them."

Where no one would hear them? That was ominous enough to make me shudder.

"Do you remember anything else they said, any names they might have mentioned?"

She rubbed her eyes again. "No. They were starting to yell real loud, and the wind was howling all around us, so I pushed down on the door handle with my boot and wiggled out like a worm. Then Blondie came after me again and chased me all over the parking lot, while the dude in the hood drove around in his van, trying to stop me from getting away. I was yelling for help, but no one was there, and the wind was so loud, I don't know if I would've been heard, anyway.

"I finally dove under a truck, but Blondie found me there, too. That's where I left the second headband. Then I saw one of the garage doors coming down, so I ran for it. I tossed out my last headband just before the door went down, like Indiana Jones did. I guess that's when the woman gave up, because she didn't come after me."

"We need to get you down to the station," the deputy told Tara. "You can visit more with your aunt afterward."

"No, wait!" Tara cried, clinging to me. "I didn't tell you the most important part. Those creeps thought I was *you*. They called me Abby. That means you're in danger. You have to come with me so the police can protect you." Tara turned to the officer. "You'll keep her safe, right?"

The deputy replied tactfully, "We have one of the kidnappers already, Tara, and we're tracking down the other one right now, but if your aunt wants to ride with you, that's fine. We'll need to talk to her, anyway."

"Tara's parents will be here any minute," I told the deputy. "They'll want to go with her. Tara, Marco will bring me. We'll follow you there, okay?"

Tara finally nodded and released her grip on my arm. I walked to the door behind them, watching as Kathy and Jordan jumped out of a squad car and ran to sweep up their daughter in a group hug, making me all teary-eyed again. I whispered a quick prayer of thanks that it had worked out all right, then headed toward Marco.

"Feel better?" he asked, putting his arms around me.

"Relieved that Tara's okay. Do you want to go with me to the sheriff's office? They want to see me."

"Sure. I'll ask one of the deputies to drop us at the Expo Center so we can get my car. So, tell me what Tara said."

"We were right, Marco. The kidnappers were after me. The blonde must have seen you and Tara come out of the concert hall and assumed she was me. Tara got away from them before they realized their error, and when they recaptured her, they taped her mouth shut before she could tell them."

"They captured her twice and she was able to escape both times?"

"Can you believe that? Before she got away the second time, Tara heard them arguing about where to take her. The blonde was angry that the guy had driven them to the warehouse. She thought they should go where they couldn't be heard. What does that sound like to you?"

"Like they had murder in mind."

A shiver raced up my spine as Marco echoed my own

thoughts. "Someone really has a grudge against me, Marco, and who could that be but Raand?"

We picked up the Prius and drove to the sheriff's office, where I was interviewed for nearly an hour by two detectives. One of them, Adrian Valderas, was a good-looking Hispanic man a few years older than Marco. The other, T. J. Maroni, was a seasoned officer with big brown eyes, a heavy-duty mustache, and an infectious smile, who seemed far too easygoing to be a homicide investigator.

I told the detectives about the letters I'd received, the burning brick, the trashing of Bloomers, the attempted kidnapping of Nikki and Jillian, and my reasons for suspecting that Nils Raand was connected to those incidents. I directed them to Sergeant Reilly of the New Chapel police for information on the evidence he'd collected on the case.

"Anyone else you can think of who might have reason to want to harm you?" Valderas asked.

"No. It has to be Raand."

"You're sure about that?" Maroni asked.

I thought for a moment. "I guess I did help put a few felons behind bars."

Valderas readied his pen. "How many are we talking about? Two? Three?"

"More like seven."

They both gaped at me. Valderas said, "You helped convict seven felons?"

"Make that eight. And they were all involved in murders."

Valderas was speechless. Maroni pointed at me. "I remember reading about you in the newspapers. You're the florist. Old man was a cop with the New Chapel PD. Am I right?"

I nodded demurely.

"Are any of these convicts out of prison?" Maroni asked.

"I doubt it. They received long sentences."

"Any of them have family members who might be hold-ing a grudge?" Maroni asked.

"The ones who had family, no. They were relieved to hear the guilty verdicts read."

Maroni said, "Okay, Ms. Knight, one more thing and then you can go home. These protests against the dairy farm—got any more planned?"

"No."

"Terrific. I'm sure Sergeant Reilly has already said as much, but my advice to you is to lay low. If someone has put a contract out on you, let's not give him any opportuni-ties."

A contract? I shuddered, imagining snipers on the roof waiting for me to step outside.

"Thank you, Ms. Knight. We'll keep you informed of our investigation."

When I was finally released, it was well after one o'clock in the morning, and my elation at finding Tara had turned into fear for my own safety mixed with sheer exhaustion. I was so tired that as Marco and I walked to his car in the parking lot behind the sheriff's department, I glanced at the rooftop only twice to see if I was about to be sniped. Okay, three times, but that last time I could hardly keep my eyes fo-cused.

"If you don't mind," Marco said, starting up his engine, "I'm going to stop by my place and pick up a few things."

I yawned. "What kind of things?"

"Clothes."

I cocked one eye open. "Clothes?"

"So I have something clean to wear in the morning." He glanced at me. "Until we know for certain that you're out of danger, I'll bunk down at your place and spend as much time as I can with you. No one is going to harm you on my watch. Okay?"

"I hate to keep inconveniencing you."

"Keeping you safe isn't an inconvenience, Abby."

I smiled and leaned my head against the headrest. What a guy to have in my corner.

Marco's apartment occupied the second floor of a two-story white colonial in a quiet neighborhood of older homes, with big shade trees dotting the front lawns, one-car detached garages in the back, and sidewalks cracked by tree roots.

"That's strange," Marco said as we pulled up to the curb behind my Corvette. "Rafe's home. He's supposed to be working at Down the Hatch until two in the morning."

Hmm. Rafe was home. My car was there. . . . "How does Rafe get to work?"

"I've been taking him. Why?"

"No reason. Just wondering." *And sighing in relief.* I stopped to give the bright yellow hood a loving rub and got a thick smudge of dirt on my glove. "I'm sorry you're so dirty," I whispered, gazing through the window on the passenger side.

"Are you talking to your car?"

I scoffed, which was always better than telling an outright lie.

Upstairs, we found Marco's youngest brother, twenty-one-year-old Raphael Salvare, sprawled on the sofa, watching a movie on TV. Rafe was a younger version of Marco, dark hair, dark sensual eyes, olive complexion, and trim build. He was slimmer than Marco, but every bit as engaging.

"Hey," he said, grinning at me. "What's up, Hot Stuff? Where have you two been?"

I flopped down on one of Marco's cushy blue recliners and closed my eyes. If Marco wanted to tell him about the kidnapping, fine. I was too beat.

"Why aren't you at the bar?" Marco asked.

"Oh, yeah," Rafe said. "I need to talk to you about that."

Uh-oh. I opened my eyes just enough to watch as Marco hit the remote's OFF button and sat down on the sofa, forcing Rafe to swing his legs to the floor and sit up. "Talk."

"Now?" Rafe whispered. "You've got your lady here, bro."

"Abby doesn't mind. Why are you home?"

Abby *did* mind because she was *tired.* But that was okay. Family matters came first, and Marco's family had certainly had its share of problems with the youngest Salvare. Rafe had left college one semester shy of graduation, deciding he needed to find himself, but then he somehow kept forgetting to look.

His mother had put up with his laziness for a few months, then brought him with her on a visit from Ohio to see Marco and his sister Gina here in New Chapel. Ultimately, Mama Salvare left Rafe with Marco in the hopes he could straighten out his brother. Marco, being a dutiful son, had put Rafe to work at his bar doing menial labor, hoping to prove to Rafe that he needed to finish school and find a career. So far, though, Rafe seemed content to bus tables and do kitchen duty.

What he didn't like was being questioned. "Chill out, man. I have a new job, a *real* job. I start tomorrow. I was going to tell you this evening, but you left before I had a chance."

"That's great, Rafe," Marco said, clapping him on the shoulder. "Congratulations, man! Where?"

"Hooters."

I pressed my lips together so I wouldn't laugh.

"Doing what?" Marco asked.

"I'm learning how to bartend," Rafe said. "I hear the tips are awesome. I even get some benefits."

With his looks, I was betting on it. I glanced at Marco and saw the great effort he was making not to snap something like, *You can learn bartending at Down the Hatch!*

"Well?" Rafe asked. "Aren't you proud of me?"

"Yes," Marco said slowly. "Yes, I am. You got out there and found something on your own." Marco gave him a smile—at great effort—then rose. "Look after things here, okay? I'll be staying at Abby's apartment. I just stopped to pack a bag. And by the way, I wouldn't tell Mama about your new job."

"Not a problem. And I wouldn't tell Mama about your new living quarters." Rafe flicked the TV on and flopped back on the sofa. "You kids have fun."

Marco grumbled all the way to my apartment, until I woke up enough to grumble back, "If you don't want Rafe working at Hooters, just say so. He should know how you feel."

"I can't rain on his parade."

"Is his parade made of sugar? You're supposed to be his mentor."

"He needs my approval right now. I have to be supportive."

Marco called it supportive, but I called it being dishonest. If I hadn't been so spent, I would have told him so.

When we pulled into my parking space at the apartment

building, Marco scanned the area before he let me get out of the car. Then, keeping a sharp eye on our surroundings, he hustled me into the building. Once inside the two-bedroom apartment, we were greeted by our furry white beast, who came galloping up the hallway, excited to have playmates.

"Are you going to keep me company tonight, Simon?" Marco asked, crouching to scratch the cat behind his ears. Marco was the only male Simon trusted. The furball had disdained my former fiancé, Pryce, which he demonstrated by puking on Pryce's loafers. It wasn't the main reason Pryce broke our engagement, but it probably came in a close second.

"Simon isn't allowed into my bedroom anymore," I said. "He snores."

"I thought I'd camp out on the sofa tonight," Marco said, reeling me in for a kiss. "It's a better defensive position if someone breaks in."

"I've got some great defensive positions myself," I murmured between kisses.

He tilted my head up. "I thought you were exhausted."

"I am. So maybe you can sing me a lullaby before you hit the sofa?"

The corners of Marco's mouth curved up in that sexy way of his. "I might be a little off-key."

"No, Salvare, you always hit the right notes. Let's get you set up out here first."

While I pulled an extra sheet set, pillow, and blanket out of my closet and made up his bed, Marco unpacked his shaving kit and toothbrush, and set his bag at the end of the sofa.

"Do you want to put your duffel bag in my room?" I asked.

"Nope. It's fine there."

Well . . . it wasn't fine there. It protruded into the hallway, which anyone could plainly see. But I let it go. Marco was there to protect me. If he wanted his duffel bag close by, then that was where it should be.

We tiptoed past Nikki's door and quietly closed my bedroom door so she wouldn't hear us . . . singing. We made beautiful music, after which I fell asleep with a smile on my face.

I woke up the next morning to Nikki screaming.

CHAPTER NINE

My first thought was that someone had broken into the apartment, overpowered Marco, and entered Nikki's room by mistake. I threw back the covers, grabbed my hand mirror from my dresser to use as a weapon—*Seriously, take a look at yourself, felon! Do you like what you see?*—and flew into the hallway, nearly colliding with Nikki, who was standing in front of the closed bathroom door, trembling all over.

"Why didn't you warn me Marco was here?" she shrieked loud enough to make my ears ring. "I thought he was an intruder!"

"I'm sorry, Nik," I said, following her up the hallway. She had on her purple robe and furry purple slippers and was shaking her hands as though trying to fling water off them. She tripped over Marco's duffel bag and landed on her hands and knees.

"We came in really late last night," I said, helping her up, "and I forgot to leave a note. Besides, you're not usually up this early."

"Well, I am today—thank you very much for the near heart attack. I have an eye doctor's appointment in an hour. Does that bag have to be in the middle of the hallway?"

I pushed Marco's belongings to one side with my bare foot. "I'm really, really sorry."

Note to self: Duffel bag is going into the hall closet. My apartment; my rules.

Still griping, Nikki stormed through the living room with me right behind. She wasn't normally a grouch in the morning; then again, she rarely rose before ten. She worked afternoon shifts as an X-ray tech at the county hospital and usually didn't get home until close to midnight.

The bedsheets, I noted, had been folded and stacked at one end of the sofa.

Nikki opened the front door and picked up the newspaper, then unfolded it and headed into the kitchen. She stopped with a gasp. "Tara was kidnapped? From the concert?"

She held up the newspaper, whose big bold headline screamed the news: ONE DEAD IN TEEN KIDNAPPING.

I snatched the paper from her, scanning the article for information. Included in the piece was a photo of a female with short auburn hair, with a caption underneath that identified her as Charlotte H. Bebe. If that was the blond kidnapper, Tara had been right about the wig.

Nikki grabbed the paper from me. "Would you tell me what happened?"

I really wanted to read the article, but Nikki's exasperated expression changed my mind. "If you'll make coffee, I'll give you the entire story."

"Deal."

While Nikki measured out the grounds and filled the coffee machine with water, I gave her the rundown, slipping over to the fridge for the coffee creamer. Then, over cups of freshly brewed java, I read the newspaper article, giving Nikki the main points.

"It says the dead woman has been positively identified as Charlotte H. Bebe, thirty years old, and police are searching for her boyfriend, Dwayne Hudge, who is being called a person of interest."

Marco came in, freshly showered and shaved. "Sorry, Nikki. Didn't mean to scare you."

"No harm done," she said pleasantly. "Want some coffee?"

What? No harm done? Could have fooled me.

Marco took a cup from the cabinet and held it out. "Thanks."

"How about some toast to go with it?" I asked.

"Got any oatmeal?" he asked.

"Sorry," I said. "We're all out. We have toast."

"Cream of wheat?"

I shook my head. "Toast."

"Farina?"

What was it with Marco and mushy breakfast food? "Until one of us can get to the grocery store, all we have is toast."

"No eggs?"

"I think I saw a packet of oatmeal in the back of the cabinet," Nikki said, and began digging through a shelf filled with risotto, macaroni and cheese, instant rice, and canned soup.

"Toast is fine," Marco said.

Nikki stopped rooting and glanced at me, rolling her eyes.

"How will this bodyguard duty work?" Nikki asked him, as I dropped two slices of whole wheat bread into the toaster. "Are you two going to hang out here until the other kidnapper is caught?"

"I can't do that," I said. "I have a business to run."

"We'll handle it like we have the past few days," Marco said. "I'll take Abby to Bloomers and pick her up after work. If she has any errands to run, Lottie or Grace can do them, or I'll take her. We just have to make sure she's never there alone."

Never? I thought about that as I watched the bread to keep it from burning. While I deeply appreciated the measures Marco was taking to keep me safe, I knew I'd miss having time to myself. It was when I did my best work. In fact, I got a bit testy without it.

Marco picked up his cup, took the toast I offered him, and headed for the living room.

"What a great guy," Nikki said.

"He's my hero."

Hearing the TV, I called, "Hey, Marco, I usually listen to the *Today* show while I'm getting ready for work."

"Hmm," he said. Then I heard a sports talk channel come on.

"Well," Nikki said, "won't this be fun?"

CHAPTER TEN

*S*weat beaded on the large man's forehead as he ducked his head to climb into the rear seat of the black limousine. The other man waited there, eyes hidden behind mirrored shades, facial expression as inscrutable as marble. The glass partition had been raised so the driver couldn't hear them.

"First of all, let me say how sorry I am," the large man said as the limo pulled away.

"You failed. There is nothing more to be said about it."

"But I can explain."

"I don't want an explanation. It's enough that I must now step in, which is exactly what I wanted to avoid."

"But see, you don't need to step in. I know how to fix things."

"Now? It took you how many tries to figure it out?"

"What I mean is, I understand that I should've taken care of the problem myself. It's just that I didn't want to risk having her see me. She knows my face."

"So, instead, you hired stupid people to do the job for you? Did I not make it clear that time is of the essence? Did I not stress that finesse would be required?"

"It isn't easy to find someone who—"

"Shut up. I'm tired of your excuses. Now we have one dead and another who could lead the police to me through you. I must think what to do about that."

"Okay, look, forget about my cut of the action. Just let me fix this."

The other man slammed his fist against the door. "I said shut up!"

The big man eased a handkerchief out of his pocket and dabbed his brow as he glanced out the side window. Was it his illness or his nerves causing him to sweat so?

He noticed the driver had turned the car into a wooded area just beyond the city limits. As they drove deeper into the forest, he wondered if he'd make it out alive. He eyed the door handle, gauging his chances of making an escape.

The car pulled to a stop before he could act. The driver got out and came around to open his door. The big man glanced fearfully at his seatmate. "What's going on?"

"Get out."

"Okay. Sure." He'd be glad to hoof it home, no matter the frigid temps outside.

He stepped from the car and turned to see the driver bring a crowbar down on his skull. His last thought was that he should have known better than to trust an ex-con.

As Marco drove me to Bloomers that morning, I called my brother's house to see how Tara was faring.

"She didn't sleep well," Kathy told me. "She kept having nightmares, some about you. Tara's really afraid for you, Abby."

"Assure her I've got an around-the-clock bodyguard. Does Tara know about the blonde's death?"

"Not yet. I haven't had the heart to tell her. That's on

tap for later this morning. I don't want her to hear the news from her friends. She's showering now or I'd put her on."

"I just wanted to see how she was doing. I'm so sorry for what I put all of you through."

"I know you are," Kathy said. "We'll be fine. You just take care of yourself."

I put away the phone and blew my nose.

"Everything okay?" Marco asked as he pulled up in front of Bloomers to let me out.

I blinked a few times to clear away the tears. "It will be. I've got a strong family."

I slid from the car and hurried inside Bloomers, where a welcoming party had gathered: Lottie, Grace, my mom and dad, and Sergeant Reilly. Starting with my mom, each woman hugged, then inspected, and finally admonished me about being extra vigilant, paying attention to my surroundings, not taking candy from strangers—okay, not the last one, but they *were* treating me as though I were five.

Marco rapped on the door, and Lottie let him in. He accepted Mom's hug—she was a kindergarten teacher; hugs were built-in—shook hands with my dad, then stepped to one side to talk to Reilly.

When the women hustled off to the parlor to set out coffee and scones, I knelt down beside my dad's wheelchair, knowing he'd been waiting his turn to talk to me. "How are you doing, Dad?"

"Never mind about me. How's my girl? Are you really all right?"

It had been nearly four years since Dad had taken to a wheelchair, yet I still found it difficult to accept. He'd been such an active, vibrant man—a graceful dancer, nimble bowler, strong swimmer—before a drug dealer shot him in the leg during a drug bust. A subsequent operation to remove the bullet had caused a major stroke that paralyzed Dad completely in one leg and left him with limited use of the other.

My mother, brothers, and I were devastated, yet Dad refused to let his handicap prevent him from enjoying life. In true Irish spirit, he made the most of what he still had and joked about what he didn't. Although his courage inspired me, the senselessness of the crime, and the fact that the drug dealer was back on the street nine months after his conviction while my dad was sentenced to a lifetime in his chair, gave me a deep hatred of injustice.

Now Dad put his hands on either side of my face, gazing at me as though memorizing my features. We shared not only the genes for red hair and freckles, but also a deep bond of understanding, making words often unnecessary. His thoughts were all there in his expression: He was extremely relieved the kidnapping had been unsuccessful, both for my sake and for Tara's, and worried that next time the kidnappers might get it right.

"I'll be okay," I assured him. "Marco has promised to keep me safe. Yep, he'll be guarding me pretty much twenty-four/seven now."

Saying it that way sounded so—infinite.

"That's a lot of time to spend with one person," Dad said. "Are you up to it?"

I knew what he was really asking. He was aware that Marco and I were close to making a commitment, but he also knew that I had qualms about taking that step. "I guess this will be a good test . . . except I was never a great test taker in school."

He tugged my earlobe. "Listen up, Abracadabra. This isn't about memorizing facts and spewing them back. It's about finding a person you trust and enjoy doing things with."

It had been a long time since Dad had used my old nickname. He'd given it to me when I was a kid because whenever there was work to be done, I'd disappear. "And Marco is that person. It's just that—I don't know—I'm still nervous about taking such a big step."

"It's understandable that you'd be gun-shy. But don't overthink this, okay? You have a tendency to do that, you know."

"I can't help it, Dad. I get that from Mom. And I think we'd better can this discussion because she keeps looking our way like she wants to know what we're talking about."

"Gotcha. Once this case has been solved and you have some free time, drop by the house so we can have a real talk."

"I'll take you up on that." I glanced over at Marco, and he gave me that little half grin that always made my heart beat faster. Why was I so skittish? Marco had so many positive qualities, having him in my life all the time should be a piece of cake.

Since the shop wouldn't open for another forty-five minutes, the seven of us sat around a table in the parlor sampling Grace's freshly baked cranberry scones and gourmet coffee, while Marco and I recounted the evening's events. Mom and Dad had already been to Jordan's house that morning to see Tara and hear Kathy's version. Now they needed mine.

After I finished, we turned to Reilly to update us. Unfortunately, there wasn't much to tell. All they knew about the dead woman, Charlotte Bebe, was what had been in the newspapers. An autopsy was scheduled for later that morning, and her boyfriend, Dwayne Hudge, was believed to be in South Bend, Indiana, where he had family. Police expected to have him in custody shortly, and Nils Raand had been brought in for questioning.

"That's all I'm at liberty to tell you," Reilly concluded, leaning back in his chair.

"Come on, Reilly," I urged. "Tell us something that might be in the newspapers tomorrow."

Reilly eyed me, as though weighing his options. "Can I have more coffee, please, Grace?" He waited until Grace had refilled his cup, then, after a moment's consideration, said, "Two items came to light that tie Nils Raand to the kidnappers. The first is public knowledge, so there's no harm in telling you. Charlotte Bebe worked at Uniworld until two weeks before her death."

"I knew we'd find a connection!" I said.

"It was a big factor in the decision to bring Raand in," Reilly said.

Marco frowned in thought. "I'm surprised Raand would hire someone to kidnap Abby who had such an obvious connection to Uniworld."

"Maybe he wasn't as smart as he thought," Lottie said.

"What other item came to light?" I asked Reilly.

"It's evidence," he said. "I can't say anything about it."

"But it's my case," I argued. "Why shouldn't I be privy to the evidence?"

"Because it relates to the crime committed last night," Reilly said, "and that's not your case. It's Tara's."

"Does that mean they'll share it with my brother and sister-in-law?"

"When the time comes," he said cryptically.

"What does that mean?" I asked.

"It means forget it," Dad said. "I know how the prosecutor's office works."

"Look," Reilly said to me, "all I can tell you is that if and when the evidence affects the investigation on your matter, they'll share it with you."

What if *if and when* was never? Didn't I have the right to know who was trying to kidnap me? Gearing up for further argument, I opened my mouth, but the look on Reilly's face said, *Don't even think about it.*

I glanced at Marco for support, but he gave a quick shake of his head, as though to say, *Don't press the issue.*

Fine. I knew someone who could clue me in—Deputy Prosecutor Gregory Morgan, aka Nikki's boyfriend. I glanced at my watch. Morgan would be in his office. Maybe I could slip into the workroom and give him a call to catch him before any hearings dragged him away.

I stuffed the last bite of scone in my mouth and wiped my fingers on my napkin, my mind busily turning over various ways to get Morgan to give up the info. He'd grown more reluctant to share with me of late, fearing the constant information leak would be traced back to him. Morgan wasn't the brightest bulb in the chandelier, but he did catch on eventually, so I had to keep my tactics fresh.

"Abigail," Mom said, snapping me out of my thoughts, "I think you should stay with us until the police have the culprits in custody."

I nearly choked on a cranberry. Had she really just suggested I live in the same house with her? Had she forgotten my law school days, when we fought over whether a plate had to be rinsed before being placed in the dishwasher? How to wrap the hair dryer cord? How many times a pair of jeans could be worn before they absolutely had to be laundered? And those were just a few of our thousands of points of disagreement.

Before I said something rash, such as, *You'd have to shoot me first*, Dad said, "Maureen, she has a bodyguard."

"A bodyguard?" Mom glanced at me in surprise. "I didn't see anyone guarding you."

Marco raised his hand. "That would be me."

Mom regarded Marco with some uncertainty; Lottie and Grace looked pleased; and Reilly sipped his coffee, trying to stay above the fray. Dad, however, was watching me. At his wink, I gave him a thumbs-up.

"Our daughter is in good hands, Maureen," he said.

"We'd better get ready to open," Lottie announced, standing. "It's almost nine."

That ended the discussion. Reilly thanked us for the goodies and left. Mom cautioned Marco to take very good care of me, after which Dad told Marco he had every confidence that he would, and they left. Then Marco departed, too, but not before extracting promises from Grace and Lottie that they wouldn't leave me alone in the shop.

"And you," he said to me, tapping the end of my nose with his fingertip, "have to promise not to leave Bloomers without an escort."

"No problem," I said. "I'm not in any hurry to make myself a target."

"Good girl." He gave me a kiss and left.

I shut the door and glanced around at my lovely little flower shop. It had been more than a week since the break-in, and I doubted whether anyone could tell it had ever happened. Now I just had to make sure it never did again.

Grace was in the parlor preparing for our usual batch of morning customers, and Lottie was taking inventory of the glass-fronted display case against the back wall of the shop, so I went through the purple curtain and settled at my desk to dial the prosecutor's office. But just as I was about to punch in the courthouse number, the phone rang.

I answered with my usual, "Bloomers Flower Shop. How may I help you?"

An overly chipper male voice said, "Well, good morning there, honey. Is the owner of your business handy?"

I got that a lot. Trying to make myself sound older, I said, "How may I help you?"

"I have a shipment of exotic lilies coming in next month, with the best prices you'll find anywhere. You won't want to miss out on this opportunity—"

Another salesman. I hung up on him. I hated cold calls. I dialed the courthouse before anyone else tried to get through on my line. "Mr. Morgan, please," I said to the secretary. "This is Abby Knight."

"Abby, how are you?" Morgan asked a few moments later. "I just got a full report on what happened last night. Is your niece doing okay?"

"She's still traumatized, and I'm a little shook up myself, which is why I'm calling. I'll feel so much better when they find that other kidnapper and lock him up, along with whoever else was involved. So what do you know about the evidence the cops recovered last night?"

There was a pause, and then he answered in his best imitation of a prosecutor's voice, "As much as I need to know."

So he wanted to play it coy. Fine. I loved a challenge.

First rule of coyness: State your question as a known fact. "Then I'm sure you're not surprised that the evidence ties Nils Raand to the kidnappers."

"Which evidence are you talking about—the flowers or the note?"

Flowers? Note? They'd collected *two* pieces of incriminating evidence?

"Wait a minute," Morgan said. "How did you hear about the evidence? Okay. Never mind. I suspect I know, but I don't want it confirmed. Better for all of us."

Rule two: Pave the way with flattery. "You're a wise man, Greg Morgan. I can see why Nikki thinks so highly of you."

"She does?"

Rule three: Be authoritative. "Would I say so if it weren't true? Now, about the flowers, are we talking bouquets, baskets, something sent to him by one of the kidnappers . . . ?"

"I thought you knew about the evidence."

Rule four: Don't admit ignorance. "Actually, I knew about the *other* evidence—the, um, note to Raand—"

"Don't you mean *from* Raand?"

"That's what I meant. The note from Raand."

Morgan was silent for a moment. "You didn't know about either one, did you?"

Rule five: Punt. "With what the cops recovered from the scene, plus the threats against me, and the break-in at my shop, the prosecution has to be building a case against Raand, right?"

"You can stop fishing, Abby. You know I can't discuss the case with you."

Rule six: Make it easy for him. "I'm not asking for a discussion, Greg, just a yes or no."

"Same thing."

"Not."

"Yes."

Wait. He'd lost me. "Yes, it's the same thing, or yes, they have a case?"

He sighed sharply, clearly growing exasperated with me. "Yes."

"To both?"

"Yes!"

Finally! Rule seven: Leave him with a glow. "Okay, Greg, I'll stop pestering you. I can tell you've got way more important things to do than talk to me, but thanks for giving me a few moments. Nikki's a lucky girl to be . . ." What? Dating Morgan?

I decided to leave it at that.

I hung up the phone just as Lottie brought in a message for me. As she handed me the slip of paper, I said, "I just confirmed with Greg Morgan that the other item of evidence Reilly told us about this morning is actually two items, and they do tie Raand to the kidnappers. The prosecution is building a case against him even as we speak."

"That's good news."

"Yes, it is. I'm positive Raand was behind all the threats I received, so why wouldn't he be behind the kidnappings?"

"Sweetie, the fact that you're asking me makes me think you're having a few doubts."

I sighed. "I hate to admit it, but you're right. Marco brought up something earlier that I keep pondering, and that's why Raand would hire someone who'd worked for him."

"That's not so hard to believe. She wasn't working for him when she died."

"Okay, but even so, I've seen Nils Raand in operation, and both times he struck me as a calculating, meticulous, no-nonsense type. So why would he hire two obviously inexperienced people to do any type of work for him, especially kidnappings?"

"Then how do you explain the evidence?"

"I can't—unless it's purely circumstantial. That's why I want to find out more about it. Unfortunately, I have a feeling Morgan isn't going to be of any more help there."

"But, sweetie, if it wasn't Raand behind the kidnappings, who would it be?"

"Don't I wish I had an answer to that. I'd prefer to think the kidnappers cooked up the scheme themselves, since one of them is out of the picture now, and the other soon will be. The only problem is, what would they kidnap me for? My mortgage? Flowers?"

I was still holding Lottie's message, so I stopped to read it. "Another sales call? How many does that make this week? Seven?"

"You weren't around last winter, but they usually start flocking in around this time of the year for the all-important pre-Easter sales. This fella had some awfully good prices, though, so I told him you'd be in this afternoon, if he wanted to call back. If you don't want to talk to him, I'll just have him drop off his catalog."

I pinned her message to the bulletin board. There weren't enough hours in my day to accomplish all I needed to do. The phone rang, and I answered with my standard greeting.

"Hey, Buttercup," Marco said. "Turn on the news."

I turned to whisper to Lottie, "Would you turn on the radio?" While she hurried to the back counter to switch on her radio/CD player, I said to Marco, "What's up?"

"The cops found Dwayne Hudge hiding in his uncle's basement in South Bend. He was just booked into the county jail. It's on now. I'll wait."

Lottie and I listened to the news reporter tell us the exact same thing Marco just had. "Well, that's a relief," I said.

"Maybe now we'll find out if Raand was behind the kidnappings."

"I'm sure he was smart enough to lawyer up. I'll let you know if I hear anything more. Everything cool there?"

"Everything's fine. Well, except that I've been thinking about the kidnapping attempts."

"Go on."

"You saw how Raand behaved at that meeting. He was so icy cold, I wondered if he had a pulse. His warehouse operation was efficient, as was his secretary, and his office was neat to the point of being sterile. Which is why it seems unlikely that Raand would hire two bumbling people to do anything for him."

"That thought occurred to me, too."

"So we're on the same page with this."

"You bet. Raand's shrewd. He wouldn't have hired them himself. He probably had a go-between to put a layer of protection between him and the kidnappers. All the more reason not to take any chances until we know for sure who was at the helm."

"True."

"Good. I'll be down at noon with sandwiches. Should I bring some for Lottie and Grace?"

I had him hold while I checked; then I said, "Lottie is going out for lunch, and Grace is on a tuna salad diet. Would you make mine a turkey sandwich, please?" I gave him a phone kiss and hung up.

Lottie was just about to turn off the radio when we heard, "In other news, Assistant City Attorney Peter Chinn was hospitalized early this morning after apparently suffering a concussion from a fall on ice. No word at this moment as to his condition."

"Peter must be hurt pretty bad to be hospitalized," Lottie

said, switching the radio off. "He has diabetes, you know. That certainly can't have helped his condition any."

"How do you know these things?" I asked in amazement.

"You'd be shocked at what I pick up from other parents at my boys' school functions. It's a real gossip fest. Did you know Peter is from Portland, Oregon? And that he's single?"

Didn't know. Didn't care. Peter wasn't on my list of favorite people. "Maybe I should take a bouquet of flowers to him at the hospital as a gesture of goodwill," I said, "and as a reminder that we're still waiting for that permit."

"Sweetie, I like the way you think."

I made a mental note to work on that later. For now, however, I had to concentrate on business. So while Grace worked in the coffee-and-tea parlor and Lottie took care of customers in the shop, I pulled the top order from the spindle and began to ready my supplies, humming happily as I worked.

A floral arrangement for the Walshivers' dinner party. Cool. Gloria Walshiver, one of our loyal customers, wanted the arrangement made with both traditional and nontraditional elements, so I opened one of the big walk-in coolers and surveyed my stock. For the traditional elements, I pulled pale pink peony stems, then added red saucer magnolias, white spider mums, and aspidistra leaves. Nontraditional elements? Glossy red anthuriums fit the bill. Also, I'd been dying to use herbs in an arrangement, especially dill, which was so feathery and fragrant. What else was I itching to use?

Anemones. That was it. Anemones just felt romantic to me, perfect for Valentine's Day. I searched among the bucket of flowers only to discover we had run out. I wrote a note to

Lottie asking her to put them on our next flower order, then looked for a substitute.

Twenty minutes later, I had a wonderfully aromatic dinner table display for the Walshivers' party. I wrapped the arrangement, tagged it, put it in the second cooler, and started on the next order. By the time Marco came down at noon, I had finished seven more orders and was almost done with the bouquet for Peter.

"Food's here," he announced, carrying in a big sack. He put it on the worktable and began to unload the contents. "I told Lottie to give us ten minutes to eat; then we'd come up front so she could take her lunch break. Grace should be able to take hers when Lottie comes back. Does that sound like a plan?"

Yes. *His* plan.

"Here's your sandwich." Marco handed me a big, greasy bundle of something wrapped in white butcher's paper.

I sniffed suspiciously. "Is it turkey?"

"The turkey didn't look good today. I thought you'd like the pork cutlet instead."

He thought wrong. But what could I say? It was free, and the delivery boy was sexy. I watched him take out two small bags of salt-and-vinegar potato chips and put one in front of me. "You like this kind, don't you?"

Wrong again. Wasn't going to complain, though. Not one word of complaint. Didn't want to seem ungrateful. Not going to think about adding to Marco's minus column, either. But if I were to think about adding to it, the word *presumptuous* might have to go on it. Bad Abby for thinking about it.

"Did you just zip your lips?" Marco asked.

I stopped unwrapping the greasy sandwich. "What?"

"It looked like you made that motion to zip your lips."

I gave him an innocent gaze. "Why would I do that?"

"Maybe because you don't like the chips."

I shrugged apologetically. "I eat only the baked kind." Which he should have remembered from our romantic weekend in Key West. He eyed my bag, as though fearing I might toss it in the trash, so I pushed it toward him. "Be my guest."

Being hungry enough to eat just about anything, I downed half the sandwich, then wrapped the rest for another day— actually for another person. Marco and I went up front so Lottie could take her lunch break and found her on the phone and Grace in the parlor, bustling between several tables of customers, pouring tea and coffee and replenishing plates of scones.

"Our regular supplier is out of anemones," Lottie told me as she ended her call. "I'll have to shop around for another source."

"Didn't we place an order for anemones recently?" I asked.

"That was a few weeks back," Lottie said. "Now that I think about it, I don't recall receiving that order. I'll have to check the records."

"Aren't anemones sea creatures?" Marco asked.

"Flowers, too." Lottie shook her head, chuckling. "When I first came to Bloomers all those years ago, I placed an order for *an-ee-moans*. There was dead silence on the other end of the line; then the guy started laughing. 'You're saying it wrong. It's *a-NEM-o-nee*, like *an enemy* said backward.' Well, you can imagine my embarrassment. There I was, trying to act like I knew what I was doing—"

The phone rang and she picked it up. "Bloomers Flower

Shop. How can I help you?" She listened a moment, then said, "Hold on." Then she handed me the phone. "Detective Maroni."

I took the receiver from her. "Hi, Detective. This is Abby."

"I'd like you to come down to the sheriff's office to take a look at a lineup. Can you be here in an hour?"

CHAPTER ELEVEN

Marco drove me around the square to the tan brick building on Indiana Street that housed the sheriff's department. It was located next to the New Chapel Savings Bank and across from the entrance to the courthouse. Once inside the building, we went through security; then I was taken to a room no wider than a hallway, where I sat in front of a one-way glass mirror, Detective Maroni beside me.

"Any questions before we start?" he asked.

I nodded eagerly. "Did Dwayne Hudge confess to the kidnapping?"

"I meant questions about the lineup."

"Oh, I understand how that works. What I need to know is whether Hudge was operating independently or hired to do the job."

The detective gave me a look of disbelief.

"Don't worry," I assured him. "As I mentioned in my interview, I've helped with investigations before, and after all, this is my case, too, so I'd appreciate it if you'd brief me."

He rose and said into an intercom, "We're ready."

Fine. I'd get my information somewhere else.

Six men, all of similar height, weight, coloring, and clothing, down to their hooded sweatshirts, filed into the room on the other side of the glass, then turned to face the glass. Behind them, height markings were painted on the wall.

"Take your time," Detective Maroni told me. "If you want to hear a voice or have them say a phrase, let me know. Mainly, we need to know if you've seen any of these men in your shop or outside your shop, or otherwise near your person."

I studied the men for several minutes. "I've seen number three before. His face is very familiar."

"Okay. Anyone else?"

I took a long look at each one. "Just number three."

He stood up. "Well, then, thanks for your time."

"Is the third man Dwayne Hudge?"

"No, he's one of my deputies."

No wonder he looked familiar. Number three was the cop who'd threatened to arrest me if I led the protesters onto Uniworld property.

Okay, then. Feeling a bit foolish, I left the room and found Tara waiting outside with her mom. Tara seemed relieved to see me and gave me a fierce hug. "Was it scary?"

"Not at all," I told her. "They can't see you behind the glass. You can only see them."

The detective called her in then, allowing Kathy to accompany her. I sat down on a bench against the wall just as Marco strode up the hallway toward me. He radiated such virility, confidence, strength, and genuine concern for me, I couldn't help thinking that I'd made a mistake starting a minus column. I'd delete it the moment I got back to the shop.

He sat down beside me. "How did it go?"

"I wasn't much help. I picked a cop out of the lineup."

"Don't sweat it. That happens. People see cops around town in uniform, but don't recognize them in regular street clothes."

"That was probably it."

"Ready to go back to the flower shop?"

"Tara's in there now. I'd like to wait to see how she does."

"No problem."

I leaned back against the wall. "I tried to find out if Hudge had confessed, but Detective Maroni didn't want to share that information with me."

"Did you really expect him to?"

"Abby. Hi!" Jillian cried, sailing toward me. She was bundled into a stylishly short white faux fur coat and warm Ugg boots, with a jaunty new beret on her head. "You'll never guess why I'm here."

"For a lineup," I said as Jillian eyed the bench, trying to decide if it was clean enough for her posterior.

"For a lineup," she said one second behind me. "Wait. How did you know? Is that why you're here? Not you, Marco. I know why you're here. I heard about your—wink, wink—bodyguard duties."

Marco had his arms folded across his chest and was staring up the hallway in the opposite direction, pretending not to be there.

Jillian wedged herself in between us, causing Marco to sidle to the far end of the bench. Then she nudged my boot with the toe of her Ugg. "Kind of a sneaky way to move in together, isn't it, Abs? I mean, why not just get married and be done with it? That's what Claymore and I did. You have to step off the cliff one of these days. Right, Marco?"

I grabbed her boot at the ankle and tried to wrestle it off her foot, while she held on to the bench to keep from sliding onto the floor. "Jillian, if you say one more word about us getting married—"

"Let go of my Ugg!"

"—I'll tell Claymore you've decided you're ready to have babies. Lots of them."

It was merely a guess that Claymore had broached that subject, but it had the effect I wanted. My cousin sucked in her breath in horror. "You wouldn't!"

I released her boot. "Try me."

She glared at me as she tugged the boot in place, but when I merely glared back, she finally said grudgingly to Marco, who was now standing a few feet away trying to be invisible, "I'm sorry. I take it all back."

Marco gave her a nod, and went back to not being there.

Jillian decided to remedy that. "Seriously, Marco, if you and Abby want to live together, it's cool with me. I won't say another word about it." She winked at me.

"That's it," I said, pulling out my phone.

The door opened and the detective ushered Tara and Kathy out. "You did an excellent job," the detective said to Tara. He saw Jillian and wiggled his finger at her. "You're next."

As though she'd been called to the stage to accept an award, Jillian smoothed back her hair, moistened her lips, and followed the detective into the room.

As soon as the door closed behind them, I hopped up from the bench and went over to Tara. "How did it go?"

"She was very brave," Kathy said, stroking Tara's hair. "Weren't you, honey?"

"I identified the kidnapper," Tara told me, her voice a bit shaky from the ordeal. "The scuzzball was number five in the line."

"Are you sure it was him?" Marco asked.

Tara nodded. "I didn't recognize him until the detective asked him to put up his hood and turn to the side. Then I was pretty sure it was him, because I could see his profile whenever he was talking to Blondie. But just to be sure, I asked the detective to have him say what I heard him tell Blondie right before I got away. Then I knew it was him."

"What did he say?" I asked.

"'You're a dead woman.' He kind of screamed it at her."

"Did you hear any more of their argument?" Marco asked.

Tara nodded again. "The scuzzball called Blondie a double-crosser and accused her sister of turning Blondie against him. Then Blondie called him crazy and stupid, and then he yelled back that she was a dead woman. But the detective said that was too much to have him repeat, so instead he asked him to say only the last part—about her being a dead woman."

Tara turned to me. "Did you know Blondie died? Mom said they found her body outside one of those garage doors at Uniworld, and that maybe a semitruck crushed her, but I'll bet the scuzzball ran her down." At a buzzing noise, she pulled a cell phone from her pocket. "Is it okay if I text now?" she asked her mom.

"I guess so," Kathy said.

While Tara sat on the bench, tapping out her message, I said to my sister-in-law, "Did the detective mention anything about the evidence they found?"

"Only that they were analyzing it. Detective Maroni said he'd let me know when he had any updates."

"Would you let me know if he calls you?" I asked.

"Sure."

Tara put away her phone. "Can we go home now? My stomach feels funny."

I glanced at the door where Jillian would emerge shortly and said, "Mine, too. We'll walk out with you."

As we headed back to Bloomers, I mulled over Tara's revelations, trying to fit them into the puzzle. "Marco, what do you think Dwayne Hudge might have meant when he accused Blondie—I mean Charlotte Bebe—of double-crossing him?"

"That Hudge was afraid Charlotte's sister had convinced her to cut him out of whatever their deal was."

"Do you remember Tara saying that they were arguing about where to take her? Charlotte wanted to go somewhere they couldn't be heard, remember?"

"Sure. That's why we thought their intent was to kill Tara—you."

"But if Charlotte was planning to double-cross Hudge, maybe her true intent was to kill *him*. And if Hudge suspected that's what Charlotte's intentions were, that would give him a motive for running her down."

"True."

Terrific. We were on the same page again. "I wish we could sit in on Hudge's interview. I really want to know about those two pieces of evidence that tie Raand to Hudge and Charlotte."

"What two pieces of evidence?"

"I forgot to tell you I called Greg Morgan today. So much is going on, I can't remember who I told what."

"Morgan talked to you about the evidence?"

"Sort of. Anyway, he said the cops had recovered two pieces of evidence that linked Raand to the kidnappers—a note and flowers. I got it out of him that the note was from Raand, but he wouldn't say who the recipient was or how flowers fit into the picture, so maybe Reilly can help there."

"We can't keep asking Reilly to divulge information from the police files, Abby. He's taken too many chances for us."

"Not on this case."

Marco gave me a frown. "Don't."

"Don't what?"

"Go there. Leave Reilly alone."

Our page numbers were not lining up now. "Then what do you suggest we do to get more information?"

"Why do we have to do anything?"

"For my peace of mind."

Marco glanced at me. "You're going to work this like a dog with a bone, aren't you?"

"Can you blame me?"

He drummed his fingers on the steering wheel. "Okay, here's an idea. I'd be highly surprised if Hudge had enough money to hire private counsel, so he'll ask for a public defender. And who is the county's public defender for major crimes? Your old boss, Dave Hammond."

"And of course Dave will need to hire an investigator, and that will be you."

"Now you're getting the picture."

"Then you'll need an assistant, and that will be me. So let's get moving on this. I should have some free time this afternoon to . . ."

Marco frowned.

"What now?" I asked in exasperation, as we pulled up in front of Bloomers.

"Let's not jump the gun. Hudge has to have his initial hearing first. Then if he qualifies for a public defender, we can get moving on it."

"Are you kidding me? We're talking a week, at least, and I'm really tired of checking the roof for snipers."

"Snipers?"

"All I'm saying is that I want to know *now* who I'm dealing with and whether I'm still in danger. I don't think that's an unreasonable request."

"I didn't say it was unreasonable."

"Think of it this way. If we can prove that I'm no longer in danger, you'll be off the hook as a bodyguard. You'll be able to resume your normal duties at Down the Hatch instead of hanging around Bloomers, bored out of your mind."

"Are you trying to get rid of me?"

"What? No. Of course not."

The corners of Marco's mouth curved up in a sexy grin. "You're sure about that?"

I leaned across the console to gaze into his eyes. "Not on your life would I want to get of you, Salvare."

"You mean *your* life, don't you"—he leaned toward me for a kiss—"Fireball?"

Marco had started using that nickname on our romantic getaway, and it still had the power to heat up my blood. "You want to see fire?"

"Do you need to ask?" He met my lips in a passionate kiss that swept me back to that dreamy, steamy weekend we spent in Key West only a month before. Then, nibbling a trail along my jaw, he murmured, "I don't want you to worry about Hudge and Bebe. You take care of your flower shop, let me take care of protecting you, and let the cops handle the investigation."

"Mmm," I replied, my eyes still closed, my thoughts taking a leisurely stroll along the white sands of Smathers Beach.

"If Dave Hammond gets the case," he whispered in my ear, "then we'll talk about getting involved. In the meantime, I have to head down to the bar to see if my new bar-

tender showed up today. I'll give you a call in a bit to see
how everything is, okay?"

"Mmm." The warm sand massaged my bare feet; a tropi-
cal breeze lifted my hair . . .

He straightened, all business now. "And remember, if
you have to go out for any reason, call me. I'll take you.
Not a problem. And make sure the ladies don't leave you
alone for even a minute. You've got your cell phone on,
right? You're carrying it with you at all times?"

Great. We were back to the warnings again. Visions of
the tropics faded to the stark white snowy backdrop of New
Chapel. "Yes to everything. Don't worry. I'll be here working away."

I could tell Marco was about to add another instruction,
so I unbuckled my seat belt and got out. "See you later."

Inside Bloomers, Grace was working alone because Lottie had been asked to come to the station and view the lineup,
too. When Lottie returned a short time later, she reported that
she had picked out the phony UPS man who, it turned out,
was none other than Dwayne Hudge.

When we had a few minutes between customers, I filled
my assistants in on what Tara had revealed about the kidnappers' argument, and how it had most likely led to Charlotte's death.

"I knew that phony deliveryman was up to no good,"
Lottie told us. "I never suspected he was a killer, though. We
can breathe a little easier now that Hudge is in custody."

"But we shan't let down our guard until we know who
hired him," Grace added. "As Confucius said, 'Better be de-
spised for too anxious apprehensions, than ruined by too con-
fident security.'"

"Good one," Lottie said, applauding.

When I finally made it back to my workroom, I discovered that none of the orders I'd finished that morning had been delivered because there'd been no one available to deliver them.

Yowzers! We had to get them out! The only problem was that Lottie had begun helping a young couple select flowers from a wedding catalog, and Grace was waiting on three tables full of women downing scones and cups of espresso. I hated to butt in on a job Lottie had started, and I still couldn't operate the espresso machine, so no way was I going to take over in the parlor. That left asking Marco to come back, so I quickly called the bar.

Gert, a longtime waitress, answered in her gravelly voice, "Down the Hatch."

"Hi, Gert. It's Abby. Is Marco busy?"

"He sure is, hon. Just went into a meeting. Want him to call you back when he's finished? Should be an hour or so . . . unless this is an emergency or something."

An hour? The shop would close in two hours. I couldn't afford to wait that long, but I also didn't want to pull Marco away from something important. "Never mind, Gert. I'll see him later."

Damn! It was so frustrating not being able to leave on my own . . . unless I wasn't the one leaving.

CHAPTER TWELVE

"What are you doing?" Lottie asked, startling me.

I was standing in front of the mirror in the bathroom, swaddling my head in a black wool scarf that was already starting to itch. "I'm disguising myself so I can make deliveries."

"No way, José. My orders are to make sure you don't leave here alone."

"But we need to get these out."

"Well, we're too busy right now for one of us to go with you, so get on that phone and call your bodyguard."

Lottie could be a real pain at times. I began to unwind my turban. "I did call Marco. He's busy, too."

Lottie held out her hand, and I placed her wool scarf on it. "I'll make the deliveries," she said. "You stay with Grace. And by the way, that salesman I told you about left a price list. It's on your desk. You might want to take a look at it. The prices on orchids are the best I've seen this year. The Wilmar Galaxy Star? Under six dollars."

"Abby?" came Jillian's shrill voice from the other room.

Lottie gave me a nudge. "There's another reason you need to stay and I need to leave."

With a weary sigh, I marched forth to deal with the diva and found her standing in front of the armoire, looking among the gift items, muttering, "Grace said it would be right here."

"Hey, Jillian, how did you do at the lineup?"

"I picked out the driver of the van," she said, intent on her search. "Naturally I couldn't ID the guy in the ski mask."

"I'm pretty certain the guy in the ski mask was actually a woman named Charlotte Bebe."

"Hmm." She felt along the top of a high shelf, clearly not paying attention.

"Didn't the person who grabbed you talk in a hoarse whisper? And have thin arms?"

"I guess that would explain why the creep took my expensive beret." Jillian gave up with a huff and put her hands on her hips. "Where is the new brooch your mom said she made? Claymore's secretary's birthday is today. She's old. She likes gaudy jewelry. The brooch sounds perfect for her."

Ignoring her unintentional slam, I showed her where Grace had put it, except that the brooch wasn't there. "That's odd. It was here last Friday."

"Does that help me *now*?" Jillian asked, her hand on her hip.

"Hang on. It has to be here somewhere."

While Jillian looked on, tapping the toe of her boot on the tile floor, I hunted all over the shop and finally went into the parlor to ask Grace. She slipped away from her customers long enough to help me hunt, but once again, the brooch had vanished.

"Great," Jillian said. "This is exactly what happened last time I wanted to buy a brooch."

"You can always give her a beautiful floral arrangement," I said.

"I want something unique, Abby. Flowers aren't unique. I'll just have to call Claymore again and tell him to come up with something himself."

The bell over the door jingled and in walked Tara. She wore a puffy orange down jacket, jeans, black gloves and boots, and a backpack on her shoulder. "Hey," she said, swinging her load onto the decorative bench in the corner. "What's up?"

"Your collar," Jillian said, and straightened it. She leaned back to study Tara, then arranged a lock of her hair to cover one eye. "Now all you need is a dab of lip gloss. . . ."

"I'm good, Aunt Jillian," Tara said, ducking out of reach. She and Jillian were actually first cousins once removed, but Tara preferred to remove her a little further. She opened her backpack and pulled out a manila envelope. "Mom forgot to give these to you, Aunt Abby."

"How's your stomach feeling?" I asked her, opening the envelope.

"Why?" Jillian asked, eyeing Tara warily. "Do you have the flu? Are you contagious?"

Tara shrugged. "Maybe. Lots of bugs going around school."

Jillian immediately distanced herself. "Okay, then. I hope you're better soon. Gotta run." She blew kisses and dashed out the door.

"She's such an easy target." Tara cupped her hands around her eyes to gaze into the glass-fronted display case. "I almost feel bad about doing that."

Tara was so much like me, it scared me. I removed the contents of the envelope—a half dozen samples of wedding invitations, and a newspaper advertisement of a sale at a bridal salon—and immediately put them back with an exasperated sigh.

"They're from Aunt Portia, too," Tara said, referring to my brother Jonathan's model-thin wife, "but she didn't have the strength to stuff the envelope. Mom says if she'd eat more than a teaspoon of applesauce a day, she might have more energy." Tara took a yellow daisy out of the case, tucked it behind one ear, and checked her reflection in the glass. "How's this for a junior bridesmaid look?"

"The next customer who needs a junior bridesmaid, I'll give them your number."

Suddenly, Tara gasped, then swung around, staring saucer-eyed out the bay window. "It's Spook Face," she whispered, and quickly looked away.

"Nils Raand? The guy from the Home and Garden Show?"

Tara barely nodded. "I saw his reflection in the glass. He's watching us. Don't look!"

"I have to look." I moved toward the bay window and peered cautiously outside. "Where is he?"

"On that bench across the street. He's staring right at us! Call Unc. Hurry."

I spotted Raand. He was sitting alone on the bench, dressed in a light gray topcoat, one arm draped across the back of the bench, one leg crossed over his knee. Despite his casual posture, he was clearly and intently watching the shop, like a cat watching a mousehole. Was he waiting for me to come outside? Did he want me to see him? Was he trying to unnerve me? Because it was working.

I stepped back behind the counter to pick up the phone, but dialed Reilly's number instead of Marco's. As I waited for him to answer, I said to Tara, "Did you call Marco Unc?"

"You won't let me call him Uncle Marco," she said, trying not to move her mouth.

"Raand can't hear you, Tara."

"He might read lips."

"Reilly, hi, it's Abby. Nils Raand is sitting on a bench on the courthouse lawn watching my shop."

"That's not against the law, Abby," Reilly said.

"But I think he's trying to intimidate me."

"Still, unless you can prove it . . . Look, tell you what, I'll drive by and make sure he sees me eyeball him. If that doesn't do it, I'll walk over and have a talk with him."

"Thanks, Reilly. You're the best." I hung up and said to Tara, "Cops are on their way."

Tara turned her head just enough to see out the window; then she relaxed. "Never mind. He left."

I ran to the window to look out. Not only had Raand left the bench, but I couldn't see him anywhere on the courthouse property. I searched people getting into cars parked around the square but caught no glimpse of him. Thank goodness both of us had seen him. If it had been only me, I might have thought I'd imagined him.

By the time Marco came down to Bloomers to get me at five thirty that evening, I'd had a full day and was ready for a quiet evening. Reilly had stopped by to tell me he hadn't located Raand and to ask if I was sure I'd actually seen him. After assuring him that Tara could back me up, I asked him to make out a report for the theft of my mom's brooch. Since it was the second such theft, I thought it important to do so. No one had notified Mom yet. None of us wanted to be the one to break the news.

"Losing one brooch I can almost understand," I told Marco on the ride home, "because it wouldn't be difficult to lift a small piece like that. But then to have the second one stolen makes me think it's more than a coincidence. And then to spot Nils Raand watching us through the window on the same day . . ." I shuddered. "Why would he do that? Is he playing games with me?"

"I don't know, but next time you see him, call me. I can be there sooner than the cops. Is Tara okay?"

"A bit shaken. She had Kathy pick her up right after Raand left."

"Are you okay?"

"A little unnerved, which I'm sure is what Raand wanted."

Marco was mulling something over. I could see his jaw muscles working. "Was the brooch the only item stolen both times?"

"As far as we can tell, yes."

"And both times, it was Jillian who wanted to purchase a brooch?"

"Yes, but she didn't know anything about the first one until Grace told her. Why? What are you thinking?"

"Maybe Jillian is the one playing games."

"By stealing Mom's brooches? Why would she do that?"

"Think about it. You wear a beret; Jillian wears a beret. You wore a brooch; then she wanted to buy a brooch. You were engaged to an Osborne; she got engaged to an Osborne. See where I'm going with this?"

"Yes. You're saying my cousin is a thief with bad taste in men."

"She likes to copy you—that's all I'm saying."

"If she wanted the brooch, she has the money to buy it."

"Maybe it's more fun to make you look for it. It's something to keep in mind, anyway. By the way, did Jillian tell you whether she identified anyone in the lineup?"

"She picked out Hudge as the van driver. And Lottie picked him out as the UPS guy."

Marco shook his head. "I can't believe how inept Hudge was to let Jillian see his face. It's as though he never considered she might ID him."

"So wouldn't you think that after Hudge and Charlotte botched the first attempt to kidnap me, Raand would find someone else? Or if not, then surely after the second failed attempt? It bothers me that he continued to let them try, because it seems out of keeping with Raand's character."

"I'm with you on that. Raand was surely savvy enough to realize that the more those two screwed up, the more likely they were to be caught and lead the police back to him. Still, we can't discount the evidence Morgan mentioned. If it decisively connects Raand to the kidnappers, then he's their guy."

"I'd feel better knowing what that evidence was."

"You just have to have a little patience, Abby, while the detectives do their job. In the meantime, I'm doing my job—keeping you safe."

At my apartment building, Marco pulled the Vette into my assigned parking space and shut off the engine. "We're home. What's for supper?"

I was supposed to have supper ready?

"Just kidding," he said. "I brought food." Then he reached for a bag in his backseat.

As long as it wasn't more greasy pork, it worked for me.

Marco took out a package of ground beef, a jar of spaghetti sauce, and a pound of whole wheat pasta and set them on the counter. "Perfect," I told him.

Then he pulled out a thick mailing envelope and set it

on the counter, too. "From my mom. Take a guess what's inside."

"Another bridal magazine." I opened it up and showed him. "I stand corrected. It's a pattern book for bridal wear. She's branching out."

"Now her comment makes sense. She said to tell you she's an excellent seamstress."

"Your mom wants to make my gown?"

Marco shrugged. "I'm only the messenger."

"Tell her I said thanks—again." I opened the front hallway closet and tossed the pattern book onto the growing pile of wedding-themed magazines.

Marco washed his hands at the sink. "If you show me where the ingredients are, I'll whip up a salad."

I pointed to the refrigerator.

"How about a knife?"

I pointed to the knife block on the counter.

"Olive oil?"

I pointed to the cabinet where we kept our supplies. "Are you new in town?"

"How about spices?"

"Same cabinet. Wait. What spices do you put in a salad?"

"Italian spices, I guess."

"Seriously? I use sea salt and black pepper."

He reached for the phone. "I'll call my mother and find out what she uses."

I grabbed the phone from him. No way did I want Francesca Salvare to know I was a bland, uninspired cook. Her meals could rival those of the best chefs in Italy. I opened the cabinet and searched among the spices, pulling out oregano and basil. "Italian spices. There you go."

While Marco tore lettuce and chopped tomatoes, I browned beef in a skillet and cooked the pasta. It wasn't easy for two adults to work in a small galley kitchen, so we found ourselves constantly bumping into each other, until soon the bumping became more deliberate, more sensual . . . and then more than just the pasta was cooking in that kitchen.

CHAPTER THIRTEEN

"**A**bby," Marco murmured, his breath hot against my throat as I sat on the edge of the counter, my legs wrapped around his hips, "it's burning."

"Same here," I panted.

"The beef, Abby."

Oh. Right.

Fortunately, we were able to save our meal from total annihilation. And once the candles were lit, the wine was poured, and the food was on the table, I was ready for a relaxing meal with my hero. We sipped wine, smiling at each other across the glow of the candle. "So," I purred, "what do you have in mind for dessert, Hotshot?"

With an apologetic glance, Marco explained that he'd taken on a new PI case and would have to leave soon to do surveillance work.

"So you'll be gone all evening?"

"Right. And you'll need to decide whether you want to come along on the stakeout with me or find someone to stay here with you."

Those were my choices? Be babysat or hunch down in

Marco's car in the dark for hours on a cold, workday evening? Not a chance. "I choose to stay here but I don't need a sitter. No one is going to get past that new dead bolt you installed on our door."

"Locks aren't foolproof, Abby. I'd feel better if someone was here with you. How about my sister?"

Right, and spend my evening watching Gina change diapers and make comments about how she is positive Marco wants to be a daddy soon? "No, thanks, Marco. Your nephew's bedtime is eight o'clock. I wouldn't want to disrupt their schedule when it's not even necessary for someone to be here with me."

"Okay, then how about Jillian?"

"How about I jump out the window?"

"Abby."

"Marco, I'll be fine. Stop treating me like I'm helpless."

He thought about it while he finished his wine. "You're right. You're anything but helpless. Let's clear the table; then I need to get going."

An hour after Marco left, he phoned. "Everything okay?"

"You bet. I was just doing some research to see if I could locate Charlotte's sister."

"Abby."

"I'm bored, Marco. I need something to keep my mind occupied. Anyway, there are two Bebes in the phone book but neither is related—"

"Sorry to interrupt, but I have to take some photos." The line went dead.

At eight thirty, he phoned again, asking quietly, "How's it going?"

"Still bored," I said. What I didn't say was how frustrated I was, as well. Except for the article about the kidnapping in yesterday's paper, I hadn't found anything on the Internet about Charlotte or any Bebe relatives.

"Sorry, Sunshine. I'm on the move. I'll give you a call later." He hung up.

Not sure whether to be grateful to him for checking on me or annoyed that he felt the need, I continued my search. Finally, I located a listing for C. H. Bebe in Maraville, a city a half hour away, but when I dialed the number, there was no answer and no machine to pick up.

My intercom buzzed, startling me. I debated about pretending I wasn't home, then decided I'd be safer letting my visitor know someone was in residence. I answered with a terse, "Who is it?"

"Reilly," came the crackly reply.

I started to buzz him in, then decided I'd better play it safe. "Give me your name, rank, and serial number."

"Sergeant Sean Reilly, and you don't know my serial number, so how would you know whether I was telling the truth?"

"Badge number, I mean."

"You don't know my badge number, either. Would you just let me in? I'm freezing my ass off out here."

Yep. It was Reilly. I buzzed him in, then waited by the door. Once he was visible in the spyglass, I unchained and unlocked the door. "What's up, Reilly? Why aren't you in uniform?"

"Marco asked me to stop by after bowling tonight."

Unbelievable. Marco had called a sitter after all. "Listen, Reilly, you don't need to stay. I'm fine by myself. Marco is being a worrywart."

Reilly rubbed his chin. "The thing is, I owe him a favor and I'd like to pay it off. So I'll stay a while and then get out of your hair, okay?"

Hmm. As long as he was there, maybe I could get him to divulge more information. "Sure. Come on in. Would you like a beer?"

"Sounds great."

"Hey, take a look at my computer screen, would you?" I called from the kitchen.

I grabbed a Bud Light from the fridge and took it to him. Reilly had already seated himself in front of my monitor and was reading the information I'd pulled up.

"You're researching Charlotte Bebe? Why?"

"Because I thought if I located her sister, she'd tell me if Raand was behind the kidnappings."

"Just like that she's gonna admit that she or her sister was involved in an illegal activity?"

"Haven't I persuaded you to tell me things you really didn't want to?"

He scowled at me. "Pull up a chair."

I did so, and then watched as he typed in a Web address. "Okay, here's the site you need—GDS2, a desktop search tool."

I leaned in to take a closer look. "Wow. That's good to know."

"But you're wasting your time with this search because the prosecutor has already decided to go after Raand. And between you and me, I wouldn't be surprised if the guy isn't in chains this time tomorrow. Done and done."

"What will the charge be?"

"Conspiracy."

"Does the prosecutor have enough on Raand to charge him?"

"Are you kidding? Our DA? You know what he's like. He could indict a ham sandwich, as the saying goes."

Boy, did I know that. In times past, District Attorney

Darnell had gone after both Marco and me based on circumstantial evidence. From a prosecutor's standpoint, it was
always politically advisable to find the likeliest suspect and
arrest him—or her—quickly, so the jittery public felt safe again.
Unfortunately, that meant once a person was in Darnell's
crosshairs, guilty or not, look out.

"What if Raand isn't the guy?" I asked.

Reilly gave me a perplexed look. "You can't stand the
guy. Why are you even bringing that up?"

"Because I keep thinking about the incompetence of the
kidnappers, and somehow I don't see Raand hiring them."

"Maybe he had someone else hire them. You know,
delegate?"

I sighed. "Marco mentioned that, too."

"But you're not convinced, so you'll keep poking into
things until you tick someone off."

"I might be convinced if I knew what the evidence
was."

Reilly pushed back the chair, grabbed the bottle of beer,
and made himself comfortable on the sofa. "Any games on
TV tonight?"

I plucked the remote from the coffee table and held it
out of reach. "Can't you tell me one little thing, such as whether
you saw anything in the file about a note from Raand?"

"Why do you do this to me? I knew I should've found
another way to repay Marco, but no. I have to be Mr. Nice
Guy."

"How about Charlotte Bebe's autopsy report?" I asked.
"I mean, there's no harm in saying what the cause of death
was, is there? Please?"

Reilly sighed. "If I tell you that, will you drop the subject and give me the remote?"

"Yes."

"Massive trauma to the chest and head."

"Caused by—?"

"A vehicle."

"Type of vehicle?"

Reilly glowered. "The tread pattern and size of tire are the type normally used by a van or SUV."

"A van like the one Dwayne Hudge drove?"

"No way of knowing."

"But it wasn't semitrailer tires, right?"

"Right."

That was proof enough for me. Hudge ran down his partner. He must have truly believed Charlotte and her sister were going to double-cross him. That meant finding Charlotte's sister just became my number-one goal.

Reilly held out his hand, so I tossed him the remote. "Here you go."

I went back to the computer, typed *Bebe* in the GDS2 search box, and came up with a long list of names, none of them local. I stared at the list, tapping my fingers on the desk. Now what? Track down each one of them? I sighed in frustration.

A ding alerted me to an incoming e-mail, so I clicked on it and saw a letter from one of the PAR members, wanting an update on the dairy farm protests.

I replied, *The dairy farm is set to open in two weeks, but I need someone to take over temporarily, as I am . . .* What could I say? A potential kidnap victim? Under house arrest by my boyfriend? Banned from group activities? Sniper-phobic? *. . . incapacitated. Please advise.*

That was vague enough. I hit SEND, and went back to the search engine to see what I could find about Nils Raand. A half hour later, I'd uncovered nothing but what was on the Uniworld Food Corporation's Web site. In a single paragraph, it stated that Raand had started in the mail room and worked his way up the corporate ladder to management, where he was now in charge of Uniworld's Midwest Distribution Center. To me, it sounded way too hokey to be true, almost as if Nils Raand were a fictional character.

Maybe that was why I couldn't find anything. Maybe Nils Raand was an alias.

"Hey, Reilly, I know I promised to drop the subject, but isn't there any way you can take a peek in the Raand file for me?"

Silence. I turned to look and found him sound asleep, mouth open.

Some sitter.

Reilly was still asleep and Marco hadn't yet returned when I finally decided to hit the sack. I fell into a sound but not restful sleep, my dreams filled with snipers, chases down dark alleys, missing brooches, and screaming women. Oh, wait. That scream was real.

I shot out of bed and tore from my room, the morning sun temporarily blinding me as I stumbled into the hallway and collided with Marco, who had a towel around his middle.

"What happened?" I asked, squinting.

"I didn't know Nikki was in the bathroom. I went in to shower."

Didn't anyone know what a closed door meant?

I almost asked him that, but, seriously, *all* he had on was a towel wrapped around his hips. The rest of him was bare and hard-muscled and unbelievably sexy. However, since I was unshowered and unbelievably hungry, I headed for the kitchen. "What time is it?"

"Almost seven o'clock." Marco opened the front door to retrieve the morning newspaper. I hoped the Samples across the hall weren't on their way out their door to walk their Chihuahua. Mrs. Sample was given to hysterics.

I got out the orange juice and set it on the counter. "Want some juice?"

"Sure, thanks." Marco came up behind me and slid one arm around my waist. "You're pretty hot in the morning, with your messy hair . . . bare legs . . ."

And morning mouth. I poured two glasses of juice, took a sip from one, and handed the other to him over my shoulder. While he drank it, I started measuring out coffee grounds.

The bathroom door opened; then a bedroom door slammed. Nikki was angry.

Marco downed his juice and set the glass on the counter. "I'd better get dressed and go apologize."

"I wouldn't do that. Nikki went back to bed and will be sound asleep in a few minutes. She was probably half awake when it happened anyway."

"No kidding?" Marco called from the other room.

Definitely kidding. Nikki would be angry until tomorrow morning. "Do you want toast with your coffee?"

I held my breath, hoping he didn't go through the mushy breakfast list again. Instead, Marco appeared dressed in jeans and a white undershirt, walked to one of the cabinets, and took out a box of instant oatmeal.

"I picked this up last night. Want me to make you a bowl?"

"Okay." Marco was really on the ball. I could handle having a guy around who paid attention.

He took out two packages and opened them into bowls.

"The word on the street is that Nils Raand will be arrested soon."

"I heard that, too. From my sitter."

Marco was wise enough to look sheepish as he heated water in the microwave. "I guess I should have mentioned Sean was coming over last night."

"I guess. You didn't need to send Reilly here. He slept most of the evening, anyway."

"Reilly owed me. It was no big deal."

Maybe for them.

Marco kissed my cheek. "Have to keep my woman safe."

His woman. Aw. My caveman hero. "By the way, Reilly told me that Charlotte's cause of death was massive trauma to the head and chest from tires like a van would have made, so it's pretty clear that Hudge ran her down."

"Yet another stupid move on Hudge's part."

"Also, I did some research on Nils Raand, but other than a short bio on the Uniworld Web site, there is nothing out there on him. Nada. I find that highly suspicious. And by the way, Reilly showed me a new Web site for digging up information on people."

"If it's the site I'm thinking of, I showed it to him."

"Oh." I poured him a cup of coffee. "You showed it to him and not me?"

Marco finished stirring the oatmeal, then handed me one of the bowls. He gave me another kiss, this one on top of my head, then picked up his cup and went around the corner to sit at the dinette table. Through the pass-through, I watched as he opened the newspaper and began to read as he wolfed down his breakfast.

He'd totally ignored my question.

"Marco?"

"Hmm?" came his mumbled reply.

I took back what I thought about him earlier, because he wasn't paying attention now.

"Okay if I drive?" I asked Marco, as we walked across the parking lot toward the Vette.

"Better if I do."

"Better why?"

"Just better."

New word for the minus column: *autocratic*. "How is it better?"

"Safer for you. Defensive driving is one of the skills I learned in Ranger training."

Hard to argue that one, but I had to give it a go. It was only a ten-minute trip, after all. With a forlorn sigh, I said, "I really miss driving my Vette."

Marco glanced at me and his gaze softened, no doubt because of the heart-wrenching look of sadness on my face. He handed me the keys. "I guess it won't hurt."

Defensive whining was a skill I learned in kindergarten.

I got behind the wheel, pulled the seat forward, adjusted the rear- and side-view mirrors, and turned on the engine. I ran my hands along the steering wheel, familiarizing myself with its feel. I patted the dash, whispering, "That's my baby. Listen to your engine purr. Mama is back!"

"Seat belt," my caveman said.

"I was just about to do that," I said sweetly.

"Watch that post behind you."

The post I'd been watching for a year now and had yet to hit? I backed out of the space in one smooth motion, glanced at Marco to see if he'd noticed, then drove across the lot and paused at the street to check for cars.

"Careful. The road looks icy."

I gripped the wheel tighter but didn't reply. Make that, I didn't *trust* myself to reply. How did Marco think I made it to work each day? Blindly hitting posts and sliding across icy streets? Had he always been that bossy and I just hadn't noticed?

"Why aren't you wearing that flower pin on your beret anymore?"

"My mom still has it."

"I kind of liked it."

"You did?"

"The red brought out the blush in your cheeks."

He noticed a blush in my cheeks? "Thanks. That's really sweet of you to say so."

How had I ever thought Marco was bossy? He was merely watching out for my well-being in that self-assured Army Ranger way of his. I had to stop being so critical and start appreciating his finer points. Maybe if I weren't under such a cloud of worry, it would be easier.

To demonstrate my appreciation, I started to reach across the seat to take his hand, but he made a sound through his teeth as though an accident were imminent.

I yanked my hand back. "What?"

He pointed to the cross street. "Two hands on the wheel at an intersection. Defensive driving, remember? Taking your focus off the road for even a second is long enough for someone to charge through and broadside you."

I was on the verge of pulling off the road and letting him drive when his phone rang. He slid it out of his pocket and checked the screen for a name. "It's Reilly," he said, then pressed the phone to his ear.

Good! That would distract him for a while. Maybe I could get all the way to the shop before he finished.

"Hey, man," he said to Reilly, "I was going to give you a call later. Thanks for stopping by the place last night. We really appreciated it."

Did not.

"So what's up?" Marco asked. He listened for a moment, then said, "You've got to be kidding. I don't believe it! How the hell did it happen?"

"What happened?" I asked.

Marco covered the phone with his hand. "Dwayne Hudge is dead."

That was a distraction, all right.

CHAPTER FOURTEEN

Dwayne Hudge was dead? No way. He couldn't be. The cops had him locked up in the county jail. He was surrounded by guards. They had the wrong guy.

"Thanks for letting me know. Keep me posted, okay?" Marco flipped the phone closed. "Damn. The detectives never even got to question him."

"I don't believe it."

"That he's dead?"

"That the body they have is Hudge. He's in jail, for heaven's sake. He's got guards." I glanced over at Marco to see him giving me a look that said, *Do you seriously think I could be wrong about this?*

"Hudge is dead, Abby."

"Did he hang himself?"

"He was stabbed."

"Oh, my God! In jail? Who stabbed him?"

"No one is saying. One minute Hudge was leaning up against the bars of the holding cell; next minute he was on the ground, bleeding out. By the time someone alerted the guards, and they got to him, he had no pulse. Whatever weapon was used, it hit his carotid artery."

"Aren't the inmates searched for weapons before they're processed?"

"Of course they are. Sometimes, in a prison situation, someone manages to slip in a shiv, but Reilly said the guys in the holding cell were clean." Marco hit the dashboard with his hand. "Damn it. Twenty guys were in there with him at the time, and all of them swear they saw nothing."

"If none of the men in the holding cell had a weapon, then obviously someone outside the cell killed him."

"Except that the only people outside the cell were the jail guards. Some are former cops."

"But someone at that jail has to know something or have seen someone."

"You're right. The detectives are going to have their hands full. But the coroner should be able to determine the weapon from the edges of the wound. That could help ID the murderer."

"Do you think it's possible someone wanted Hudge silenced?"

"*Someone* being the mastermind behind the kidnapping? Sure, it's possible. Probable, in fact."

"So now the only person who knows who hired Hudge and Charlotte is Charlotte's sister, which means the cops better find her soon before she's the next one murdered. And what's to stop the killer from coming after me next?"

Marco reached across to rub my shoulder. "Me. I'm not going to let anything happen to you, Abby. My main job right now is to keep you safe. We'll let the detectives worry about Charlotte's sister."

When he put it like that, how could I argue? "Thanks, Marco."

"I'll make sure someone is with you this evening while I'm out, too."

Not another sitter! "Honestly, Marco, I'll be perfectly safe in my apartment."

He pointed toward the curb. "Pull up in front of Bloomers. I'll escort you in."

Before I could protest that he was being a little too protective, he was on the phone with Lottie. "Abby is feeling a little nervous so I'm going to walk her to the door. Be ready." He glanced over at me. "Okay?"

A moment later, Lottie and Grace were standing guard in the doorway, checking up and down the sidewalk for any signs of danger, while Marco hustled me toward the shop. I felt absolutely ridiculous.

Still, I glanced up at the roof.

No sniper.

As soon as we were in the shop, Marco left to park the Vette and Lottie locked the door behind us; then the women sat me down in the parlor to hear the news about Dwayne Hudge. Afterward, they both assured me that the man behind the kidnappings would be crazy to come after me now, knowing he was being sought by both city and county police. I agreed with them, and we all breathed sighs of relief. We weren't fooling anyone, of course, but none of us wanted to say so.

Marco was just putting away his cell phone when Lottie let him in the front door. He strode into the parlor and sat down with us at a table. "I've made arrangements to be here with you all day. My head bartender is back on duty, so that frees me up."

"I'm so sorry to put you through this, Marco," I said. "I'm sure you have things you'd rather be doing than hanging out here all day."

"No problem, babe. I'll keep busy. Ladies, if I get underfoot, let me know. I'll be as unobtrusive as possible."

Lottie patted his hand. "Don't you worry about that. We just want our Abby to feel safe."

"Coffee?" Grace asked, holding up the pot.

"Sure." He turned a chair around to straddle it, sampled the coffee, pronounced it delicious. "I've been thinking," he said to me. "If Nils Raand is arrested, as Reilly believes will happen soon, Raand will use Uniworld's local counsel— Chinn, Knowles, and Brown. Dave Hammond won't be involved."

"Which means you won't, either," I said glumly. And since Marco had nixed Reilly and Morgan, that left one source—Charlotte's sister. But there was no way Marco would let me help search for her now.

"Speaking of Chinn," Lottie said, "we've got flowers to be delivered to Peter."

"Is he still in hospital?" Grace asked.

"Yep," Lottie said, "and no one's saying how bad his condition is."

"Poor man," Grace said. "He must have suffered quite a concussion. He's rather a large fellow, isn't he? Probably none too firm on ice. What a shame."

"Something's been bugging me all morning," Lottie said to Marco. "Nils Raand knows the cops are watching him, right? Especially after Tara was found at Uniworld. It sure doesn't seem to me that he'd be foolish enough to sneak into the jail and stab Hudge. Does it to you?"

"Or that he'd sit on a bench in full view of everyone on the town square to goad Abby," Grace pointed out.

"You're right," Marco said. "It doesn't make sense. But I doubt Raand would have killed Hudge himself. He'd most

likely hire someone. In any case, you have to view this from
a prosecutor's perspective. If the DA is convinced Raand
masterminded the kidnappings, and then the remaining kidnapper is murdered, that would only reinforce his case against
Raand. Remember, the DA is looking for a quick conviction. As Abby and I have learned, a determined prosecutor
doesn't need much more than a motive to go after someone."

"Not that I'm a fan of Raand's," Lottie said, "but what if
he wasn't behind the kidnappings? Wouldn't it make sense
for the cops to widen their search for the murderer, just to
make sure they look at all likely suspects?"

"It makes sense, but that's not how it works. Cops follow orders from the DA." Marco drained his cup. "Would
any of you mind if I used the computer? As long as I'm
here, I might as well make good use of my time."

"Go right ahead," Lottie said. "Just yell if you want anything."

"I'll be right on the other side of the curtain if you need
me, Abby." Marco headed out of the parlor, but at the doorway paused to say to me, "I'll let you know as soon as I get
someone lined up for this evening."

"Okay." I blew him a kiss, waited until he was out of
sight, then turned back with a sigh. Another babysitter. My
life was so wonderful.

Lottie leaned across the table to scrutinize me. "This is
taking its toll on you, isn't it?"

I leaned my chin on my palm. "Is it that evident?"

"You do seem rather tense about the cheekbones, dear,"
Grace said, "as though you've been clenching your jaw a
lot. Having nightmares, are you?"

I nodded sadly. "I guess I'm just not used to having a
man around all the time, driving me everywhere, watching

over me, telling me what I can and can't do. My dad worked swing shifts as a cop, so he wasn't home that much, and my brothers were always out playing sports. Most of the time it was just Mom and me."

Lottie and Grace glanced at each other. Then Lottie said, "I meant the kidnapping attempts were taking their toll. Odd that you thought I meant Marco."

I tried to laugh. "Oh, right. The kidnappings."

Grace leaned toward me, too. "Is there something you'd like to share with us, dear? Having second thoughts about furthering your relationship with Marco?"

"Absolutely not. Marco is a great guy. Look at the sacrifices he's making to keep me safe."

"It's perfectly natural to have a few doubts, love," Grace assured me. "Right, Lottie?"

"Hell, yes. Every path has a few puddles. Remember, sweetie, deep, abiding love doesn't happen overnight. It takes time—as long as there's more to your relationship than sex."

That was a discussion I definitely wasn't ready for. Fortunately, the phone rang, so I thanked them for their advice and fled.

"Bloomers Flower Shop. How may I help you?"

"Good news," Mom sang out. "The brooches are done. I finished last night."

"You made more brooches?" I glanced at the doorway, where Lottie stood with a sheepish grin.

"I told her someone bought her last one," Lottie whispered.

"Didn't you get my message?" Mom asked. "I made a dozen more. I'll run them by during my lunch hour."

Yippee?

*   *   *

Two things happened at noon: Mom brought in twelve glossy anthurium brooches to replace the one she believed we sold, and Reilly stopped by to tell us Nils Raand had been charged with conspiracy, as predicted, and taken into custody. But instead of feeling any sense of relief that I no longer had to fear Raand, and that my mom had found an avenue for her creative talent, both events vexed me.

Vex number one: We now had a dozen more of the odd little brooches to sell. If no one bought them, Mom would be hurt. If I ended up buying them myself, then stashing them in the basement, Mom would be thrilled, but my conscience would poke me mercilessly, plus I'd be out a hefty piece of change. Neither scenario looked good, but I couldn't come up with any other to take its place.

Vex number two: It was possible that Nils Raand could be found guilty of conspiracy—proven by evidence collected by the police—and sentenced to prison. That would be a good thing. On the other hand, Raand could be found innocent, also proven by evidence. That would be the justice system working as it was supposed to—unless the detectives didn't renew their search for the real conspirator afterward.

And then there was another possibility, that the prosecutor would ignore evidence that didn't lead to the outcome he wanted, which was to get Raand convicted—something he'd been known to do. That would basically suck air, because then Raand would be punished for a crime he didn't commit, the true criminal would be loose, and I could still be a target.

All the more reason for searching for Charlotte Bebe's sister. But how could I get Marco to agree with me?

"Abigail," Mom said, shaking me out of my gloomy thoughts, "what do you think of the latest batch?" She was beaming as Grace set out a mirrored tray and placed her brooches on it. "They came out very well, didn't they?"

"Lovely," Grace said.

"You've outdone yourself once again, Mom," I said, gazing at the tray of heart-shaped red leaves with their yellow spadix in the centers. My niece's original assessment was right. The brooches did look like . . . well, whatev. "The only problem is, after Valentine's Day, sometimes gift items like these brooches don't sell well. Just so you understand."

"Thanks for the warning, honey, but considering how quickly the last one was snapped up, I have every hope these will move fast, too. Do you mind if I hang on to the original, though? I want to show it to your aunt Corrine at the country club Friday night. I thought she might want me to make some brooches for her women's club benefit raffle."

"No problem. Keep it as long as you like." To be honest, I didn't care if I ever saw another anthurium brooch again, even if mine had brought out the blush in my cheeks. Makeup worked for me. But dinner at the country club? Not so much.

I hated trying to figure out which water glass was mine, how to keep my napkin from sliding off my knees, and how to get a bad piece of meat out of my mouth without anyone noticing, but I dutifully attended our weekly family dinners there because they were important to Mom. In her eyes, belonging to a country club was the epitome of class.

Thanks to my genius brothers, Jonathan and Jordan, who had joined the club as soon as they'd finished their medical residencies and established practices, Mom's dream had been partially realized, even though she and Dad couldn't afford the fees on his police salary, and Mom wasn't a member herself. Every Friday evening she gathered the Knight clan at the club to show off her highly skilled surgeon sons and her highly, um, freckled daughter.

"Abigail?" Mom asked, jerking me into the present. "Did you hear a word I said? Will you be bringing Marco to the country club with you on Friday night?"

Right. Last time we went, my family and Marco's family, whom my mom had secretly invited, threw us a surprise engagement party. The problem was that we weren't engaged. My aunt had seen me in a jewelry shop and assumed I was picking out a ring instead of what I'd actually been doing—investigating a murder.

Unfortunately, our families wouldn't believe us, so Marco and I had ended up promising to announce our engagement soon. They were still waiting, and not patiently. Which reminded me that Marco and I hadn't had that discussion yet.

First things first. Knowing Marco was within hearing distance, I took Mom's arm and walked her toward the door. "Unfortunately, Marco won't be able to make it. He took on a new PI case and will probably have to work straight through the weekend." Exaggerations did not count as lies.

"Can't he make an exception for one evening?" Mom asked.

"I'll ask, but don't count on it."

"Would you like me to ask him?"

Dear God, no. Marco wouldn't turn down an invitation from my mother for fear of offending my family. "I'm not sure I'll be able to make it, either, sadly. I'm way behind on my work here at the shop. I'll probably have to put in a few late evenings to catch up." Probably didn't count as a lie, either.

Mom looked appalled. "I'm so sorry, honey. I know how you love our get-togethers."

I shrugged, trying to look dejected. "That's the price a business owner pays, Mom. So, what time do you have to be back at school?"

She checked her watch. "Oh, phooey! I've got ten minutes to get back. Let me know what Marco says, okay?" She blew me a kiss, waved at Grace, and left.

"You won't be able to hold off taking Marco to the family dinner forever," Grace said.

"I don't need forever, only until Marco and I figure out our future."

Presuming, of course, I had one.

I headed into the workroom, where Marco was doing some research on the computer for his PI case. Draping my arms around his neck, I watched the monitor over his shoulder. "I was just thinking."

"It's never good when you start a sentence that way."

"If the DA is successful in getting Raand convicted, but Raand isn't the mastermind behind the kidnappings, the true culprit will still be out there and may come after me."

"Your point being?"

"That we should make a concerted effort to find out what the DA's evidence is. As Grace always says, 'Forewarned is forearmed.'"

"Abby."

"It wouldn't do any harm for me to call Morgan again, would it?"

"You've already trolled that pond. Morgan's not going to cooperate."

"Don't be such a pessimist. I have ways of making him talk."

Marco muttered something about me needing to have patience, but I had no time for that conversation. Leaving him to his computer work, I used the kitchen phone to dial the prosecutor's office, only to learn Morgan was in conference with the prosecutor.

"How long will he be?" I asked his secretary. "It's important I talk to him."

"It'll be a while," she said. "He and the prosecutor will be going straight into a meeting with Attorney Knowles."

"Knowles, of Chinn, Knowles, and Brown?"

"That's correct."

"Attorney Knowles represents Nils Raand, right?"

"That's correct, as well."

I had a strong hunch what that meeting was about. "Okay, thanks. I'll talk to him another time." A time when Morgan would be fully informed and ripe for the brain picking.

I hung up and quickly phoned Nikki, catching her before she left for work. "Hey, Nik, are you going to be seeing Greg this weekend?"

"We're having dinner together Friday night. Why?"

"Tell me you're not going to the country club again."

"Not for a long time. I'm still having nightmares about my close brush with the kidnappers. We're going to the new Greek restaurant instead."

Moussaka but no Mom. Perfect. "Want to double date?"

I caught movement from the corner of my eye and turned to see Marco leaning against the doorjamb, shaking his head slowly.

"Hold on, Nik." I covered the phone. "What?"

"If you have any ideas of pumping Morgan for information over dinner, forget it."

"How do you know that's what I had planned?" I whispered.

"I heard you call the prosecutor's office."

Make that *over*heard. Giving Marco a scowl, I said into the receiver, "Hold on another minute, Nikki."

I covered the phone again and whispered, "With Dave out of the picture, and with your ban on asking Reilly to help, Morgan is our best resource."

"So you're going to pump your best friend's boyfriend over dinner on a double date? That's kind of tacky, not to mention that you can barely tolerate Morgan."

"I think I should learn to like him, though, for Nikki's sake."

"You don't have a problem with taking advantage of Nikki's friendship?"

"It's what girlfriends do for each other, Marco."

He tweaked my nose. "You're cute when you're desperate."

"So, we're on with Nikki and Morgan for tomorrow night?"

"As long as you're not going to quiz Morgan."

I sighed in frustration. "Do you have a better plan?"

"Are you going to keep Nikki waiting?"

"Hey, Nik? Do you mind holding?" I listened a moment, then said to Marco, "Go ahead."

"She's going to hold?"

"No, she hung up." I replaced the receiver. "How do you propose I get the information?"

Marco shoved away from the doorjamb and headed into the workroom. "You already know my answer to that."

And wasn't accepting it. All I could see was more days of being confined to the shop or having a sitter at my apartment. More days of having to negotiate to drive my own car. More days of waking to Nikki's screams.

Wait. An idea was forming.

We had flowers to deliver to Peter Chinn at the hospital, and Marco hated hospitals. If I could convince Marco to let Lottie drive me there, I could arrange a quick stop at the prosecutor's office afterward. Plus, as long as I would be seeing Peter, I might be able to persuade him to push through my door and ramp projects.

And my mom thought her sons were the geniuses of the family.

"Lottie, are those arrangements ready to go?" I asked, returning to the workroom.

"They will be in about five minutes, sweetie."

"Hey, Marco," I said, draping my arms around his neck, "since I know you hate hospitals, how about if I help Lottie deliver flowers there today?"

"How about if I help her instead?" he asked, his eyes on the monitor.

"But I love making deliveries. I miss that."

"Okay. Then you and I can make the deliveries."

Rats. That wouldn't work.

"Lottie, dear," Grace said, coming through the curtain with a tea tray, "didn't you say earlier that you wanted to stop by the nursery to see Paula's new baby?"

Lottie and I stared at Grace in befuddlement. I had no idea who Paula was, and by the look of it, Lottie didn't, either. Then I caught a mischievous gleam in Grace's eye and understood. There was no Paula. Grace knew in that uncanny way of hers that I needed to get away from Marco for a while and was doing what she could to help.

"Oh, that's right!" I chimed in. "Paula had her baby."

Lottie caught on. "Then we'll have to stop by the nursery to see the little darlin'. I'll take real good care of our gal here, Marco. We'll pull right up to the hospital's lower level entrance so we can unload our deliveries right where the guard is. Abby can even sit in the back of the van where no one can see her. We'll be back in less than an hour."

That was called teamwork.

"What do you say?" I asked Marco.

He gave me a look that said he wasn't completely buying it. "You really want to go?"

I nodded. "I really want to go."

"You're not nervous about leaving the safety of the building?"

Well, of course I was nervous. I wasn't a total moron. Still, in a show of bravery, I shook my head. My desire to be free from whoever had *initiated* the kidnappings was stronger than my fear of *being* kidnapped.

"Okay," he said with great reluctance.

I wanted to high-five my girls, but that would have been too obvious. Instead, Lottie and I waited until he'd gone back to his Internet search; then we huddled inside the walk-in cooler, ostensibly to gather the arrangements, but really to giggle together like naughty schoolmates.

"I don't know this Paula person," Lottie whispered, "but maybe we should take flowers to her anyway." She slapped her knee, chortling. "Poor Marco. He doesn't have a clue, does he?"

CHAPTER FIFTEEN

Ten minutes later, I was riding shotgun in the rented minivan we used for deliveries, drawing vertical lines in the condensation that had formed on the glass. Seated behind the wheel was Marco, who, as it turned out, had a clue after all.

"So what was your plan?" Marco asked, pulling out of the alley. "Make your hospital run, then get Lottie to stop at the courthouse afterward so you could talk to Morgan?"

I drew crosshatches through my lines, tic-tac-toe style. "Possibly."

He reached over to run his thumb under my chin. "Sunshine, don't you trust me to get the job done?"

"Yes. But you hate hospitals, so I thought—"

"Are you sure you trust me?"

I heard the hurt in his voice and turned to reassure him. "Of course I trust you. Haven't I always relied on you to get the job done?"

"Abby, I've had to pull you out of more than a few dangerous situations because you *didn't* rely on me. You're impetuous. You rush into things without thinking them through."

"Not true. I'm just a fast thinker."

"A good PI has to come up with a strategy, set it in motion, and watch for results. That takes patience."

"But I don't work like that."

"I've noticed."

"Try to understand it from my point of view, Marco. You know how I love being independent, but right now I feel like a prisoner, unable to come and go as I please without someone always there watching me. And that's not going to change until we find out who was behind the kidnappings. So what are my options? Let the DA make his case against Raand and hope he's got the right guy? Or take immediate action ourselves?"

"My being around all the time makes you feel like a prisoner?"

Was that all he got out of my impassioned speech? "I didn't say you were the cause of my feelings. Whoever planned the kidnappings is the cause."

"This bodyguard arrangement isn't permanent, you know."

Great. Marco was stuck on the prisoner concept. "I know it's not permanent." I drew more vertical lines in the condensation. "I just wish I knew how long it would be until I wasn't in danger anymore."

"I don't know what to tell you, Abby. It is how it is. I'm doing my best to keep you safe."

I drew a box around my lines. "What if the true mastermind is never found?"

"Seriously, Abby, if you have a problem with me being around all the time—"

"No! Absolutely not! I love your being around. It's different, certainly, but . . ."

He lifted an eyebrow. Yikes. Was I making it worse? And in all honesty, why wasn't I enjoying Marco's company more? What normal, red-blooded twenty-seven-year-old woman wouldn't want a hot guy like Marco, the love of her life, the man of her dreams, keeping a protective eye on her at work—sitting at her desk and hogging her computer not withstanding—as well as bunking down in her apartment? In her small apartment. That she already shared with a roommate and a cat.

Why did my window drawing look like bars on a jail cell?

I used my coat sleeve to erase my artwork before Marco saw it. Stress, I assured myself, was causing me to think irrationally. Once everything went back to normal, so would our relationship.

"Listen, Marco. I don't mean to sound ungrateful or unwelcoming. You're merely hearing the voice of a frightened, frustrated florist." I smiled at him and reached over to squeeze his hand. "I really do appreciate you. Bear with me, okay? I'll try not to be such a pain."

"I know losing your independence is hard on you, Abby. Hell, I'd feel the same way." He squeezed my hand back. "We'll get through this together."

"Thanks for understanding."

"No problem. And I found someone to keep you company this evening."

Not another sitter!

"Rafe is working the day shift this week, and since he doesn't have wheels, he'll be bored stiff. If I can drop him at your place, I won't have to worry about him getting into trouble. You okay with that?"

More than okay. Ecstatic. If I decided to get out and do a little sleuthing, Rafe would be putty in my hands. "I suppose," I said, trying to sound resigned.

*   *   *

Marco pulled the minivan up to the rear entrance of the hospital so we could unload the two large boxes of floral arrangements. The entrance opened onto the hospital's lower level, where the laboratory and X-ray departments were located, accessible up the long hallway past the bank of elevators. Close by was the physical therapy center; through large glass windows I could see therapists working with patients.

As I waited inside for Marco, I heard a rapid *tap-tap-tap* of high heels striking the cement floor and glanced up the hallway to see a slender woman in her thirties, with big honey blond hair and an oversized, shiny gold tote bag slung over one shoulder, heading toward the entrance. I studied her as she approached. She seemed very familiar. I was sure I'd seen her recently. A flower shop customer perhaps?

As she passed, she glanced at me and did a fast double-take before hurrying on. She was probably trying to figure out how she knew me, too.

When Marco came in, we carried the boxes to the bank of elevators and rode up to the second floor.

"We're taking these to Peter Chinn in room 203," I told him, after checking the tag on one of the arrangements. "That should be at the other end of the hallway."

"You didn't tell me you were delivering flowers to Chinn."

"I didn't think it mattered."

"You're not going to harangue Chinn about your back door and ramp, are you?"

I scoffed. "He's injured, Marco. Of course I won't." Not on this visit anyway. Maybe a few subtle hints, but no haranguing.

"Then why not leave the flowers for the nurses to deliver?"

"They're busy and understaffed. And as I told you, I enjoy making deliveries."

"I'm surprised you're allowed into the patients' rooms."

"They didn't used to let me, but now that they know me, they usually do, unless the patient is seriously contagious, requests privacy, or is in the intensive care unit."

"How about the maternity ward?"

"I'm allowed."

"So did you bring those flowers for Paula?"

I glanced at Marco. *Damn.* He knew we'd made her up. I could see it in the slight upward turn of the corner of his mouth. "Busted," I said, and he shook his head.

"You're so transparent, every thought and emotion plays out on your face."

"I'm trying to correct that."

"Don't do it on my account. I like your face just the way it is."

As a courtesy, I stopped at the nurses' station to tell them my destination and get their approval. "No problem," one nurse said, waving me on. She barely gave me a glance. Marco, however, was another story. As was typical with most every female, all three nurses stopped what they were doing to watch him. In fact, two of the nurses couldn't take their gazes off him—or his hot pockets. I was surprised they didn't form a conga line behind him.

A loud moan came from one of the rooms as we trundled the boxes up the hallway.

"I hate hospitals," Marco grumbled.

"So you've mentioned. You were an Army Ranger, for heaven's sake. You've seen worse."

"Why do you think I hate hospitals?"

We stopped in front of 203, a private room. The door was open, but I knew better than to walk in without announcing myself, especially to a male patient. I called, "Floral delivery," but nobody answered.

"Would you look to see if Peter's presentable?" I asked Marco. "I don't want to embarrass him."

Setting the box on the floor outside the door, Marco walked to the end of a short hallway, past a bathroom, to see into the room. He peered around the corner, stared for a moment, then turned around and came out. "That's not Peter Chinn."

"Isn't this 203?" I checked the ticket Lottie had written for the delivery. "Oh, wait. Lottie makes sloppy numbers. I'll bet this says 208."

Marco had a contemplative frown on his face as he picked up his box and carried it back up the hallway. "I don't know who was in that room, but he reminded me of Tom Harding."

"Tom Harding?" The former owner of Tom's Green Thumb Nursery and Greenhouse, otherwise known as the first man I helped send to prison? No way. "Harding got a twenty-year sentence, Marco. If he were ill, wouldn't he be in the prison's infirmary?"

"Yes, he would. And the man I saw was heavily bandaged, so I'm sure it was a mistake."

We carried the boxes to 208, where I called, "Floral delivery," and, after receiving no response, Marco once again stepped inside.

He backed out quietly. "This is Chinn's room, but it looks like he's sleeping. Why don't you leave his flowers with the nurses? They can bring them down later."

"I hate to put that task on them. Maybe Peter's just resting his eyes. Make some noise."

Marco scowled. "No way."

I sighed. Sometimes you just had to do things yourself. Holding my box, I announced myself again, then walked up the short hallway and peered around the corner. The assistant city attorney was propped up on several pillows, eyes closed. A television mounted on the wall was tuned to CNN, and behind him, a heart monitor made a steady blip across the screen.

"Floral delivery," I called again.

Peter turned to gaze at me through half-closed lids. "Okay," he said in a singsong voice.

I waved Marco in, but he refused to set foot in the room, so I put down my box and went back for the other one. "See how simple that was?" I said to Marco.

"Just put the flowers out and come back," Marco said. "I'm leaving in two minutes."

Right. Like he could go without me. Maybe it would do him good to get a sample of what my life was like, unable to travel anywhere on my own.

"And no haranguing!" he whispered as I headed inside.

"I'll put these on your bedside table and window ledge," I said to Peter, dispersing the arrangements. "Would you like to read the cards that came with them?"

"Okay," he responded in the same dopey manner as before. I had a strong hunch he was sedated.

"How are you feeling?"

He pointed to the back of his skull. "Got a concussion."

Oh yeah. Sedated. "From a slip on the ice, right?"

He didn't reply. I studied him as I laid the gift cards on the tray table. He had his lips pressed together like a child with a secret. Hmm. What was that about? Was there more to his accident than the public knew?

"Was that how you got the concussion, Peter?"

"Not supposed to say."

I moved closer to his bed. "For legal reasons?"

He frowned, as though he was trying to remember.

"Abby, let's go," Marco said from the hallway.

"One minute," I called. I turned back to Peter. "Do you remember falling on the ice?"

He plucked at the blanket, as though he were getting agitated; then the blips on his monitor got closer together, so I backed off. "That's okay, Peter. Just keep getting better. Anything I can do for you before I go? Pour some water? Turn up the volume on the TV? Run the next planning commission meeting?"

He pursed his lips into a pout. "I rang for the nurse, but she hasn't answered. She brought me tea but forgot my honey." He sounded like a sad little boy.

"Do you want honey?"

He nodded.

"I'll be right back." I dashed into the hallway and glanced around.

"Let's go," Marco said.

"I need to find honey first." I saw a trolley cart parked down the hallway and made a beeline toward it.

"Honey who?"

Only a male would assume that referred to a woman. I found a box of honey packets on the cart, grabbed a handful, and showed him. "*Actual* honey, made by bees, for Peter's tea."

"Hey, it was an honest mistake."

"How many women named Honey do you know?"

"One, and so do you."

"Do not."

"Sure you do. Honey B. Haven. Tom Harding's girlfriend."

I came to a sudden stop. Honey B. Haven? Wait a minute. Was that the woman with the ginormous hair whom I'd seen leaving the hospital? Because if that was her, seeing both her and someone who looked like Tom Harding was an awfully big coincidence.

"Marco, I thought I saw Honey downstairs when we came in. Do you think it's possible Tom Harding *is* a patient here?"

"There'd be cops outside his door, remember?"

"Then you think it's a coincidence that Tom Harding's girlfriend was here?"

"There are all kinds of reasons for people to visit hospitals. Maybe she was visiting Paula and her new baby. Now, let's take those packets to Peter and leave."

"How about this instead?" I shoved the packets into his hands. "You take these to Peter. I'm going to see who's in room 203."

Without waiting for his response, I hurried up the hallway, only to stop short of entering the room. What if the man in that bed was the same jerk who had tried to do away with me?

Ridiculous, my little voice of reason whispered. *Do you see any cops?*

Not a single one. I took a breath and slipped inside. A large man lay beneath a blue hospital blanket, tubes in his nose and mouth, an IV in his hand, and a heart monitor behind him making slow blips across the screen. The top of his head was swathed in bandages, and his eyelids were purple and swollen, yet he did bear a striking resemblance to Harding, who was a big man—craggy-featured, thick-bodied, ham-handed, and intimidating, with eyes that were cold and a gaze that was remorseless. I'd never forget his piercing stare, or how I'd gotten entangled with him in the first place.

Through a series of events, the main one being the purchase of a box of what I thought was fertilizer, I had been able to tie Harding to a murder—make that a murder and an attempted murder (mine)—that got him sent to prison for a very long time. I knew he'd been sent away. I was in the courtroom when the sentence was read and he was led out in handcuffs. Thus, the man in that bed could not be Harding. Still, he bore a strong resemblance. Could he be a brother?

I slid his bedside chart from the holder, flipped open the cover, and focused on the name at the top. *Patient: Thomas Harding*.

I gripped the chart, staring at the name in disbelief. Tom Harding!! Why wasn't he under guard? Where were the police to keep him from escaping?

I heard footsteps coming toward the room and quickly slid the chart back in place. As I turned to go, I glanced once more at the huge form lying so deathly still.

Harding's eyes were open.

CHAPTER SIXTEEN

I froze, unable to draw a breath. Wide-eyed, all I could do was stare back. Where was my bodyguard when I needed him?

A sudden recollection flashed into my mind—the two detectives quizzing me about possible enemies.

"Anyone else you can think of who might have reason to want to harm you?"

"Not off the top of my head, but I did help put a few felons behind bars."

"How many are we talking about? Two? Three?"

"More like seven."

"You helped convict seven felons?"

"Make that eight. And they were all involved in murders."

One of those eight lay right in front of me.

Harding's puffy eyelids fluttered shut. I watched him for a moment longer, then filled my lungs with air. Had he recognized me? Was he even conscious?

I ran from the room straight into Marco's arms. "It's him," I said breathlessly. "It's Harding."

"Are you sure?"

"I saw his name on the chart! Why is that man here without cops?"

Marco ushered me away from the doorway and said quietly, "I don't know what he's doing here, but I sure as hell intend to find out."

As we started toward the central nurses' station, I said, "The nurses won't be able to tell you anything unless you're family."

"Okay, I'll call Reilly. There's a lounge on this floor somewhere, isn't there?"

He pulled out his cell phone, but I pushed his hand down before a nurse saw him. "You can't use that in here."

"Then let's go outside."

We did a quick walk to the elevator and rode down to the basement. Outside the back entrance, Marco made his call while I paced, shivering in spite of my warm coat. Seeing Harding was like being caught in a bad flashback, making me relive the terror that man had caused me.

Take it easy, Abby, my little voice of reason said. *If Harding is hooked up to all those tubes, with no cops to watch him, the man must be near death. He can't hurt you. So forget about him. Stay focused.*

"Sean," Marco said, jolting me out of my musing. "Hey, man. I have a favor to ask. Abby and I just delivered flowers to the hospital, and who should we see but Tom Harding. Yeah, formerly of Tom's Green Thumb. Right. That's what I thought. He seems to be a patient here but he doesn't have any guards. Yes, I'm serious. Will you look into it? Thanks, man."

Marco closed his phone. "Done."

"When will he get back to you?"

"As soon as he can. Are we finished here now? Can we head back to Bloomers?"

I nodded, my heart still racing. Wasn't there something I'd wanted to do after making the deliveries?

"Are you okay?" Marco asked, glancing my way as we headed toward the minivan.

"A little rattled."

"Don't worry about Harding. He's obviously not a threat."

"That's what I've been telling myself, Marco, but I'd feel a whole lot better if I knew for sure Harding wasn't going to wake up tomorrow, throw back that blanket, and leap out of bed crying, 'It's a miracle! I'm alive. Now I have a score to settle with that meddlesome florist.'"

"Abby, come on. You saw the guy. He's got tubes in every orifice."

Still, as we headed back toward Bloomers, I couldn't stop thinking about Harding. "When the detectives interviewed me, they asked about enemies, specifically the ones I'd helped put behind bars and whether any had been released. Now I can't help but wonder whether Harding was behind the kidnappings. Remember the death threats he shouted at me after I testified against him? Maybe he's trying to make good on them."

"Harding didn't look like he was in any shape to mastermind anything."

"Yeah, now. But how about before he was admitted? I'll have to ask Nikki to take a peek at his medical chart."

"Are you sure an X-ray tech has open access to medical records? You don't want her to get into trouble."

"She won't if she's careful."

At Marco's skeptical glance, I said, "It's what girlfriends do for each other, remember?"

"How about leaving Nikki out of this and letting me worry about your safety? That's why I'm here. Or don't you trust me on that, either?"

"Marco, I trust you! I know I'm overreacting. It's just not often I run into a man I hoped I'd never lay eyes on again—and vice versa."

Marco reached over to squeeze my hand. "Forget about Harding, babe. Let it go."

As if it were easy to forget that the man had tried to kill me.

Remembering one of Grace's stress-buster tips, I drew in a deep breath while imagining Tom Harding inside a big balloon. Then I let out all the air in my lungs with a *whoosh*, sending the balloon with Harding in it up to the sky to be carried off by a strong breeze.

"Okay, Tom Harding is out of my head," I reported.

"Good girl."

After another deep breath, I said, "I'm back on track. Focused."

"That's the way to do it."

"So let's stop at the courthouse to have a little chat with Greg Morgan, see what he'll tell us."

"Not gonna happen."

Fine. I knew a Salvare who would be more than happy to oblige.

Marco's cell phone rang as he was ushering me into Bloomers, so he headed toward the workroom to take the call. Since there were customers browsing, I motioned for my helpers to follow me behind the counter, where I whispered to them the account of my hospital visit. They were horrified to learn that Harding was no longer behind bars.

"And get this," I said. "Remember Harding's girlfriend, Honey B. Haven? With the big hair? I saw her coming out of the hospital. She must have been visiting him."

"His young chippy?" Lottie exclaimed, then clapped a

hand over her mouth when a customer gave her a quizzical glance.

"Honey B. Haven," Grace said, shaking her head. "What parents in their right mind would burden a child with such a name?"

"If I remember what came out during Harding's trial," I said, "Honey worked at a strip club before she met Harding. Maybe that was her stage name."

Grace cleared her throat and took hold of the edges of her cardigan.

Here it came, her quote for the day.

"As Logan Pearsall Smith once said," Grace began, " 'Our names are labels, plainly printed on the bottled essence of our past behavior.' Now, *what,* I ask you, does the name Honey B. Haven say about *her* behavior?"

Lottie snorted. "Maybe she should've called herself Honey *Mis*behavin.' "

"Did she recognize you, Abby?" Grace asked.

"I think so," I said. "She did a double take."

"You know," Lottie said, "now that you mention her, I could swear I saw a woman who looked like Honey in the shop last week."

"That's weird, because I thought I caught a glimpse of her, too," I said.

"I can't imagine Tom Harding's girlfriend setting foot in Bloomers," Grace said. "Not after Abby was instrumental in sending her man to prison. Don't you remember the hateful looks that dreadful creature was giving Abby during the trial?"

That was a memory to treasure.

"Maybe Honey was buying flowers to take to her jackass boyfriend," Lottie said.

"Here?" I asked. "Why not at Harding's former business, Tom's Green Thumb? Or even the grocery store?"

"'Tis indeed a puzzler," Grace said.

"Here's a thought," I said. "What if Harding was behind the kidnappings, and Honey stole the brooches?"

"But why single out the brooches?" Grace asked.

Marco walked up behind us. "Can I guess what this conversation is about?"

The shoppers brought a silk flower arrangement to the counter, so Grace, Marco, and I stepped away while Lottie rang them up.

"Since we have a bit of a lull," Grace said, "shall we repair to the parlor for some tea?"

"That was Reilly on the phone," Marco said as we gathered at a table with a fresh pot of tea. "He told me that after Harding was sent downstate to a prison facility, they had so much overcrowding, he was returned to our county jail to wait for an opening. While he was at the jail, he was diagnosed with lymphoma, but because the sheriff's budget can't afford long-term treatment for prisoners, he was quietly OR'd and transferred to the hospital."

"What's OR'd?" Lottie asked.

"Released on his own recognizance," Marco explained, "making Harding responsible for the cost of his medical care. In between treatments, he's allowed to recuperate at home. If and when he recovers from his illness, he'll go back to prison."

"All those bandages on his head are from his cancer treatments?" I asked.

Marco shrugged. "I don't know anything about lymphoma."

"Well, I don't care how sick he is," I said. "It doesn't seem fair to let him out of jail on his own recognizance. He should have guards."

"Marco, love," Grace said, "would you explain how it's possible for a man serving a twenty-year prison sentence to be released after a mere six months? Even an ill man? As Abby pointed out, that doesn't seem fair."

"Here's how the system works in Indiana," Marco said. "Every person sentenced to prison goes first to a central reception center to be evaluated for assignment to the appropriate facility. In Tom's case, the facility where he was assigned was severely overcrowded. Since this was Harding's first offense, someone decided he'd be a good candidate to return to the county jail to wait there.

"And by the way, most of the prisons in this state are overcrowded and getting worse by the day, but the cost of building new facilities is more than our current economy can handle, so there are a lot of inmates being OR'd."

"Is Harding being monitored at least?" Grace asked. "An ankle bracelet, perhaps?"

"I'm certain he's being monitored," Marco said. "He's just not in jail."

"So it's all about dollars and cents," Lottie said with a disgusted shake of her head. She started to sip her tea, then cocked an ear toward the doorway. "Was that the bell over the door?"

We stopped talking to listen. Lottie got up, walked to the doorway to glance around the shop, and came back. "Nobody there. I must be hearing things."

Grace clucked her tongue. "OR'd. I never knew such a thing was possible."

"I wish I didn't know," Lottie added. "It doesn't give me

a warm, fuzzy feeling. . . . Okay, now, did anyone hear *that* jingle?" She got up to look around the shop, returning a moment later. "I don't know what I keep hearing."

"Would anyone care for more tea?" Grace asked, rising.

At that moment, the bell jingled with gusto, but Lottie kept sipping her tea.

"I'll get it," I said, and stood up, causing Lottie to glance at me in surprise.

"Was that for real?"

"Yes, Lottie, dear, that was real," Grace said.

Lottie heaved a sigh of relief. "Thank goodness. I thought I was losing it."

Three of our regular coffee customers peeked into the parlor. "You're still open, aren't you?" one asked.

"Yes, we are," Grace said, going into action. "Do come in and sit down. We have lovely pecan scones today."

Break time over, Lottie stayed up front to man the shop while Marco returned to my computer, and I gathered supplies for the next order.

"What's this?" he asked.

I glanced at the shiny, credit card–sized object in his hand. It was pale green with the image of a pink hibiscus on the front. "Where did you find it?"

"On your desk." He turned it over, revealing printing on the bottom.

"Aloha Florals, Limited, Maui," Marco read. "Keahi Kana, sales associate, with a telephone number."

"Must be his business card."

"Kind of thick for a business card." Marco examined it, then pressed a button on one edge and a beam of light came from the other. "It's a pocket flashlight."

He handed it to me, and I switched it off and on again. "Perfect for my purse. It feels good, too, silky smooth. Looks like it's made from crushed seashells."

Lottie came through the curtain and saw us playing with it. "Oh, I forgot to tell you, that salesman I mentioned yesterday—the one offering those great bargain prices on exotics—left that for you. He said to give him a call if you're interested in placing an order."

"Determined, isn't he?" Marco said, returning to the computer screen.

"That's a salesman for you," Lottie said. "Always trying to push something, always with an agenda, always schmoozing with clients, yakkity-yakkity-yak all the time. I can't imagine living like that."

The bell over the door jingled, prompting Lottie to grab the basket she had come for and return to the front, still grumbling to herself.

"I can imagine it," Marco muttered.

I stowed the flashlight in my purse, then studied the next order. *Okay, here we go. An anniversary bouquet for delivery tomorrow morning.* I glanced at the clock on the wall. One hour before closing. Plenty of time for me to do the bouquet.

Or . . .

I could try to find out why Harding was in the hospital.

Hold it, Flower Girl. Tom Harding isn't going anywhere anytime soon. So let's focus on our career so it doesn't fall into the toilet, okay?

Sometimes that voice of reason wasn't reasonable at all. If Harding was dying, would it hurt to find out how long he had? Ghoulish or not, I wouldn't breathe easy until Harding's balloon had passed way beyond *my* stratosphere.

I slipped into the kitchen, lifted the receiver from the

base on the wall, and punched in Nikki's cell phone number. She'd be on duty in the X-ray department, so I hoped she'd have time to slip up to the second-floor nurses' station and take a peek at Harding's chart.

So as not to be overheard by Hot Pockets, I stretched the cord all the way over to the hallway that led to the basement and sat down on the top stair. I hated corded phones, but at least this cord was long.

My call went straight to Nikki's voice mail. *Damn.* I forgot the hospital rule that the employees had to keep their phones off during work hours. Now what?

There was a tug on the cord. I glanced around and there stood the light of my life, arms folded, gazing at me speculatively. "What are you doing?"

"I was . . . ordering your birthday present. I didn't want you to hear what I got you."

"Ordering my present? Really. Do you know when my birthday is?"

"Well, of course I know!"

He lifted an eyebrow, waiting.

Marco's birthday was—*damn!* How could I have forgotten it?

Oh, wait. I knew this one. It was three days before Nikki's. "July fifteenth." I smiled.

"You're ordering a present five months in advance?"

"Well," I said, my mind working at warp speed, "it takes that long to . . . be . . . manufactured."

"Manufactured?"

"Actually, made by hand. Don't ask me any more questions about it, because I won't answer. It's a surprise."

A surprise to both of us.

"Well," I said, rising, "now that *that's* done, I can get back to work." Ignoring Marco's questioning gaze, I replaced the receiver and returned to the workroom, making straight for the walk-in cooler. I stepped inside and began to pull stems for the order.

Okay, back to the Harding puzzle. Nikki wasn't answering her phone, so either I'd have to wait until tomorrow and hope she had time to do a little detective work during the afternoon, or I could drop by the hospital tonight to ask her in person. So, do it sooner or later?

A no-brainer for sure.

With only thirty minutes to go before we turned the sign to CLOSED, I got a call on my cell phone from my cousin, Jillian the pest.

"Hey, Abs? Your mom said she made more brooches, but before I make the trip down to Bloomers again, you *do* have one I can buy, right?"

"I do. In fact, I have twelve brooches, Jillian."

"I don't need to buy twelve. Just one."

"I didn't say you had to *buy* twelve. What I meant was—never mind. Do you want me to gift wrap one for you?"

"That'd be awesome. Do you have gold paper?"

"No, floral."

"How about silver?"

"Floral, Jillian. When did you see my mom?"

"I was having lunch with my mom when your mom called about dinner at the club tomorrow night, and she mentioned making more brooches. She also said to remind you to bring Marco."

"Marco can't make it tomorrow."

"Wink, wink," Jillian said.

"No, seriously, Jill, he has to work on a PI case."

Jillian huffed. "How are you two ever going to make a

marriage work with you spending your days at Bloomers and Marco spending his nights doing two other jobs?"

That was an issue we hadn't tackled yet, and I wasn't about to get into it now with Jillian. I carried my cell phone into the shop, heading toward the armoire to pick out one of the brooches. "Are you going to stop by for the brooch before we close?"

"Yes, if you're sure you *have* a brooch for me."

"I told you, Jillian, I have twelve—"

Make that none.

CHAPTER SEVENTEEN

The mirrored tray was empty. Where did the brooches go?
"Hold on, Jillian." I glanced around at Lottie, who
was rearranging the flowers in the glass case. "Did you sell
any brooches today?"

"No, why?"

"I can't find them."

"You gotta be kidding me." Lottie took a look for herself, then headed toward the parlor. At the doorway, she
asked, "Gracie, did you put the brooches somewhere?"

"On the mirrored tray."

"They're not on the tray now," Lottie said.

Grace came out of the parlor to help us search the shop;
then the three of us stood in front of the armoire, staring at
the empty tray as if somehow the brooches would magically
reappear.

"I'll be doggone," Lottie said. "Someone swiped 'em
again."

"Do we have a thief with an anthurium fetish?" Grace
asked.

"Abby!" the phone squawked.

"Jillian, I'll have to call you back." I hit the END button and set the cell phone on the armoire.

"What the hell is going on with these brooches?" Lottie asked.

Marco came through the curtain. "Something wrong?"

"The damn brooches are gone," Lottie said. "All twelve of 'em. Now, how could someone get a dozen brooches out of here without us seeing a thing?"

"Remember when you thought you heard the bell jingle?" Grace asked Lottie. "Is it possible someone slipped in and nicked them?"

"But I looked twice and didn't see anybody," Lottie said.

"Still," Grace said, "it's odd you heard the jingle twice, isn't it?"

"Did you just discover they were gone?" Marco asked.

"Jillian called about them," I said. "Otherwise I probably wouldn't have noticed until tomorrow."

"Perhaps," Grace said, "our thief slipped in while we were preoccupied with the Harding matter, hid behind the counter, emptied the brooches into a bag, and slipped out again."

"Sneaky devil," Lottie said. "I'd sure like to get my hands on him."

"Or her," Marco said.

We all turned to gaze at him, but I guessed at once what he was going to say. "Honey B. Haven?"

He shook his head. "Jillian."

"It wasn't Jillian!" I cried.

"Then why is it," he posed, "that each time your cousin inquires about a brooch, you can't find it? You search all over the shop, then decide it's been stolen. Next step is for Jillian to come in and raise a stink over it, so that you're tripping all over yourself trying to make it up to her."

"I do not trip all over myself. I just feel bad when she comes down here for nothing, not to mention that someone is stealing my merchandise."

"Maybe that's the idea," Marco said. "She wants to make you feel bad."

"Surely Abby's cousin wouldn't be so cruel as to steal as a practical joke," Grace said.

"And it's not like she can't afford to buy the brooch," Lottie added.

"Marco's theory is that Jillian is playing with my mind," I explained with an eye roll.

"Mind games?" Grace asked. "For what purpose?"

"I get what Marco means," Lottie said. "Jillian wants to be like big cousin Abby, and at the same time she resents Abby for it because she sees herself as superior. So this is her way of getting back—playing little mind games."

"Jillian isn't that clever," Grace said flatly.

"That would be a pretty sick joke, even for her," I said.

Marco lifted an eyebrow. I was always amazed how much he could convey with that tiny gesture. "It's worth investigating before we file a police report, isn't it?"

"How do you plan to investigate?" I asked warily.

"To start with, I'll have a little talk with her."

"Talk," I asked, feeling a sliver of panic in my gut, "as in interrogate?"

"I wouldn't go that far," Marco said, "unless I have to."

"Oh, Lordy," Lottie said, rolling her eyes.

"Questioning Jillian would be a very bad idea, Marco," I said. "She's a lot shrewder than she looks . . . or acts . . . or talks. If you start quizzing her about the brooch, she'll know right away you suspect her of stealing it."

"She has that animal cunning," Grace added.

Marco sighed impatiently. "I know how to do my job."

"You don't understand," I said. "It's not Jillian who concerns me as much as what this could do to my already tarnished reputation in the family. I mean, they're still trying to figure out how I got booted from law school. Then to have the man to whom they are expecting me to become engaged treating my own cousin as a suspect in a robbery?"

"Wouldn't be good," Lottie said, shaking her head.

"Do you have any idea what they'll do if they find out you interrogated Jillian about the brooches?" I asked him. "Picture a school of hungry piranhas—"

"Calm down, Sunshine," Marco said. "Wouldn't you rather have me talk to Jillian than have the police pick her up for questioning?"

"Why? It'd be off our shoulders."

"Maybe so, but what if the police find out that Jillian's the culprit?" Marco asked.

"Again, Marco. Off. Our. Shoulders."

He took the phone from the shelf and hit REDIAL, then held it up high when I tried to get it from him. He turned his back on me to say, "Jillian. Hey, it's Marco. Would you come down to Bloomers? It won't take long. Yep, it's about the brooch. Thank you."

He hit END and gave me the phone.

I blinked rapidly, trying to fire up my stunned brain cells. "You asked Jillian to come here?"

"It's always better to confront in person."

"But here? Where I am?"

"And where I am."

Where I wished he wasn't at that moment.

I sank onto the wicker settee next to the armoire and leaned my head back with a groan. Marco was going to confront drama queen Jillian Ophelia Knight-Osborne. In my shop. I would pay for this forever.

*   *   *

When Jillian breezed in fifteen minutes later, Lottie came to let us know, then said, "Grace is cleaning the coffeepots in the parlor and I'll be in the kitchen . . . hiding."

Marco got up. "Let me handle it."

"No problem," I said. "I'll just retire to the cooler until the furor dies down."

"There's not going to be a furor. I know how to deal with your cousin."

"Right. Thaw me gently."

Marco shook his head and stepped through the curtain into the shop. I eyed the cooler, then sighed and followed him. It wasn't often I got to witness someone self-destruct.

Jillian was standing in front of the counter, arms folded, wearing a short black-and-white leopard print swing coat, red cashmere beret, shiny red tote bag, and black patent boots. She glanced from Marco to me. "Where's the brooch? Do you have it wrapped yet? I'm in a hurry."

"Nice beret," Marco said, leaning his hip against the counter.

I stared at him, trying to get him to see the pleading look in my eyes: *Don't do this, Marco*. He ignored me.

Unable to resist a compliment, Jillian took off her beret and patted it. "Thanks. I got it to replace the one that was stolen."

"Reminds me of Abby's," Marco said.

She glanced at me. "You have a beret?"

There was my opening to firm up our cousin bond and possibly salvage Marco's standing with my family. I gave her a playful punch. "Come on, Jilly," I said, using the nickname I'd given her when we were little. "You remember my Kelly green wool beret that we got last St. Patrick's Day at Target."

"Stop," she cried, looking horrified. She hated to admit to shopping anywhere but on Chicago's Magnificent Mile. "I remember, okay?"

"Abby was wearing the brooch on her beret before her mom borrowed it to make copies," Marco added, watching her closely. "Remember now?"

Jillian studied my head. "S.O.R.'ing."

Wonderful. She was making up words again. "Translate," I snapped, then quickly added with a smile, "please?"

She huffed. "S.O.R. Sort of remembering. Don't you text?"

"Sort of remember more," I said.

She pressed her fingertips to her temples and closed her eyes. "Okay, I think I remember seeing you wearing your green beret when you were on the news after someone hurled that brick through the door. And yes, I do remember seeing the brooch on it. You were standing outside the shop, right? Holding a press conference or something?"

Marco gave me a scowl. "Yeah, an impromptu press conference just after she was told to keep a low profile."

Jillian's eyes opened. "There. Satisfied?"

"That certainly does it for me," I said. "Thank you for being so helpful!"

"I have a question," Marco said.

"Can't you save that for another time?" I asked him. "Sweetheart?"

"Can you describe the beret that was stolen from you?" Marco asked.

"Why?" Jillian asked skeptically. "Don't tell me the cops actually found it."

"This is for my own investigation," he replied.

"Oh. Well, it's hand-stitched black Italian leather, and I hope you have better luck than the police, because my dad brought it back from Naples, Italy, for my twenty-first birthday, and I'm very attached to it."

"Your twenty-first birthday," I said, "which was five years ago, whereas I bought my beret last year." I gave Marco a pointed look. "So Jillian had hers *first.*"

He tipped his head, acknowledging my point.

Jillian glanced at her watch. "Okay, it's been fun reminiscing, but I really need to pay for the brooch and go."

"Just one more question," he said, giving her a hint of a smile.

I groaned inwardly. Couldn't Marco let well enough alone?

"Who are you buying the brooch for today?" he asked.

"Me," she said. "The way Abby's mom has been raving about them, I decided I should have one. Why? Does it matter?"

"If the brooch is for you," Marco asked, neatly side-stepping her question, "why do you want it wrapped?"

Jillian sighed, as if the answer was obvious. "Because Claymore is giving it to me as a surprise."

I smiled at Marco. From the bemused look on his face, I could tell he was ready to call it quits. I was vindicated!

"Now, can I have my brooch, please?" Jillian said. "I want to open my present at dinner." She pulled a credit card from her wallet and held it out. "Use this. I just paid it off."

Marco moved aside. "That's Abby's department."

What? Leave me to clean up his mess? I scowled at him. Some bodyguard he was.

Trying to portray abject wretchedness, I said to my cousin, "I am *so* sorry to tell you this, Jilly, but it seems we don't have any brooches after all. They were stolen."

All sounds from the coffee-and-tea parlor ceased. Obviously Grace was eavesdropping. Only the ticking of an anniversary clock on the shelf behind me could be heard as my cousin absorbed the news, as if the shop itself were holding its breath.

Suddenly, Jillian's nostrils flared, her hands curled at her sides, and her lips pressed into a hard line. "Then *what* am I *doing* here?"

"Well," I said slowly, trying to think of how to pacify her, "you're here because . . ."

"*I* asked you here," Marco said, fixing her with his most sincere gaze.

What was he doing? He wasn't going to tell her his real reason, was he? Never mind; I couldn't take any chances. "That's right—Marco asked you here because I need your help."

Jillian's lips plumped into a perplexed pout. "Let me see if I understand this. Marco asked me to come over because *you* need my help?"

"Yes! Knowing how enlightened you are about fashion," I continued, "and how socially connected you are, we—I mean I—thought you'd be the perfect person to keep an eye out for someone wearing one of the stolen brooches."

Jillian tapped the toe of her high-heeled boot on the floor. "Is that so? And you couldn't tell me this on the phone? I had to drive here through snowdrifts, in this subarctic cold?"

Three inches of snow did not constitute a drift, and the temperature was thirty-three degrees Fahrenheit. Still, I was in no position to debate it. I shrugged. "But then we wouldn't have had this chance to visit."

Jillian drew in a deep breath. She let it out slowly, as though composing herself. Or maybe she was sending me up in a balloon. Whatever it was, she managed to say in a civil tone, "While it may be true about my fashion expertise and well-fixed social position, if you will remember, except for that one blurry image of your beret on the news, I have yet to *see* any of the missing brooches! Every time I've come here, they've been gone.

"But wait," she cried dramatically, "not just gone. *Stolen! Filched! Purloined!* Right out from under your nose! And not once but three—count them—*three* times. I mean, come on, people. Buy a security camera. This is getting tiresome!"

Huffing indignantly, she whipped out her cell phone, gave me one last dirty look, and headed for the door. "Hi, Claymore? You won't believe what Abby did this time."

The bell jingled behind her.

Marco's eyebrows were higher than I'd ever seen them. But it wasn't like I hadn't warned him. "I've never seen her turn on you before," he said in wonder.

"That could have been you, dear," Grace said to Marco, as she and Lottie came back into the room from different doorways.

"You should be grateful, Marco," Lottie said, winking discreetly at me. "Abby took the bullet for you."

"The main thing is that Jillian doesn't know you suspect her," I told Marco. "I think we're safe as far as the family goes."

"Boy oh boy, Jillian was madder than a wet hen," Lottie said with a chuckle. "I could feel it through the curtain. Woo-ee!"

"But we're still missing the brooches," I said, "so we'd better file another police report. I'll call Reilly and see if he's around to take the report." I glanced at Marco to see if he was in agreement, but he was headed for the workroom like a man on a mission.

I made the call, then went to tell Marco. He was working at the computer, typing words into a search box, while Lottie finished a silk flower arrangement at the worktable behind him.

"I left a message for Reilly. What are you searching?" I asked, leaning over his shoulder.

Marco was concentrating, so his answer came out in bursts. "Jillian mentioned the brooch—news conference—checking something."

He had typed *flower brooch* into the box, and was resting his chin on his hand, reading through the links, so I prompted him to fill in the blanks. "Jillian mentioned seeing the brooch on my beret at the news conference and you're researching flower brooches because . . . ?"

"It got me to thinking about who else might have seen it."

"What do you mean? Like a professional brooch thief?"

"Where did you say you got it?"

"It was lying loose in a box of orchids, but I called our supplier in Hawaii and he didn't know anything about it. He said to keep it unless I heard otherwise."

Marco scrolled through the links on the first page. "Two and a half million results. We have to narrow the search."

"Try anthurium brooch," I said.

He typed it in, glanced down the list of links, then clicked on *Hawaiian collectibles: Antiques and Hawaiiana.* Up popped a page full of photos of flower pins, pendants, and brooches in a variety of materials. I watched over Marco's shoulder as he scrolled down the page.

"There's an ivory anthurium brooch," I said, pointing to the image on the screen. "That looks a lot like the one I found."

Marco clicked on the photo, but all it did was enlarge it. "I'll have to get in touch with the dealer to find out more about their brooches. The pieces on this site are all collectors' items."

"Maybe the one you found is a collector's item, too," Lottie said.

"If it were valuable," I said, "you'd think it would be packaged in a cushioned box."

"Maybe a woman packed the flowers and didn't realize her brooch fell into the box," Lottie offered.

Marco dialed the phone number on the Web site's home page, then held his hand over the receiver. "It's an automated menu. I have to leave contact information." He removed his hand and gave his name and cell phone number, then left a brief description of the brooch.

"Here's a thought," Lottie said. "Remember when the phony delivery man came by for a package he claimed was delivered to us by mistake, and that man turned out to be Hudge? Maybe we did get someone else's package and he came to pick it up."

"So you're saying Hudge pulled off those kidnappings to get the brooch?" I asked.

Marco turned to look at Lottie. "When did Hudge come here?"

"Right after the flower shop was trashed," Lottie said.

"Why don't I remember that?" Marco asked.

"You were checking out the other rooms for damage when we discussed it," Lottie said. "Sergeant Reilly was making out a report, and I said I wondered whether the damage was the result of a plain ol' robbery instead of Uniworld trying to retaliate."

The phone rang and Grace caught it out front, then came back to say that Reilly was on the line. Marco picked it up at my desk. "Hey, Sean. Yes, Abby did call. Right, and this time twelve brooches were taken. Three brooch-related thefts. We've definitely got something going on here, so we'll need to file a police report. Sure. I'll hold."

"Abby," Lottie said, "Gracie and I are going to close up shop now."

"Okay," I said. "See you tomorrow."

Marco glanced at the clock. "Five o'clock? Damn. I haven't been down to the bar yet."

Reilly came back on the line, so Marco turned away to talk to him while I cleaned up the worktable. As I brushed bits of leaves and blossoms into the plastic-lined trash can, I started thinking back over the times my mom's brooches had turned up missing. The first theft happened after I appeared on our local cable TV news station. Was that a coincidence or, as Marco mentioned, had someone with a reason to care spotted the anthurium on my hat? Was it possible Dwayne Hudge was working for a jewelry thief?

Marco ended his call and got up. "Reilly said no viable fingerprints were collected when Bloomers was trashed, and right now they don't have any leads."

"You mentioned that someone might have spotted me wearing the brooch. What if Hudge and Charlotte were hired to get it back?"

Marco's eyebrows pulled together. "I guess it would explain the theft of the brooches, although I still think Jillian should be a suspect."

"It would also explain why Jillian's beret was snatched."

"But it doesn't explain why they kidnapped Tara. She wasn't wearing a beret."

"We were dressed alike. Maybe they were planning to hold me until I gave up the brooch."

"That would be risky."

"They were bunglers, Marco. And I just remembered something else. When Jillian was nabbed, she said the kidnapper told her to give *it* up. Do you remember that? The brooch has to be what they were after."

"We could speculate all evening, and I wish I had time for that, but Reilly is sending officers to take the report and dust for prints, so while they're here, I've got to run down to the bar to check on things and get my accounting done, or there won't be any paychecks to hand out this week. I'll be back afterward to take you home, pick up Rafe, and drop him at your place so I can squeeze in a couple of hours of work at the bar before I start on my PI case."

I was exhausted just thinking about all he had to do. Poor Marco, dealing with stolen brooches, kidnapping attempts, wayward younger brothers, his bar, my crazy family, and me, in addition to his private investigator work. He really was my hero.

But we absolutely did have to discuss the issue about our conflicting work hours. Soon.

As he stood there in his fitted shirt, tight jeans, and worn boots, his dark hair curling around his ears, a five-o'clock shadow on his handsome face, I couldn't resist slipping my arms around his waist. "You go to a lot of trouble for me, Salvare."

That was all it took to get his juices flowing. His eyes darkened in that seductive way of his and one corner of his mouth quirked. "You know what I always say about paybacks." Then he dipped his head down for a deep, smoldering kiss—that was interrupted a moment later by a sharp rap on the front door.

Marco gave me one more quick kiss, then strode through the curtain to let in the cops.

Chapter Eighteen

By six o'clock that evening, I was at home, dead bolt and chain in place, just finishing the last bite of a turkey sandwich, when two handsome Salvare men showed up at my door, one a younger, slightly thinner version of the other.

"Hey, Hot Stuff," Rafe said, sauntering into my apartment, "your bodyguards are here." He winked at me. "Looking good, as always."

"Thank you, Rafe," I said, rolling my eyes at Marco. Rafe was a shameless flirt.

"Hey," Marco called to him from the doorway. "Remember what I told you."

"No prob, bro." Rafe continued into the living room and turned on the TV, putting himself out of sight and earshot.

"Did the cops find any prints?" Marco asked me.

"Nothing useful. Just smudges, probably most of them mine, Lottie's, and Grace's. How the thief was able to scoop up a dozen brooches without us hearing anything still alarms me."

"Have you told your mom yet?"

"I did, and of course Mom took it as a sign that she should make more. She wants us to lock her next batch in the glass case where we keep the crystal figurines. She said she's going to call the pawnshops in the area to let them know to watch for her brooches."

"At least she wasn't upset." Marco drew me against him. "I've got to get going."

"I wish you didn't have to work these late evening hours, Marco."

"Sometimes it can't be helped. I don't plan to do it forever."

"Can we kiss on that?"

With a little grin playing at one corner of his mouth, Marco tilted his head, his lips meeting mine in a kiss that got hotter by the second.

"Sure you can't stay?" I murmured dreamily, as he nibbled his way along my jaw.

He pressed his lips in the hollow behind my ear, a spot he'd discovered made me go weak in the knees. "I wish." Then he tilted my chin so he could gaze into my eyes.

"Are you going to lecture me now?" I asked, still in my stuporous state.

"Yes, so pay attention."

"You can be bossy at times."

"Don't let Rafe talk you into leaving the apartment. I told him he's your bodyguard tonight, and your safety is in his hands until I get back. Got it?"

"Word for word." I leaned into him for another kiss and Marco happily complied. Then he tilted my chin up again.

"Don't wait up for me. It'll be late by the time I pick Rafe up and drop him off at home again."

"Okay." Or maybe I would wait up and surprise him.

We shared one more long kiss; then he had to go. "Remember what I told you," he called as he started down the hallway.

"And *you* remember that a closed bathroom door means you have to knock before entering."

He gave me a thumbs-up. Then I shut the door, slid the chain into place, and headed for the living room. Time to put my plan into action.

Rafe was sprawled on the sofa, watching TV. I blocked his view. "Do you really want to watch a basketball game all evening or would you rather take a field trip with me?"

Rafe swung his legs to the floor. "A leaving-the-apartment type of field trip?"

"I need to pay a visit to Nikki at the hospital."

"She's sick?"

"No, on duty. Nikki works there. I need some information from her."

"Whoa. Back up, Freckles. Marco gave me strict instructions to stay *here* with you. He'll kill me if I let you leave."

I sat down beside him. "That's not what I heard Marco say. He told *me* you were going to be my bodyguard this evening."

Rafe looked confused. "So?"

"So he didn't say you were going to be my babysitter. There's an important difference. Sitters watch their charges in a home. Bodyguards protect their charges everywhere. Do you see what I mean?"

"Well, yeah, except he said not to leave here."

Rafe was such a babe in the woods. "Marco's exact words to me were 'Don't let him talk you into leaving the apartment,' which you're not. Again, an important difference."

A light went on in Rafe's head. He hopped off the sofa with a devilish grin. "I'm ready when you are."

* * *

In the parking lot, I discovered that Marco had taken his Prius, leaving me my bright yellow Vette—not exactly camouflage material. Not enough to deter me from my mission, either. Thinking it would be better if I wasn't seen behind the wheel, however, I made the mistake of letting Rafe drive, then held on to my seat with a white-knuckled grip as we sped away from every stop sign and light between apartment and hospital. In between hanging on for dear life and ordering him to drop his speed, I explained the purpose of our trip.

"Damn! I don't blame you for wanting to be sure Harding's on his last breath," Rafe said.

"So how about slowing down even more so we're not about to draw *our* last breath?"

We parked on the top floor of the hospital garage—less chance of being seen—then took the stairs to the main level and crossed the street to the hospital. I steered Rafe toward the X-ray department in the basement and asked the volunteer at the sign-in desk for Nikki.

A few minutes later, Nikki and another tech came out of a doorway in the back, both women dressed in green uniforms. "Abby, is everything all right?" Nikki asked.

"We're fine," I said as Rafe gazed appreciatively at the attractive girl at Nikki's side. "I just had a question for you."

Rafe held out his hand to Nikki's coworker, turning the full force of his charm on her. "Hi, I'm Rafe Salvare. And you are . . . ?"

The young woman blushed as she took his hand. "Erin Sells."

"An X-ray technician, I see," Rafe said.

Nikki took me aside to whisper, "Is he your sitter tonight?"

I held my index finger to my lips to hush her. "I have to ask a really big favor, Nik. Tom Harding is a patient on the second floor, and I need to know why he's been admitted."

"Harding's here?" she whispered, her eyes huge. "I haven't seen any cops on that floor."

"He isn't being guarded. He was released because of his health. It's a long story that I'll tell you later. Right now, I really need to know how bad off he is. Can you help me out?"

"I'd like to, Ab, but I can't get into the filing cabinet up there without permission. I could be sanctioned for doing that."

"Can't you just glance at the chart at the foot of Harding's bed?"

"That contains only his immediate information, like current meds and dosages, temperature and blood pressure readings. Everything else, including his medical history, is kept in a file at the nurses' station."

"There's no way you can sneak a little peek for me?"

Nikki wrinkled her forehead, looking worried. "I don't know, Ab. . . ."

"If you don't feel safe, then forget it," I said.

"Well," she said, "maybe if the nurses weren't around, I could take a fast look."

We managed to drag Rafe away from Erin, then took the elevator to the second floor and waited while Nikki checked out the nurses on duty. She came back moments later to report that there were two presently at the station.

"Now we need a diversion," I said.

"I could take off my clothes and streak past them," Rafe offered.

"And wind up in the psych ward," Nikki said.

"Or jail," I said. "How about if I stage an accident on the landing between floors? Rafe, you can run to the nurses to get help for me, and while they're away, Nikki, you can take a look at Harding's chart."

Nikki thought it over, then shrugged. "We can try."

We stepped into the stairwell next to the elevator bank to check out the scene of the so-called accident. I hurried down to the landing and sat down on the cold metal, making sure to twist one leg under me. "How does this look?"

"Perfect," Nikki said as I rose to brush myself off. "I'll watch for the right moment, then send Rafe back here to signal you to get into place."

We high-fived each other. A door opened above and footsteps came our way, so we scooted up the stairs and waited outside the door until Rafe peered in and declared it clear.

"What should I do if someone finds me before the nurses get there?" I asked.

"Moan," Nikki said, "loudly. And don't let anyone move you until the nurses examine you. As soon as I take a look at the chart, I'll come to the stairwell and let you know."

"Okay, sounds like a plan." I watched them head out the door; then I dashed down to the landing, hoping we hadn't forgotten anything.

As the minutes ticked by, I began muttering, "Hurry up, hurry up," and checking my watch—it was almost seven o'clock—until Rafe finally appeared and motioned for me to get into position. Then he dashed away, and I arranged my legs to look as though I'd slipped down the last few steps, hoping no one else stumbled upon our staged scene.

Suddenly, the door above me opened, and I heard Rafe say, "She's down there."

I moaned and rubbed my right ankle as the nurses hurried down the steps toward me. One of the nurses, a woman whose name tag said *Teresa Warner*, crouched down to examine my right leg. She felt along my calf and shin, probed the bones in my ankle, and turned my foot. I gasped for effect, but not enough to raise any big concerns, or so I thought.

"I think I just bruised something," I said, wincing. "Rafe, help me up."

"We need to get you to X-ray," Teresa said. "You might have a broken bone."

Oh no! That would require time and money I wasn't willing to spend. "I'm sure I'll be fine. Rafe, would you help me up, please?"

"No, don't do that," the other nurse said, dashing up the stairs. "I'll call for assistance."

I glanced at Rafe and gave him a *help me now* look.

At that moment, Nikki came through the door, saw me, and cried, "Abby, what happened?"

"I missed a few steps," I said as Nikki raced down the stairs toward me. "Teresa thinks I might have a broken bone."

"Let's get you down to X-ray," she said. To Nurse Teresa she said, "I know these two. I'll take responsibility for them."

Rafe scooped me up and started down the stairs, calling back, "X-ray's in the basement, right?"

"I'll show you," Nikki offered, leading the way.

I glanced over Rafe's shoulder at the stunned nurse. "Thanks, Teresa. You've been a great help."

"You're a lot heavier than you look," Rafe grunted, setting me down at the bottom. He wiped the sweat off his brow with the back of his hand.

"Thanks for that."

"Come on," Nikki said, pushing on the door that led into the basement hallway. She took us to a waiting area filled with people, where we huddled in a corner to hear Nikki's report.

"Harding's not dying from cancer," she said quietly. "His lymphoma is in remission."

"Then why is he here?" I asked.

"According to his chart," Nikki said, "Harding has multiple contusions, abrasions—"

"In English, Nikki," I said. "The condensed version."

"He's in a coma."

"A coma? From what?"

Nikki shrugged. "There's nothing in the file about how he came to be in that condition, only what his condition is—severe trauma to his head, a crack in his skull, concussion, cuts, bruises, frostbite on his hands and face . . . Right now, he's at high risk for dying."

"When I saw Harding," I said, "his eyes were open. Was he in a coma then?"

"Yes. That's actually a common occurrence. The eyes are open, but we don't know if the person actually sees anything."

"Here's what I want to know," I said. "If Harding pulls through, will he be released or stay on for further cancer treatment?"

"Unless further tests show the cancer is flaring up, or he needs physical therapy from his head trauma, he'll be released."

That was not what I wanted to hear. "Did you happen to notice when Harding was admitted?" I asked.

"This morning."

"What about for his cancer treatment?"

"Gee, I glanced at the file so quickly, but I believe he was transferred in about four weeks ago. I know he was released after five days of treatment. He'd probably be due back soon for follow-up blood—"

"Nikki," we heard someone whisper. I glanced around and saw the other X-ray tech, Erin, motioning to her.

"I'll be right there," Nikki called back. "I've got to go, Abby."

"Promise me you'll keep an eye out in case Harding does recover and is released."

"Of course."

"Thanks for your help, Nik," I said, giving her a hug. "I know you took a risk for me."

"You'd do the same for me."

Make that I'd *done* the same for her.

I turned to look for Rafe and saw him leaning against the wall, flirting with Erin. "Rafe," I called. "Let's go."

As he started toward me, Nikki said, "Wait, Abby. I just remembered something."

I grabbed Rafe's coat sleeve before he could head back toward Erin. "How about pulling the car up to the door, Romeo?"

"Will do," Rafe said, then winked at Erin and strode toward the door.

"Slowly!" I called before turning back to Nikki. "What did you remember?"

"H. Bebe was listed on the initial admission form as Harding's contact person."

"Charlotte H. Bebe?"

"It just said H. Bebe. I figured it was either her or a relative." Nikki showed me the digits she'd jotted on her palm. "Here's the number if you want to look it up."

"Better yet," I said, moving closer to the exit, "I'll call and see who answers. It certainly wouldn't be Charlotte." As I pulled out my cell phone and punched in the number, I said to Nikki, "Do you realize that if H. Bebe *is* Charlotte, we'll have a link between Harding and the kidnappers?"

"Hello?" a female voice said in my ear.

Yikes. I hadn't planned what to say. "I'm, um, looking for a friend of mine. To whom am I speaking, please?"

"Just tell me your friend's name," came her curt reply.

"Charlotte."

The woman's voice became brittle. "What is this? A sick joke?"

"No! Not at all. I just—"

The line went dead.

"What happened?" Nikki asked as I slid my phone into my purse.

"The woman on the other end accused me of playing a sick joke on her."

"She wouldn't say that unless she knew Charlotte was dead."

"It must be Charlotte's sister!" I hit REDIAL, hoping I could keep her on the phone long enough to explain why I'd called, but this time it went straight to voice mail.

Nikki's pager beeped. She glanced around at Erin, who was gesturing for her to hurry. "I have to go, Ab. See you at home." As she trotted up the hallway, she called back, "Are we still on for our double-date dinner tomorrow night?"

"Sure are."

"That'll be fun."

For some of us more than others.

Outside, I found Rafe waiting with my car. I slid into

the passenger seat and showed him the number on my palm. "I need to find out who this woman is."

"Let's get to a computer," he said.

Back at my apartment, Rafe headed toward the fridge for a beer, while I hung my coat on the back of the chair. "If we can find this H. Bebe's address, Rafe, and it isn't far from here, are you up for another field trip tonight?"

"Just say the word."

"Let's not bother Marco with the details of our evening, okay? I can tell him Nikki provided the information, but he doesn't need to know we left here to get it."

"Kind of a quid pro quo deal, then, right?"

"What do you mean?"

Rafe twisted the cap off a bottle and took a swig. "I mean, I'll keep quiet, but then you owe me a favor."

Great. Another payback. I tossed my car keys on the counter. "What's the favor?"

"I met this awesome girl at Hooters, and I want to take her out Friday night, but I don't have wheels, so . . ." He picked up my car keys and dangled them, smiling.

My stomach sank. The speed demon wanted to use my Vette? I'd walked right into that one. It was fair punishment, I supposed, for going behind Marco's back.

I took a deep breath and blew it out. "Okay. Sure. If you—"

"Awesome."

"Hold on. I was about to say *if* you promise to keep the speed below thirty-five, park far away from other cars, and not bring any food or drink inside the vehicle—or make out in it. Because if you put one dent, nick, stain, scratch, or smidge of yucky DNA matter in it—"

"Be cool, Freckles. I've never had a single car accident." He sat down at the desk and logged on to the Internet. "Give me that phone number. I'll do a reverse lookup."

As Rafe worked at the computer, my home phone rang, reminding me that I hadn't checked for messages. What if Marco had called while I was out? How would I explain neither of us answering? As I dashed to get it, I glanced at the red light on the machine, and was relieved to see it wasn't blinking. Whew. He hadn't called. He would have left a message. I'd have to be more careful in the future.

"How's it going?" Marco asked.

"Everything's fine here." I nibbled my lip, hoping he wouldn't question me about my evening. "What's going on there?"

"I'm just finishing up my ledgers; then I'm going to head out to do some surveillance. So Rafe's behaving himself?"

"Yes, he's behaving."

"I found the address," Rafe called.

I motioned for him to be quiet.

"What's happening?" Marco asked. "What did Rafe just yell?"

"He's playing a game on the computer. How late do you think you'll be?"

"Let's see. It's seven thirty now. . . . I'm sure it'll be well after midnight."

I heard the weariness in his voice and felt guilty once again for being partly to blame. "That's a long day for you, Marco. I wish you didn't have to get up early to take me to work."

"It's for a good cause. That's you, in case you forgot."

I was going to have to tear up that chart. This man was all pluses. "Have I told you lately how much I appreciate you?" ·

"I'd rather you showed me," came his sexy growl.

"Anytime, Salvare. Good luck with the surveillance."

"Thanks. I'll call you later."

Eek. What if I was out? "Marco, use my cell phone if you need to reach me, okay?"

"Sure. Are you still having trouble with your landline?"

"Well—"

"You have to keep on the phone company, Abby."

"Okay."

"Love you, babe."

"Love you, too, Marco."

I hung up and unplugged the phone from the jack, then looked at the address Rafe had printed out. "Sixteen forty-three Gray Heron Drive, New Buffalo, Michigan. Can you pull it up on a Google map?"

In a few keystrokes, Rafe brought up a map, and I leaned over to study it. "Looks like about an hour's drive from here."

"I say we go check it out," he said, starting to rise.

I pushed him back down. "Marco gave me firm instructions that I was not to let you talk me into leaving the apartment."

"But I thought—"

I put my hand over his mouth. "Wait for it. . . . Okay. I say we go check it out."

"If you insist."

This time, I drove the Corvette, but I took the precaution of wearing my black wool cap with my hair tucked up beneath it. I wasn't about to take any chances of being spotted. With my hair color, it was like waving a red flag.

We headed north toward Lake Michigan, then took Route 20 around the bottom of the lake and crossed the Indiana state line into Michigan, following the Red Arrow Highway up to New Buffalo. Using the map Rafe had printed out, we located a development called Heron Cove, where hundreds of identical town houses were situated cheek by jowl on looping streets with a golf course at the center.

Deep into the development, I finally found Gray Heron Drive. The mailboxes were at the curbs, with brass numerals running vertically down thick wooden posts to indicate the addresses. I slowed in front of the mailbox marked *1643* and studied the two-story brick and cedar town house it belonged to.

"No lights on inside or out," I said. "Either the owner isn't home or is asleep."

Rafe checked his watch. "It's not even nine o'clock yet. I'll go with not home."

I parked in a visitor's parking area down the block, and sat in the car, deciding what to do. Did I ring the bell and see if anyone answered the door? Talk to neighbors to find out the identity of the town house's occupants? What would Marco do?

Rafe opened the door and got out.

"Where are you going?" I called.

"To see who lives at that address."

I jumped out of the car, shut the door, and hurried after him. "We need a plan."

"I don't know the person who lives there," Rafe called over his shoulder, "and she doesn't know me, so what's the harm in knocking on the door?"

"But the person might know me, and that might not be a good thing."

"Then stay out of sight."

Rafe was not a chip off Marco's block; that was certain. "Wouldn't it be smarter to talk to the neighbors first?"

"That's the girly way to do it." He started up the sidewalk to the front door of 1643, so I dashed for a nearby shrub and crouched behind it—in two inches of snow.

Rafe knocked, waited, rang the bell several times, and waited some more.

"No one's home," I called. "Let's go."

"What do you know?" he said. "It's not locked."

Unlocked door? No one answering? I knew what Marco would do. He'd phone the police. I peeked around the shrub and saw Rafe step inside the house.

Exactly what I would have done.

I jumped up and ran after him. "Wait, Rafe! Don't touch anything!"

"Hello?" he called. "Anyone home? I'm coming in now."

By the time I stepped inside, the younger Salvare was checking out the living room of the narrow, two-story home. "Look at that giant TV," he said. "Someone has some big bucks."

I left the door partway open in case we had to make a run for it. "Don't touch anything with your bare fingers. You don't want to leave prints."

"I have a delivery," Rafe called, standing in the kitchen doorway.

He used the edge of his jacket to flip the light switch on. I peered under his arm and saw a kitchen filled with high-end appliances—Bosch, Viking—with lots of black marble counter space and tall, cream-colored cabinets. On the island sat a glossy red dinner plate containing a half-eaten pork chop and a mound of mashed potatoes, with an open beer bottle beside it.

"Looks like someone didn't clean his plate," I said. I pulled up my coat sleeve and used my wrist to test the temperature of the bottle. Warm. I touched the potatoes with a knuckle. Cold.

Rafe used his jacket again to open a door and peer through the doorway. "One-car garage, no car."

Front door was open, car was gone, and dinner was half eaten. "We'd better leave, Rafe. I've got a bad feeling about this."

"It'll take just a moment to check out the upstairs."

It took just a moment to fall off a cliff, too.

"Delivery," Rafe announced again, leading the way up the oak staircase. He proceeded cautiously, pausing to listen every few steps as he repeated his call.

A clock in the entryway began to chime. When it struck ten, I realized my mistake. "Rafe, we're on Eastern time here!" I whispered. "Someone could be asleep up there."

"Too late now," he whispered back, and stepped around a corner. Hearing nothing, I followed.

The first doorway opened into an opulent bathroom, with more black marble counters and double sinks, gold fixtures, a glassed-in shower-for-two, and a big Jacuzzi tub. I used a tissue to open a cabinet below one sink and saw the usual cleaning products, roll of paper towels, extra toilet paper, and the same beneath the other sink.

In a medicine cabinet in the side wall next to one sink I found an assortment of bandages, skin lotions, and over-the-counter cold remedies. The medicine cabinet on the opposite side had toothpaste, mouthwash, shaving cream, and men's deodorant.

I pulled out the drawers below the under-sink cabinets, but save for traces of loose face powder, a few long, golden blond hairs, and smudges of lipstick, they'd been cleaned out.

"Looks like two people live here," I said, "but it's odd that all the woman's products are gone and not the man's."

"Maybe she ran away with another guy," Rafe said. "Maybe her husband hasn't come home yet."

"Maybe we should leave before he gets here."

But Rafe was already through the next doorway into a bedroom decorated in beige and blue. "Don't leave prints!" I reminded him.

"Nothing in the closet or dresser," Rafe reported. "Must be a guest room."

Across the hall was a second bedroom done in pinks and purples, silks and satins, with a plump, quilted silk headboard and a pile of furry throw pillows. I opened one of two closets opposite the bed to find a row of empty hangers. Rafe opened the other closet and found men's clothing—jeans, plaid work shirts, corduroy jackets, and the like—most of it folded and stacked on shelving.

"The guy must work with his hands," Rafe said. "No suits, ties, or dress shoes."

He checked a drawer in the bedside table. "Magazine, box of tissues, phone book . . . Aw, look. A Valentine." Rafe opened it, then showed it to me.

Beneath the verse was a signature scrawled in large, heavy handwriting: *Tom.*

Harding?

"Hello?" I heard a man call from downstairs. "Who's up there?"

I glanced at Rafe in shock. He motioned for me to stay quiet. "Who's down there?"

"You first," came a male voice.

"I told you we should have left," I whispered. "What are we going to use as our excuse?"

"We got the wrong house?"

"Never mind. Let me handle it."

"Okay, but open your coat and undo a few buttons of your shirt first."

I gave him a scowl.

We crept up the hallway and peered around the corner to see down the staircase to the front hallway.

Four sheriff's deputies had their weapons aimed at us.

Damn.

CHAPTER NINETEEN

*T*he limo idled half a block away from the police station. The driver glanced in the rearview mirror. "What do you want me to do?"

"Follow them."

The driver put the big sedan in gear and eased out onto the street. Nothing easier than tailing a bright yellow Corvette. Those two showing up here had been something of a surprise, though, especially coming on the heels of that broad slipping away before she could be silenced.

The driver cast another glance in the mirror. It always amazed him how well his boss hid his feelings. It was only the clickity-click of those tiny seashells he was palming that indicated how hard his brain was working.

"Bad luck tonight, huh?" he commented, trying to make conversation.

"For now."

"What do we do about the florist?"

"Nothing for now. She doesn't realize what she has, so it will be merely a matter of looking for it where we failed to look before. Then I'll decide whether we need to do anything more with her."

The driver shook his head. "I don't know, boss. You might have a problem with her boyfriend. He seems to be attached to her at the hip."

"She will be without him sometime. And then we'll make our move."

"I am so busted," Rafe said as we sped along the Red Arrow Highway, heading for Indiana. He had the passenger seat tilted back as far as it would go and one arm flung across his eyes. "What are you going to tell my brother?"

"I'm thinking."

It was midnight Michigan time, eleven o'clock p.m. at home, where a very perturbed Salvare awaited our arrival. Thanks to a vigilant neighborhood watch group, we had spent the last hour and a half at the New Buffalo police station, answering questions and being printed and photographed, hoping and praying that my dear friend Reilly would come through for us.

Bless Reilly's heart, he did. He called a cop he knew in New Buffalo and arranged our release, although he grumbled when he learned I'd referred to him as *my extremely close friend and New Chapel police sergeant*. Still, I didn't know how I'd ever repay him.

But first I had to figure out how to explain everything to Marco.

"Okay, how's this?" I asked Rafe. "We'll say that I had to go to New Buffalo anyway because . . . Forget it. He wouldn't buy it. Do you have any ideas?"

"Honesty is the best policy," Rafe said. "That's what Mama always taught us."

"You're right." I sighed morosely. "I'll have to confess."

He sat upright. "Are you out of your mind?"

"You just said honesty was the best policy."

"I'm not rational. Don't listen to me." Rafe flopped backward against the seat. "I shouldn't have listened to *you*; that's for sure."

"Hey! You were just as eager to get out this evening as I was. Don't even start with me."

Rafe sighed. "Sorry. I just don't want Marco to send me back to Ohio."

"Why not? I got the impression you lived like a prince there."

"Who told you that? Do you seriously think my mom would treat me like a prince? Have you met the woman? She's an Italian commando. Never mind. You wouldn't understand. You don't have any idea what it's like to have your mother telling you what to do all the time, and comparing you to your older, successful brother and sisters."

Actually, I did know.

"It's not my fault I'm different than them," he muttered.

Boy, I heard that loud and clear. It made me feel even more remorseful for involving Rafe in my scheme. "Look, I do understand what you're going through, so take my advice. Do something completely different than your siblings so there won't be any way to compare the six of you."

"Like what?"

"I don't know. Surprise them. And I promise I won't let Marco send you home. I'll tell him you didn't want to come with me, but I twisted your arm, okay?"

"Awesome. Thanks. So I can still use your car tomorrow, right?"

I had a feeling I'd been played.

When I pulled into my parking spot, Marco was leaning against his Prius, arms folded, an inscrutable look on his face. Rafe saw him and groaned. "This is gonna be bad."

I took a deep breath, stuffed my anxiety inside a balloon, and blew it out. Time to face the music. I glanced at Rafe. "Ready?"

We got out and slammed the doors. "Hey, bro," Rafe said, striding around to the passenger side of Marco's car. "I'm beat. Let's go."

"Hold it," Marco said. "Come back here."

I stood beside my car, twisting my keys in my hand. Marco was one parking space away. "You, too," he said to me. "Come here."

Like errant schoolchildren, we stood in front of him, guilty looks on our faces. "I can explain," I said, shivering in the cold night air. "This wasn't Rafe's fault."

"You're cold. Let's go inside and talk about it," Marco said.

"Now?" Rafe asked. "It's eleven thirty."

Marco shot him a look and Rafe shut up.

At my apartment, I offered beers to the brothers and both accepted. I handed out the beers; then Marco asked us to sit on the sofa. He rolled the desk chair around so he could face us. "Okay, Abby, you first."

Why was I thinking *Spanish Inquisition*?

Here we go, Abby. Make it good. I began by explaining how important it was for my own peace of mind to know Harding's condition, and that I'd only been looking out for *Marco's* peace of mind when I didn't tell him I'd gone to the hospital to find out. If I *had* told him, would he have been able to concentrate on his work? No. Would he have worried? Yes. Ergo, zipped lips.

Marco said nothing.

Next, I explained that Nikki had stumbled upon the existence of H. Bebe, and that I'd felt it important to find out if she was Charlotte's sister.

Marco still had no comment.

Finally, I said it was my idea to try the front door, and having found it unlocked, I checked inside the house to make sure there hadn't been any foul play. Unfortunately, the neighbors saw us and called the police. Fortunately, Reilly cleared us. Then I sat back and waited.

Marco leaned forward. "Tell me what you learned."

"Not to leave the apartment without letting you know our plans."

"I meant," Marco said, "what did you learn when you went inside the house?"

"Oh." What? No lecture? I glanced at Rafe, and he shrugged.

"Okay," I said, "judging by the half-eaten plate of food and open bottle of beer, and no car in the garage, I got the impression that someone left in a big hurry."

"Temperature of the food?" Marco asked.

"Mashed potatoes were cold; beer was warm."

"What else?"

"Upstairs in one of the bedrooms, we found men's clothing in one closet, but the other closet was empty. In the bathroom, we saw men's toiletries but not women's, and two drawers had been cleaned out."

"There was a Valentine in the woman's nightstand," Rafe added, "signed by someone named Tom."

"It has to be Harding," I said.

"Anything else?" Marco asked.

I thought about it for a moment, then shook my head.

Marco folded his arms. "You two had quite an evening."

"I'm sorry we interrupted your PI job, Marco," I said. "I hated having to ask Reilly to get us out of jail, and I know I shouldn't have gone without letting you know. But I did it,

so yell if you want. I'm okay with that, although I think
we've had enough punishment."

He raised an eyebrow inquiringly. "Are you done?"

"I believe so, yes."

"Good. Now do you want to hear what I found out?" he
asked.

I glanced at Rafe in disbelief. To Marco I said, "Is that
it? No lecture?"

"I don't see any reason for it. I'm betting the cops
scared the living daylights out of you."

"Duh," Rafe said. "We had to chill at the police station
for ninety-two freakin' minutes. They treated us like criminals."

"We entered someone's home illegally, Rafe," I said.
"We *are* criminals."

"From now on I'm following your orders, bro, no matter
how much the Abster begs."

I turned on Rafe with a glare. "I did not beg. I never
beg, only suggest. And you are *so* not using my car tomorrow night."

"Hey," Marco said. "Let's move on. Do you want to
hear what I found out? Good. First of all, the town house is
listed as belonging to Tom Harding and H. Bebe, otherwise
known as Honey B. Haven, as joint tenants in common."

"Honey B. Haven's real name is Honey Bebe?" I asked.

"That's how it appears," Marco said. "I couldn't find any
record of a marriage to a Haven or Harding, but I did learn
that Honey and Charlotte are sisters."

"Honey B. Haven," Rafe said, chortling. "I just got that."

"When did you have time to dig up all this information?" I asked Marco.

"After Reilly phoned to tell me where you were and why."

I felt my face turning red. "Sorry about that."

"I found it a little difficult to focus after that call."

"I'm sure you did."

Rafe yawned, obviously not feeling any guilt. "I'm not needed here, am I? Would you mind if I relax for a while?"

We vacated the sofa and headed for the dinette table. Rafe immediately stretched out and flipped on the TV.

"After Reilly's call," Marco said, picking up our conversation, "I dropped by the hospital and had a chat with Nikki. When she told me what was in Harding's chart, I went back to his hospital room to get a better look at his injuries."

Marco sat back, extending his long legs. "It was obvious the man took a severe beating, so I called Reilly back and asked if a police or accident report had been made on Harding. He found out that snowmobilers had found Harding in the woods late Wednesday night, barely clinging to life. He'd apparently been out there for some time. Since his wallet was taken, they're calling it a robbery, so whether it has anything to do with the kidnappings remains to be seen. But the Bebe connection makes me suspect it does.

"Here's something else I discovered," he said, pulling out his notebook and flipping up the cover. "Honey Bebe boarded a plane for France at eight thirty this evening. She bought a one-way ticket an hour and fifty minutes before the plane departed, so this wasn't a trip she'd planned in advance. That, along with your report that her clothes and makeup were gone, says she's on the run. The question is, who is she running from?"

"Maybe the detectives asked Honey to come down for an interview, and she was afraid they were going to link her with the kidnappings."

"I thought of that, so I called Detective Valderas and told him what I'd found out about Charlotte's sister. He didn't know what I was talking about."

"Are you telling me they haven't been looking for her sister?"

"They weren't aware she had a sister," Marco said in disgust. "And after I talked to Valderas, all he'd say was that they'd check into it."

"Will they?"

Marco lifted one shoulder, his classic Italian shrug. Having been a police officer, Marco loathed to speak ill about fellow cops, but I could see the frustration in his tightly clenched jaw.

"So what do we do now?" I asked.

"We stop waiting for them to solve this case."

I wanted to stand up and cheer. Finally, we were back on the same page.

"Let's review what you saw at the town house," Marco said. He was so sexy when he was intense. "You said the front door was unlocked. Was it standing open?"

Oh no! Was it?

"No," Rafe called. "Remember, Abby? You tried the knob and the door opened."

"Right," I said, ignoring Marco's skeptical glance. "And what are the odds that a woman would leave her front door unlocked, especially after dark? It wouldn't happen."

"Was the garage attached to the town house?" Marco asked.

"Yes, accessible through a door in the kitchen."

Marco rubbed his jaw. "So I'm picturing Honey eating in the kitchen, hearing her front door open, then running out to the garage and taking off in her car."

"With her luggage already in the trunk," I added. "I'll bet you any money that after she got to the hospital and saw what happened to Harding, she decided to leave the country."

"But someone or something spooked her," Marco said, "causing her to leave sooner than she'd expected."

I sat back with a frustrated sigh. "With Honey out of the country, there's no one to say whether Raand is involved."

"Let's not get ahead of ourselves. First we need to find out whether Honey's departure and Harding's beating are related to the kidnappings, because if they aren't, we're wasting our time. We know it wasn't Raand who went after Honey because he's in police custody."

"He could have hired someone to go after Harding and Honey, maybe the same person who killed Hudge."

"But again, someone botched the job. Harding didn't die and Honey got away. And would Raand take that risk, considering the investigation is focused on him?"

"Maybe he was desperate."

Marco tapped his fingers on the table. "We need to know what evidence the DA has on Raand."

"Are you going to ask Reilly to help?"

"Nope." He closed his notebook and stood up.

"Who else is there? You nixed my grilling Morgan at dinner tomorrow."

Marco raised me up and pulled me into his arms. "I'm officially un-nixing you."

"Really?"

"Abby, I'm counting on you to do what you do best."

Awesome. "So"—I gave him a flirtatious glance—"you're not angry about Rafe and me going up to New Buffalo?"

"Don't push your luck," he said with a little quirk of his mouth. "But the next time you decide to take a road trip, would you please let me know? I hate hearing it from Reilly."

"I promise you'll be the first to know."

Marco shook his head. "It's a good thing I like incorrigible women."

"Excuse me? You mean *woman*, don't you?"

"I mean *you*." He dipped his head and our lips met, gently at first and then passionately, our bodies melding, soft curves meeting hard muscle, making me forget everything but the man against me. He sure knew how to kiss.

A few moments later, a key turned in the lock and then Nikki called, "Hello?"

Reluctantly, I broke away. "In here, Nikki. Marco and Rafe are here, too." I glanced at Marco and shrugged. "Sorry. Bad timing."

"Don't worry about it," Marco said, reaching for his jacket. "Now that Nikki's home, I'll run Rafe back to my place." He kissed me on the tip of my nose and went to rouse his brother, calling back, "You need to hit the sack, Sunshine. It's after midnight."

Ugh. He was right. I had to be up in less than six hours.

Nikki peered around the corner. "So," she said in a whisper, "everything okay?"

I knew she meant Marco and me. "We're fine. I'll tell you more tomorrow."

"Hey, Nik, thanks for your help today," Marco said, pushing Rafe toward the door. "Dinner is on me tomorrow."

"About that," Nikki said. "We'll have to take a rain check. Greg has the flu. He left a message on my cell phone about an hour ago."

Didn't it figure that the one time I had Marco's permission to be nosy, I couldn't?

Wait. Yes, I could.

CHAPTER TWENTY

Iwoke up the next morning filled with all kinds of energy. I had a plan to get the information we needed from Morgan and it involved chicken soup. My mom always kept home-made soup in her freezer. I'd just stop on my way to work to pick it up.

When I came out of the bedroom, Marco was already shaved, his sheets folded neatly on the end of the sofa. He was wearing a T-shirt and jeans, doing push-ups on the living room carpet.

"Oatmeal this morning?" I asked.

"Sure. Fifty-eight, fifty-nine, sixty . . . I'll be in to help in a moment."

"That's okay. Keep working those biceps, Salvare. The Irish chef is on duty." I was in a generous mood. It felt great knowing Marco and I were a team again. Holmes and Watson. Batman and Robin. Marco and Abby. We were unstoppable.

Marco's cell phone rang as I was pouring a packet of oatmeal in the bowl. "Would you get that, babe?" he called in between counts. "Phone's on the table."

And Nikki was sleeping, which he'd apparently forgotten. I dashed for the phone, glanced quickly at the screen, saw OUT OF AREA, and had an instant feeling of trepidation. "Hello?"

"Who is this?" a woman with a slight Italian accent demanded.

Yikes. Just as I feared, it was Francesca Salvare. "Um, just a minute, please," I said, hurrying into the living room. "Your mom!" I whispered, shoving the phone at Marco. "Don't tell her I'm here."

"But you answered," Marco whispered back.

"The last time I spoke with her, she quizzed me on my bowel habits!" I whispered. "And the time before that—"

"Hi, Mama. Yes, that was Abby. Because I was busy. Doing push-ups, Mama. I don't think she recognized your voice, either. I don't know why Rafe isn't answering his phone. I'm not at home. Yes, I know what time it is. I slept here. Why? Do I need a reason?" Marco held the phone away to draw a deep breath. "Did you want something, Mama? Yes, I gave her the pattern book. She's thinking about it."

Ye gods. How was I going to get out of that one without hurting her feelings?

Marco put a hand over the phone to whisper, "She wants to talk to you."

"No!" I whispered in alarm. "Tell her I'm leaving right now to go to work. Wait. Tell her I'm running late and have lots to do today. No, that's no good. Tell her—"

"She can't talk now, Mama. I'm sure she'll let you know when she makes up her mind. Okay, I'll have Rafe phone you later. Sure. Bye.

"Did you catch the gist of that?" Marco asked.

"Yes, and she's not going to make my gown." I headed into the kitchen, muttering, "I'm wearing jeans and a white blouse. End of discussion."

I had just stirred hot water into the oats when I heard, "Abby, you need to see this."

I put the bowls on a tray with spoons, napkins, and cups of coffee, and carried it to the living room. Marco had tuned in to the local cable TV station's morning newscast, where a reporter was talking about a press conference. I put the tray on the coffee table, sat beside Marco on the sofa, and picked up my bowl.

Marco turned up the volume, catching the reporter in midsentence. "—head of operations at the Uniworld Distribution Center gave this statement yesterday."

Head of operations? "Is this about Nils Raand?" I asked, spooning a bite of creamy oatmeal into my mouth.

"Yep. Raand bonded out yesterday afternoon," Marco said.

"He did? Then maybe Raand *is* who Honey ran from."

"It's possible."

A prerecorded clip showed a shot of the New Chapel courthouse, where microphones had been set up at the top of the steps. I watched as Nils Raand took his place in front of the mics, where a good half dozen reporters had gathered. Beside Raand was attorney Nathan Knowles in the standard-issue black wool dress coat. Raand sported a chic tan suede bomber jacket, brown pants, and shiny brown leather shoes.

"My arrest was a mistake," Raand said, "and in no way reflects on the good name of Uniworld Food Corporation. Uniworld remains one of the premier corporations in this country, dedicated to providing quality food products for everyone."

I nearly choked at that remark. "Food products laced with hormones, that is!"

"Will you be suing the police for false arrest?" a reporter called.

Attorney Knowles leaned toward the microphones. "We'll take this case step by step. Our first order of business is to clear this man's name."

A woman reporter stepped forward, a cameraman at her shoulder. "We understand there's been some controversy surrounding the opening of what has been called Uniworld's dairy factory, and, more important, Uniworld's use of bovine hormones in the operation of that factory. How would you address those issues?"

"It would be unthinkable for Uniworld to be involved in anything unethical," Raand said. "Every Uniworld product is USDA certified. What's more, we are a family-oriented company and this will be a standard dairy farm that will employ members of your own community. It is unfathomable to me that anyone would be opposed to that."

"That is such a load of propaganda," I said.

"Does this hormone controversy have anything to do with why you were arrested?" the woman reporter asked.

Knowles started to answer, but Raand beat him to it. "Yes, it does. I was arrested because of one woman's personal vendetta against me."

"I can't watch this." I started to get up, but the reporter's next question stopped me cold.

"Can you name the woman?"

"Her identity is no secret," Raand said coolly. "Her shop is there"—he pointed—"across the street. Bloomers Flower Shop. I believe you know Ms. Knight has been campaigning against Uniworld and me for some time. But her vendetta will stop now." He looked directly into the television camera, his icy glare seeming to stare right at me. "I will see to that."

At Raand's statement, a dozen hands went up and a reporter called, "Are you going to sue Ms. Knight?"

"No comment," Knowles said. "Thank you for your time." He took Raand's arm and led him toward a waiting car.

I put the bowl aside and sagged against the back of the sofa.

Energy gone.

I didn't talk much as Marco drove me to my parents' house. I was still brooding about Raand's threat against me. Didn't he realize the campaign had already stopped? Hadn't he noticed the absence of protesters?

Marco's thoughts, however, were on more immediate concerns. "Did your mom say she'd have the soup ready when we got there?"

"Do you mean like bring-it-to-the-curb ready? Right. Dream on."

I'd called Mom before we left the apartment to ask if I could have a container of her soup. Naturally, that had led to a round of questions about my health, even though I assured her the soup was for a sick friend. The only way to convince her I was fine was to let her see me.

"We won't have to stay long," I assured Marco. "Mom will be getting ready to leave for school."

"Then we'll head straight for Morgan's house," he said, glancing at me for confirmation.

"I was thinking more like midmorning. There's usually a lull at the shop then."

Marco turned into my parents' driveway and pulled up to their garage door, which they'd left open for us. Keeping a sharp eye on our surroundings, he hustled me inside the garage and through the door that led into Mom's studio.

As we circled the pottery wheel in the middle of the room, Marco said, "So this is where she makes her—" He paused as though searching for the right word.

"Art," I supplied.

The studio had once been an enclosed porch off the kitchen, but a remodel job had fixed that. Now it had a clay tile floor, and lots of counter space and cabinets to hold her craft supplies. I did a quick sweep of the room and saw traces of straw in a corner where Taz, her pet llama, had slept before she'd had the shed out back converted to a heated barn. I didn't see any brooches. Maybe she'd decided not to make more after all.

I opened the door to the kitchen and called, "We're here, Mom. Dad."

Marco followed me into the long, rectangular kitchen. Decorated in the 1980s, it had white appliances, oak cabinets, forest green laminated counters, and mauve, blue, and green floral wallpaper. A rectangular oak table with white legs and five ladderback chairs were arranged in front of a window that looked out on the backyard. There was no chair at the head of the table. That was Dad's place.

My dad wheeled himself into the kitchen to greet us. I gave him a kiss and Marco shook his hand. "Got a minute to sit down?" Dad asked us, indicating the chairs.

"Sorry," I said, "lots to do, Dad. Does Mom have the soup ready?"

"It's in the fridge," Dad said, then lowered his voice. "And just to warn you, we saw Raand's press conference on TV. Your mom"—he heard her coming and said in a normal voice—"was very upset by his statements."

"I'm furious about them," Mom said, sweeping into the kitchen with her coat over her arm. "How dare that sorry excuse for a man accuse you of having a personal vendetta against him and then make noises like he was some kind of mobster out to get you. I hope he's convicted."

Having said her piece, she kissed Marco and me on our

cheeks, whipped out the container of frozen soup, and put it in a paper sack with handles. I held out my hand to take it, but she plunked the bag on the floor. "Stick out your tongue."

"Mom, I'm not sick. The soup is for a friend."

"You'll save yourself a lot of trouble if you do as your mother says," Dad told me.

I stuck out my tongue. Mom inspected it, felt the temperature of my forehead, checked the color of my eyeballs, probed the glands beneath my jaws, and pronounced me healthy. She turned toward Marco with every intention of giving him an exam, too, but I grabbed her hand before she could lay it on his forehead. "Marco's not sick, either."

"Do you have any news on the kidnapping case?" Dad asked Marco.

"Nothing yet, sir, but I'm working on it."

"Gave up on the detectives, did you?" Dad asked.

"Unfortunately," Marco said, "they've had their hands tied."

"The DA is gung ho for Raand, isn't he?" Dad asked.

"He should be," Mom said. "Only an evil person would condone injecting bovine hormones into those poor cows and letting them suffer so. It breaks my heart to think about them spending their entire lives in that condition, and locked in tiny stalls, as well, with no room to move. On our farm, our cows were well treated and happy, and they produced plenty of milk. We didn't even have to pasteurize it, which destroys most of its nutrients, you know. It was as fresh as God intended." She glanced at my dad. "Should I tell them my news now, Jeff?"

"Why not?" he said.

She smiled. "You are looking at the new head of the local chapter of PAR."

I gaped at her, picturing her carrying a sign and calling

orders from a bullhorn as she led protesters around Uni-world's warehouse, while inside, Raand plotted her demise.

"Don't look so shocked, Abigail. I told you I wanted to help. When I contacted the president of the state organization and volunteered my services, a nice woman there said you had just notified her that you were unable to do any organizing, so she was thrilled that I called."

"Mom, I'm sure she appreciated your offer, but you heard Raand threaten me. If you organize any protests, he'll turn on you. Right, Marco?"

"Abby has a point, Mrs. Knight."

"I'm not going to lead a protest march," Mom said. "I have a better way of making sure those cows aren't mistreated." She glanced at the kitchen clock. "Now, I've got to get going."

"Aren't you going to tell us?" I asked.

Her eyes sparkled impishly. "Not yet. When the time is right."

I glanced at my dad. "She doesn't know how to build bombs, does she?"

"No," Dad said, "but her red pepper hearts can certainly ignite a few fires." He wheeled his chair toward the doorway to the living room, calling, "Marco, you've got to see this."

Mom sighed as she slipped on her coat. "He gets such a kick out of those candy hearts. Did I tell you he put them on the coffee table in a glass jar so he can tease me about them?"

"You could just toss them out."

"I'll let your father have his fun. Just wait, though, until my brooches become a must-have accessory. We'll see who has the last laugh then."

"So you're definitely making more?"

"Of course. If they're valuable enough to swipe, they must

be a hot item. You don't mind if I hang on to your brooch a bit longer, do you?"

At that moment, Marco came to the doorway with his cell phone pressed to his ear. "It'll be fine, Rafe. Let me call you back after I get Abby over to Bloomers."

He shut his phone and slid it in his back pocket. At my quizzical glance, he said quietly, "I'll tell you later."

That didn't sound good.

"Is everything all right?" Mom asked.

Marco gazed at me as he answered. "Everything is fine."

He was lying.

CHAPTER TWENTY-ONE

A s soon as we pulled out of the driveway, I said, "What's up with Rafe?"

"Mama is coming in tomorrow and he's worried."

I sympathized with Rafe. The first time I met Mrs. Salvare, she invited me to dinner, grilled me on my plans for the future, and got me drunk on wine—on purpose. A test of character, according to Marco. He said I passed, but I still had my doubts, and I still got nervous whenever she came to town.

"What's the occasion?" I asked.

"She says she wants to see how her little boy is faring. Rafe is worried that she's coming to take him back with her."

"Rafe is a grown man. Can't he just tell her he's staying here?"

"Rafe needs to grow a spine before he can do that."

"You can't just say he has to grow a spine, Marco. The poor guy has to gain confidence before he can stand up to your mother. Getting this new job on his own is a good first step."

"He dropped out of college and is working at Hooters learning how to tend bar. That may boost Rafe's self-confidence, but it's not going to inspire a whole lot of assurance in Francesca Salvare, trust me."

I saw Marco's point. Poor Rafe. No wonder he was worried. But then another thought crossed my mind. "What if your mom has an ulterior motive for coming to town?"

Marco glanced at me. "What would that be?"

"Us."

He pondered that for a moment. "You're right. We haven't made our announcement yet."

"Exactly."

"We haven't had that discussion yet, either."

With all the turmoil, I'd pushed it out of my mind. "We probably should."

"When? Now?"

Now? I'd just mentioned it. I had to prepare. "Not now. We're almost at Bloomers."

"How about at lunch?"

"Lottie and Grace will be there. Can we make it at dinner?"

"Done."

"Next problem—my mom. I have to talk her out of working for PAR."

"Abby, you know there's no way to stop her."

"I have to try. Once Raand finds out about her involvement, he'll come after both of us. I can't expose her to that. I'll confer with Dad. Maybe he can talk sense into her."

As was now our procedure, Marco phoned ahead to alert Lottie and Grace of our impending arrival, so that when we pulled up, the women were standing guard at the door, scanning up and down the sidewalk for any signs of danger. I was beginning to understand how a movie star felt as I was whisked into the store with my security entourage around me.

With the door locked firmly behind me, and Marco on his way to park the car, my first order of business was to grab a cup of Grace's coffee, then sit down with both women to fill them in on my visit to the hospital and subsequent trip to New Buffalo. They had lots of questions about Honey Bebe and Harding and whether they were linked to the kidnappings, but, unfortunately, I didn't have lots of answers.

As we were discussing Honey's disappearing act, the phone rang and Lottie got up to answer it in the shop.

"Abby," she called from the doorway, "I've got that salesman on hold. You remember the one who left you that little flashlight? Do you want to speak to him?"

"I haven't had a chance to look at his price list, but if it will stop his annoying calls, I'll take it." I had started toward the phone at the cashier's counter when Marco rapped on the door.

I let him in, and he strode past me, saying, "I think I know where I can find more information on Charlotte."

"Where?"

"Come see."

I started to follow him, but then Lottie cleared her throat and pointed to the phone, where the light was blinking. "Would you take a message, please?" I asked her. "Tell the salesman I'll try to find time later today to call him."

I followed Marco into the workroom and leaned over his shoulder as he logged on to the computer and began to type. But after a few minutes of watching him search through pages of results, I grew bored and decided to work on an order. I plucked a slip off the spindle and studied the instructions Grace had written: *Ninety-fifth birthday bouquet. Recipient—Jennie Helen Bolek. Bright colors. Fun.* I loved doing bright and fun, and for a ninety-fifth birthday, it had to be extra special.

"Take a look at this," Marco said as I gathered my tools. "It's an online job application Charlotte submitted in January for a position with Chinn, Knowles, and Brown."

"No kidding? But isn't a job application considered confidential information? How did you get it?"

Marco lifted an eyebrow.

"Okay, don't tell me, then. Was her application rejected or is that a secret, too?"

"It doesn't say, but I know how to find out."

While Marco placed a call, I stepped into the walk-in cooler to select my stems. Humming happily, I lost myself among the fresh blossoms, breathing in the soothing floral scents, absorbing the dewy moisture, feeling at peace with the world. Ah, if only I didn't have to step outside again.

Okay, bright and fun for a special birthday. Definitely some deep pink tulips, orange lilies, purple foxgloves, white mini callas, yellow daisies, bird-of-paradise . . . Hmm. A mix of blue, purple, and pink anemones would be the perfect finish . . . except I still didn't have any. Damn. I'd have to use gerberas instead.

I nearly dropped my armload of flowers when Marco spoke from behind me. "Listen to this. According to the office manager at Chinn, Knowles, and Brown, Charlotte left Uniworld to work as a filing clerk for Attorney Knowles."

"So Charlotte went from Uniworld to the lawyer representing Uniworld. That certainly establishes a strong link between Raand and the kidnappers."

"Here's where it gets really interesting. Knowles fired Charlotte two days before the first kidnapping attempt."

"Why was she fired?"

"The office manager didn't know. The only person who can answer that is Knowles, and you can bet he won't."

"Okay, Marco, I know you don't like me making giant

leaps, but here's one I can't help but make. Maybe Knowles fired Charlotte because he found out about the kidnapping plot."

"If Attorney Knowles had that information, he would have had to be forthcoming with the police. He's an officer of the court."

"Even if doing so implicated his client?"

"Knowles would have warned Raand that he knew about the plot. In that case, I can't imagine Raand giving the go-ahead to Charlotte and Hudge."

"So what do we do with this information?"

"Nothing yet. I want to see what else I can dig up on Charlotte."

I surveyed the flowers on the table, still puzzled over the anemones. "Before you do that, I need to look up an order on the computer."

I brought up a file containing my recent orders and sure enough, Lottie had put in for anemones more than three weeks ago. "There it is," I said, pointing to the monitor. "Paid in full. Now I need to find out why we didn't receive them."

I opened my lower desk drawer and removed a manila folder containing our various suppliers' information, then vacated the chair so Marco could resume his search. I took the folder to the kitchen to call the supplier in question.

"Certainly we shipped that order," the clerk there told me. "Our records indicate it was delivered on January twenty-eighth."

I glanced at the calendar hanging on the kitchen wall. That was the day we'd found the anthurium brooch in the box of orchids. But there hadn't been any other orders delivered that day. "Are you sure of the date?"

"I'm showing that the delivery was accepted by a . . . Sorry; I can't read the signature."

"Lottie Dombowski?"

"It's hard to make out. All I can say for sure is that the order went out to Bloomers Flower Shop."

"But I didn't get the order."

"You'll have to check with the delivery company. It must be their mistake."

Whoever's mistake it was, I shouldn't have to pay for it! "Thank you. I'll follow up on that. In the meantime, I need to reorder."

I placed the order, then hunted through my file until I found a delivery slip that had the UPS toll-free number on it. I dialed, and an automated voice asked for a tracking number, which I didn't have. I waded through a long menu, then hit the *O* repeatedly until finally a friendly man answered. I explained the problem, but the man kept insisting he needed a tracking number.

"I don't have a number because I didn't receive the order. Can't you search the sender's name to find out who else in my zip code area received a shipment from that company?"

"No, ma'am. I'm sorry. Not without a tracking number."

"Not even for a beautiful bouquet of flowers for that special lady in your life?"

"That would be my mother," he said dryly, "and no, not even then. I have no way of getting that information. Maybe you should call the sender."

"I tried that. Okay, how about this? Can you tell me if anyone in my zip code reported a problem with a delivery on that date?"

"If you want to report a problem, we need a tracking number."

"I just *reported* my problem! I'm asking if anyone else in my area had a problem."

"I don't have any way of checking without a tracking number."

"Okay, forget it. Thank you for your time."

"If you have any other problems, please call."

Not unless I wanted a headache, too. I returned to the workroom just as Marco's cell phone chirped. He answered crisply, "Salvare."

As I filled out a delivery tag for the birthday bouquet, Marco held his hand over the phone to whisper, "It's the antiques dealer.

"Thanks for getting back to me so quickly, Mr. Oke," he said. "I'm looking for information on a flower brooch listed on your Web site. It's a . . ." He glanced at me and raised his eyebrows.

"Red anthurium," I said. "Possibly made out of ivory."

Marco repeated it. "Can you give me a price on that? No, I'm not a collector, just an interested party. Sure, I'll hold." He swiveled the chair toward me. "Did you get your order straightened out?"

"No. The supplier claims my order was delivered and signed for."

"Yes, sir," Marco said into the phone, resuming his conversation.

"What did I sign for?" Lottie asked, coming into the workroom.

"A shipment with our anemone order in it. Supposedly, you signed for it on January twenty-eighth, the same day the orchids arrived with the brooch inside. I called UPS, but they can't tell me anything without a tracking number—which I don't have because I never received that delivery. I finally gave up."

Lottie opened one of the walk-in coolers, pausing to say,

"Well, Dwayne Hudge did come here looking for a package he said was delivered to us by mistake. I'll bet our regular guy, Joe, delivered our order to someone else and gave us the order Hudge was after."

"It shouldn't be hard to find out who got our order," I said.

"Right," Lottie said. "How many places around here sell flowers?"

She stepped into the cooler just as Marco wrapped up his phone conversation. "Use this number, if you would, Mr. Oke. Thanks for your help."

"What did he say?" I asked.

"He has to check the current market value before he gives me a quote. I have a feeling he wants to check me out more than the value of the brooch." Marco glanced at his watch. "It's ten thirty. When do you want to go see Morgan?"

"Now, if Lottie doesn't mind."

Lottie came out of the cooler carrying an armload of roses. She stopped to glance from me to Marco. "Mind what? How is it I always walk in on the middle of a conversation?"

Greg Morgan lived on the third floor of a new condominium building on the east side of town, a fast-growing area filled with lots of apartments, condos, and starter homes. His building was the typical modern brick box four stories high. It had a small entrance hall containing rows of mailboxes and a list of occupants by last name, with corresponding buzzers.

I pressed the button beside his name and eventually a hoarse voice said, "Who is it?"

"Hey, Greg, it's Abby. Nikki said you were sick, so

we thought you might appreciate some homemade chicken soup." I didn't explain who the "we" was so he'd think it was Nikki.

"Are you sure you want to come up? I might be contagious."

"Not a problem, Greg."

He buzzed us through the security door, and we headed for the elevator. As I got ready to board, Marco said, "I'll wait down here."

"Don't you want to question him?"

"I'd just be a distraction. You know how to handle Morgan. You don't need me."

"Are you afraid of catching the flu?"

"I just think Morgan will be more forthcoming without me there."

"Sure, you do." I wiggled my fingers at Marco as the doors began to close. "See you in about ten minutes."

"You're being a little overly optimistic, aren't you?"

"Fifteen, then."

Marco stopped the doors. "Do you remember what to ask?"

"About the note and the flowers."

"Get details. And ask if they recovered evidence from Hudge's van—and have a suspect."

"I've done this before, remember?"

The elevator doors were nearly together when Marco stopped them again. "Remember, you can use the information we have on Charlotte and Honey as a bargaining chip."

"Why don't you just come with me?" I asked in exasperation.

"Do you want me to come with you?"

"No!" I blew him a kiss as the doors glided shut.

I exited on the third floor and found Morgan's unit. I

knocked, announced myself, and heard the shuffle of soft soles against a hard floor. The door opened and there stood the courthouse's golden boy in a ratty old blue bathrobe tied loosely around the middle, with plaid pajamas beneath it and brown suede slippers on his feet. His nose was red, his eyes were watery and dull, and his face was pasty.

"I come bearing nutritious soup," I said with a smile, holding up the container.

He peered behind me. "I thought Nikki was with you."

I stepped inside a foyer and glanced around as I set my purse on the floor. The small front hall had been professionally decorated in shades of beige and brown, with a gorgeous, antique-style hall tree in one corner, a beautiful rosewood console table with a matching mirror on a short wall, and a thick oriental carpet underfoot. Morgan's cashmere winter coat hung on the tree, his briefcase beside it.

"Nice place, Greg," I said as he shut the front door. "Love these wood floors." I hung my peacoat on a hook, saw a kitchen through a doorway across the hall, and headed toward it. "Granite counters. Awesome."

"Thanks," Morgan said, shuffling after me.

The kitchen was airy and modern, with lots of cabinets and counter space, and even a window, something I wished our apartment had. He had room for a table, too. How could he afford a place like this on a deputy prosecutor's salary?

"How are you feeling?" I asked as I stashed the container of soup in his fridge.

"Not so good."

I glanced up as he braced himself on the doorframe, swaying as though he was woozy. "Greg, are you about to pass out?"

He shook his head, then hiccuped. "I just feel fuzzy-brained."

Not an unusual condition for Morgan. Then I spotted a medicine bottle on the counter and picked it up. "Did you take this cold remedy, by any chance?"

He nodded and hiccuped again.

"This stuff is sixty percent alcohol, Greg. How much did you take?"

Morgan held up two fingers, but said, "Three tablespoon fulls—tablespoons full."

I read the directions on the back. "You're supposed to take *one* tablespoon, Greg. One every six hours."

"It didn't seem to be working, so I kept taking it."

Great. Now I had to get information from a drunk.

CHAPTER TWENTY-TWO

"**Y**ou know what you need?" I asked. "Something in your stomach to absorb all that alcohol. How about if I heat the soup for you? It wouldn't be any trouble."

Morgan swayed unsteadily. "I think that would be a—*hic!*—good idea. I haven't eaten yet. Couldn't stand the thought of food."

I found a cooking pot and lid, and poured in a third of the container of soup, now partially thawed. I put it on the range and turned up the flame as high as it would go. "It'll be ready in a few minutes, Greg. You'd better sit down at the table before you fall over."

"Good thinking." He shuffled to the table, pulled out a chair, and carefully parked himself on the seat. He propped his elbows on the table and used his palms to keep his head up.

"Did you catch Nils Raand's news conference earlier today?" I asked, hunting for a bowl.

He nodded, then fished a tissue out of a pocket in his robe and made honking sounds as he blew his nose.

"Did you hear Raand threaten me at the end?"

Morgan stopped honking. "He threatened to harm you?"

"Yes! Well, not in those words, but Raand's intent was clear. And now my mom is joining the PAR protest, so I'm afraid he'll go after her, too."

"I wanted to keep him in jail," Morgan said, "but there's no murder charge against him, so he was able to post bond."

I stirred the soup, decided it was warm enough, and ladled it into a bowl. I found a soup spoon in a utensil drawer, a napkin in a holder, and placed everything in front of him. Morgan immediately picked up the spoon and dipped it in the soup. I glanced at my watch. I'd been there thirteen minutes. No way would I make my fifteen-minute goal.

"This tastes good," he said, liquid dribbling down his chin.

"I'm glad you like it. So, Greg, has there been any word on who murdered Hudge?"

He shook his head.

"What about the weapon? Do you know what it was?"

"Wasn't a metal blade," he said between mouthfuls. "Something smooth, though."

"Like wood?"

"No wood fibers in the wound. Wound was clean."

"Any of the inmates talking about who might have done it?"

He stopped eating to gaze at me through bleary eyes. "I've already told you more than I should have, Abby."

I pulled out a chair and sat down across from him. "But look at it from my standpoint, Greg. Three attempts were made to kidnap me, and both kidnappers are now dead, one murdered right under your nose, probably to keep him from talking. Can you blame me for wanting some information?"

He blinked a few times. "No, I suppose not."

"Then help me put some of the pieces together, okay?"

Morgan shook his dripping spoon at me. "You can't take no for an answer."

"But I already know what two of the key items of evidence are. I just need a little more information about them. It's like someone sketching a tree with bare branches and someone else painting on the leaves. See what I'm getting at? I've sketched the tree; now it's your turn."

He kept eating the soup, so I decided to keep sketching. "Okay, Raand sent a note to one of the kidnappers. Was it to Hudge?"

"Abby, please stop."

"Won't you answer just that one question, Greg? Please?"

He stopped to wipe his chin. "If I do, will you stop badgering me?"

I was about to say, *Define 'badgering,'* when all of a sudden, the napkin dropped from Morgan's hand and a sickly expression came over his face. Then his cheeks puffed out and he began making gagging noises. He clapped a hand over his mouth, shoved back his chair, and stumbled out of the kitchen. Moments later, I heard a door slam and then the sound of retching.

So much for the chicken soup cure. I picked up his bowl and spoon, left the icky napkin, and headed toward the kitchen sink to rinse them. "Are you okay, Greg?" I called.

No answer.

I scrubbed my hands with soap and hot water, stashed the rest of the soup in the refrigerator, then went to investigate. Just beyond the kitchen was a family room, and up the hallway from the family room I found a closed door.

"Greg? Are you in there?"

Silence.

I called his name again, rapped twice, then opened the

door and peered cautiously inside. I saw a handsome bathroom with tan and green striped wallpaper, an ivory marble pedestal sink, a glass-fronted tile shower, brown towels, and a shaggy brown throw rug—onto which Morgan had curled into fetal position.

"Greg?" I whispered.

His mouth sagged open and he began to snore.

I watched him for a moment and thought about nudging him awake with my shoe. But I couldn't do that to a sick man. Then I thought about his briefcase resting against the hall tree, right there where anyone could open it up and have a look inside.

I could do that to a sick man.

I called Morgan's name again, and when he didn't respond, I quietly eased the door closed, then tiptoed through the family room and into the small front hall. I knelt beside his briefcase—an expensive leather number stamped with the Bally brand name—set it flat on the floor, pushed the brass locks, and winced when they popped open with loud clicks.

I listened for a moment, but heard no noise from the bathroom, so I lifted the lid and peered inside. He had three accordion file folders in it. I didn't recognize the name on the first one. The second one, however, was labeled *Knight, Tara.*

Bingo!

The first page was the charging information on Dwayne Hudge. Beneath it were pages of statements made by the investigating officers on their initial findings, then lists of witnesses, and witness statements. I flipped through the file quickly, hunting for anything about the note or the flowers. I found the coroner's report on Charlotte, but gave it only a cursory glance. Beneath the report were more witness statements.

I heard a moan from the other room. Oh no. Was Greg coming around?

I shuffled through pages so fast I almost missed it—a photocopy of a thank-you note written in handwriting so severely straight, it looked as though a ruler had been used to keep the loops from going beyond the line. It read:

Dear Ms. Bebe,

I would like to extend a cordial thank-you for filling in for my secretary during her vacation. Your help was appreciated. A check for your services is enclosed.

Very truly yours,

Nils Raand, Agent and Dist. Manager
Uniworld Distribution Center

Encl: Check #4604

Well, that certainly didn't sound like a man who'd hired her for a kidnapping. No mention of sending her flowers, either. I read Raand's note over twice, then moved on. I'd have to analyze its significance later.

The next page was a photocopy of the check, made out to Charlotte H. Bebe, and stamped for deposit by the New Chapel Savings Bank.

I was nearly at the back of the file. There had to be something about flowers in it. Had I missed it? A receipt? A lab analysis?

A toilet flushed. Oh no! Morgan was up.

I was about to give up when I noticed a letter from the county extension agent. Quickly, I scanned the letter—a preliminary finding. It read in part: "In regard to the matter found in the tread of the subject's running shoe, the petals are consistent with those of the anemone."

Anemone?

I ran my finger across the lines of print. Whom had the shoe belonged to?

I heard running water. *Crap*. Morgan was bound to emerge any moment.

I flipped to the next page and found a letter from the prosecutor's office requesting that "the matter found in the tread of the subject's running shoe" be analyzed. And there on the next line was the subject's name: Charlotte Bebe.

Got it!

I slid the file into the briefcase just as the bathroom door opened. I closed the case and eased the locks shut, coughing to cover the clicks. Then I propped it beside the hall tree, grabbed my coat, and turned just as Morgan shuffled around the corner.

"Greg! I was just about to leave. Are you okay?"

"I guess I wasn't ready for soup."

"I put the rest in the fridge for another day, and don't worry about the plastic container. Just get into bed and take it easy. I'll let myself out."

I grabbed my purse and left, taking the stairs because I was too energized to wait. I pushed the door open at the bottom and dashed out, glancing around for Marco.

He saw me and tapped his watch. "Twenty minutes."

"And worth every one of them. Come on, I'll tell you what I learned on the way back to Bloomers."

As we headed west toward the town square, I filled Marco in. "One of the pieces of evidence that the DA said linked Raand to the kidnappers was a thank-you note Raand sent to Charlotte for filling in while his secretary was out."

"A thank-you note?"

"Yep. That's it. Not a word about hiring her for any kidnappings. Apparently he had enclosed a check with the thank-you for the days she worked—I saw the photocopy—and it wasn't a big sum, either."

"So it didn't link Raand to the kidnappings, just to a kidnapper."

"Right."

"It's weak."

"Weak is too weak a word for it. Flimsy as onionskin would be better. And the second piece of evidence, the flower, is—you won't believe this—flower petals that got caught in the treads of Charlotte's shoes."

"Petals?"

"Not just any petals. Anemone petals."

Marco glanced at me. "The flowers you never received?"

"Exactly."

"How would a person get anemone petals mashed in her shoe treads in the winter?"

"The obvious answer is by stepping in them. I find flower petals stuck to the soles of my shoes all the time. But the only anemones you'd find in February in this part of the country would be the kind sold by a florist or grown in a hothouse. There are two florists in town, the florist in the grocery store's gift department—and me. I know the grocer carries only the standards—roses, daisies, mums, orchids, violets—nothing as unusual as anemones. So that leaves one big craft and hobby store on the highway that also wouldn't stock anemones, and two garden centers with greenhouses, one of which is at Tom's Green Thumb." I raised my eyebrows. "Pretty strong coincidence, don't you think?"

Marco smiled. "You are an amazing woman."

"Thank you."

"It'd be great if we could place both Charlotte and Harding at Tom's Green Thumb. But is Harding even involved in the greenhouse operation anymore? I thought he had to sell when he went to prison."

I pulled out my cell phone and called the shop. "Let's see if Grace can find out."

Grace was a master at sleuthing out that kind of detail. I explained the situation to her and asked her to check around for anemones and inquire discreetly about Harding's involvement in Tom's Green Thumb. "You don't need to call me back," I said. "We'll be there in ten minutes."

"By the way, dear," Grace said, "that salesman called again, the one who left the flashlight? He said he's leaving town tomorrow and is planning a small reception this evening at the New Chapel Inn and Suites. He would like you to RSVP. I put the note on your desk."

"Okay, thanks, Grace. I'll take care of it later." I slipped my phone into my purse and sat back with a satisfied sigh. We were finally moving forward.

"Tell me how you got Morgan to cooperate," Marco said.

"I fed him chicken soup."

He gave me a skeptical glance. "That's it? He ate the soup and then talked?"

"No, he ate it and then barfed."

"What?"

"Morgan was being stubborn. The only information he'd divulge was that there was still no suspect in the Hudge murder and that the weapon was made from something smooth, yet not metal or wood. So after he upchucked the soup and fell asleep in the bathroom, I rifled through his briefcase."

Marco let out a low whistle. "I can't believe you went into a deputy prosecutor's briefcase and read his files."

"You can't?"

He gave me a sidelong glance. The corner of his mouth curved up.

Could, too.

"No anemones at the craft store or grocery store," Grace reported as Marco and I shed our coats and settled at a back table in the parlor. "And Samuel's Garden Center is closed for three months, reopening in March." She paused to glance at us over her reading glasses. "However, I just got off the telephone with Robin Lennox, the acting floor manager at Tom's Green Thumb, and she said—"

"They have anemones in stock," I finished, giving Marco a high five.

"In fact," Grace continued, "Robin received the shipment a few weeks back—around the end of January—even though she hadn't ordered any. She believed it to be a delivery error, although neither her supplier nor the delivery company would admit to it."

"Did Robin say anything about Harding's involvement?" Marco asked Grace.

"According to Robin, Mr. Harding is no longer officially involved in the company, yet she admitted that he keeps his fingers in the business through his lady friend, Honey, who owns controlling shares."

"How convenient," I said.

"Robin indicated she hadn't seen Mr. Harding personally since his release from jail," Grace said, "but as she was leaving one evening, she saw his black sedan parked behind the greenhouse."

"Did Robin mention when that was?" Marco asked.

"She did not. Shall I call her back, do you think?" Grace asked.

At that moment, four women came into the parlor and took seats at a table in front of the bay window, so Grace added, "After I see to my customers?"

"Thanks," Marco said, "but this warrants a trip to Tom's Green Thumb to talk to Robin in person. I'll head over there this afternoon."

"I almost forgot," Grace said. "Your sister-in-law Portia dropped these by." She put a stack of magazines in front of me. I read the spines: *Elegant Bride; Modern Bride; World Bride; You and Your Wedding; Occasion Weddings; Wedding Cakes; Wedding Bells . . .*

I pushed them aside and laid my head on my arms. "Make them stop!"

Marco's cell phone chirped, so he got up to take the call. A moment later I heard Lottie say, "This will make it all better, sweetie."

I raised my head as she placed a pizza box on the table, along with a stack of napkins and paper plates. She lifted the lid, revealing a big, cheesy pie loaded with sausage, mushrooms, black olives, and green peppers. I leaned over to inhale. Yum!

"Lunch is on me today. Dig in." She took a slice for herself and bustled away.

I was about to place a wedge of pizza on a paper plate when a small hand reached around me and grabbed it.

I turned to see Tara stuff the pointed end in her mouth. "Surprise," she mumbled through the gooey bite.

"What are you doing here? You should be in school."

"In-service teachers' meetings this afternoon," she announced, taking a seat. Her eyes lit up at the sight of the magazines. "Are you shopping for your wedding gown?"

"No. Does your mom know you're here? Because she'd probably rather not have you hanging out with me right now."

Tara pulled a magazine from the stack and began to turn the pages with her greasy fingers. "Nope. But it's okay. I saw Unky Hunky in the back. Where did you get these magazines?"

I ignored her Marco reference. "Your aunt Portia left them."

"Cool. Now we can find you a dress."

"Don't bother. I've decided to wear jeans."

"Yeah, right." Snickering, she turned the page. "No way." She turned another page. "Ug-o!" As she flipped through the magazine, I heard, "They can't be serious." "Oh. My. God." "Is this a joke?" And finally, "Awesome! This is more like it."

Tara turned the magazine so I could see it. "This gown is totally you, Aunt Abby."

I glanced at it as I took a big bite of pizza. "Sure it is, if I were a foot taller and weighed less than you."

Tara stuck her tongue out at me, then turned more pages until she found another that met her standards. "Okay, you can't say this one isn't you."

"That one isn't me."

By the time Marco returned, I'd downed one and a half slices and Tara had gone through two magazines. "Have some pizza," I said. "Lottie ordered it for us."

"That was nice of her," Marco said, taking a seat across from me. "Hey, Tara, what's up?"

"What do you think of this gown?" she asked, swiveling the magazine in his direction.

"Don't answer," I said. "It's a trick question."

"No, it's not," Tara said. "Don't you think Aunt Abby would look awesome in this?"

Marco helped himself to the pizza. "If I say yes, will I get into trouble?"

"Who was on the phone?" I asked.

"I got two calls," he said. "The first was from Rafe. He's got the afternoon shift today, so, besides needing a ride to work, he wanted me to know he won't be there to meet Mama at the apartment. I'll have to meet her."

"Wait. Your mother's coming in *this* afternoon? You told me she was coming tomorrow."

"That's because Rafe told *me* she was coming tomorrow. He said his brain froze the moment he heard her voice and everything she said after that was garbled. She's coming in around three thirty, so I told him to take my car to work. With everything else going on, I don't have time to drive him out to Maraville. I'll just use the Vette."

Nice of him to ask. At least that meant Rafe couldn't borrow it.

"Can I go with you?" Tara asked, batting her pale eyelashes at him.

"Sorry, Short Stuff. I've got too much to do. Some other time, okay?"

"Here's what you can do for me," I said to Tara. "Take the magazines to the workroom and tear out pictures of gowns that would look good on me. That's *me*, Tara, not your aunt Portia, or Jillian, or Miley Cyrus, or Hannah Montana."

"Miley Cyrus and Hannah Montana are the same person, Aunt Abby."

"I knew that."

Rolling her eyes, Tara stood up and started to reach for the magazines, then paused. "Are you trying to get rid of me?"

"Yes." I picked up the stack and held them out. "Here you go."

"Fine. I'll do it. What do I get in return?"

I reached under the table and squeezed Marco's knee so he'd play along. "Should we tell Tara now or wait until she finishes?"

"Tell her now," Marco said. "No, make her wait."

Tara narrowed her eyes at me, but she clearly was afraid to call my bluff. She took the magazines and left the room.

Marco reached for another slice of pizza. "What are you going to give her?"

"I'll have to think of something. Who was the second caller?"

"Mr. Oke, the Hawaiian antiques dealer. He asked me to take a photograph of the brooch and e-mail it to him. He wanted to know how I happened to contact him, so I explained how you found it in your flower shipment. I knew he wasn't quite buying my story, so I told him to get in touch with Reilly if he wanted to check out my credentials.

"That apparently did the trick because then Mr. Oke explained that a brooch matching that description had been stolen from a museum's display of antique Hawaiian royal jewelry on January twenty-fourth. He said if your brooch is the one in question, he'll have to notify the FBI."

"Holy cow, Marco. We've been treating that brooch as a piece of costume jewelry."

"It might be costume jewelry. We don't know yet if your brooch is the same one that was stolen, but I'll admit the timing is interesting."

"On the other hand," I said, "isn't it kind of far-fetched to think a thief would ship a valuable Hawaiian brooch to New Chapel?"

"Not all that far-fetched. Mr. Oke said there are collectors all over the world who pay exorbitant amounts of money for rare pieces, stolen or not. The collectors go through a middleman who connects them with the art or jewelry they'd like to add to their collections. Some of these middlemen are the actual thieves. They can be notoriously wealthy and are often extremely dangerous. The FBI is working on a case like that in Chicago right now, looking for a man known as the Flame."

"Art collectors actually buy stolen merchandise?"

"Are you kidding? *Museums* buy stolen merchandise. There's a big black market for art and antiquities. But do you understand what this means? If the brooch you found is actually this priceless Hawaiian jewelry, and it came in a shipment that was supposed to go to Tom's Green Thumb, then someone at Tom's is in on the theft."

"How realistic is it to imagine Harding could engineer the theft of a Hawaiian brooch?"

"He might have met someone in prison who told him about the scheme. A lot of that goes on behind bars. If Harding knew he was going to be released for treatment, he could have arranged to be the middleman, or he could have volunteered Honey for that job."

"Let's imagine that the brooch came to Bloomers instead of going to Tom's Green Thumb. Then someone on the other end had to slip it in the box and send it to him, right?"

"You got it. Which tells me the thief would be employed by your supplier, or be the supplier himself."

"I can't imagine Mr. Mikala being the thief. Lottie has been ordering from him for a long time and has never had a problem. And yes, I know you can't judge a person's moral character by that. So what do we do now?"

"The first step is to take detailed photos of the brooch and e-mail them to Mr. Oke so he can verify its authenticity. I wouldn't be surprised if the FBI showed up asking to see it, either."

"My mom still has the brooch. We'll have to stop by there after work."

Marco wiped his hands. "Okay, let's do this. I need to go down to the bar and finish some bookkeeping and cut checks for the crew. After that, I'll run out to Tom's Green Thumb and see what else Robin can tell me—like how Charlotte might have gotten anemone petals stuck in her shoe. Then I'll head over to my apartment to wait for my mom. In the meantime, you call your mom and let her know we'll be by after five o'clock."

"That's my part? Make a phone call?"

"Your part is to stay here where it's safe." Marco glanced around to see if the other customers were watching, then leaned down to give me a lingering kiss. "Tonight we'll go out for a nice meal at Adagio's and finally have that discussion. How does that sound?"

Better than dining at the country club with the wedding hunters. "It sounds perfect, except for one thing. Your mother will be here. Are you going to leave her at your apartment alone on her first night in town?"

"Oh. Right. Well, we'll just have to find time to be alone together after dinner."

"What about your PI case?"

Marco thought about it for a moment, then shrugged. "We'll make it work somehow."

Unless Marco was a magician, I didn't see how.

CHAPTER TWENTY-THREE

*S*itting on a bench on the courthouse lawn, the driver pressed the button on his earpiece to phone his boss. "The boyfriend is on the move. He's entering the Down the Hatch bar. I can see him walking toward the rear, up a hallway, into a room . . . and now he shut the door."

"And what is happening inside the flower shop?"

The driver refocused his small, high-powered binoculars. "Looks like a full house in the coffee shop, a handful of customers in the flower shop."

"Good. Keep watching the boyfriend and be ready to act. Do whatever it takes to keep him from her. We must make our move today. The risk of discovery is too great to delay any longer."

"Forgive me for saying so, boss, but how is that gonna happen? You took all the brooches she had, and none of them were the genuine article. You've searched the obvious places. She's gotta have it stashed somewhere safe."

"I don't think so. Someone has been making copies for her, and since the original can't be located, my guess is that it's being used as the model. Thus, it is a matter of learning the location of the copier."

"How are you gonna make that happen?"
"My plan is already in action."

My frustration level rose another notch as I watched Marco head out of the parlor. There had to be something I could do besides make one phone call. Musing, I packed up the leftover pizza and stowed it in the refrigerator, then stopped to check on Tara's progress.

"How's it going?"

She sighed and tossed the magazine onto her discard pile. "It'd be going a lot better if you weren't so picky. Can I take the rest home with me and look later? I'm bored."

"No." I picked up the stack and stuck them in my desk drawer. "That's how rumors get started."

"Fine. So when do I get my reward?"

"Tomorrow." I'd have to come up with something quick.

Tara gave me an obligatory hug, took a fresh daisy from the cooler for her hair, and left.

I saw a few orders on the spindle, but knew I could whip them out in no time, so I sat down at the desk to call my mom while she was on her lunch break at school. To reach her, I had to go through the school's secretary, Midge, and have her paged.

Although I told Midge it wasn't an emergency, Mom still answered with a breathless, "Abigail, did something happen? Are you okay?"

"I'm fine, Mom. I just need to let you know I'll be stopping by the house later. I have to pick up the anthurium brooch."

"Today? But I haven't finished with it yet."

"I know, and I'm sorry, but it's possible the brooch might be a valuable piece of jewelry stolen from a Hawaiian museum."

"And I'm making copies of it?" she whispered into the phone. "Am I going to get into trouble?"

Her copies weren't *that* good. "No, Mom. You won't get into trouble. But I do need to find out if it *is* the stolen brooch. So will you have it out for me, say, shortly after five o'clock?"

"I might not be home, so I'll tell your dad where it is so he can have it waiting. I'm meeting with my dissension team after school."

"Your what?"

"Dissension team. You know, dissenters. Protesters. I told the other teachers about Uniworld's plans to open a dairy farm and use bovine hormones on the cows, and all of them volunteered to help. Isn't that exciting?"

"Help you do what exactly?"

"You'll see. I've got to phone your father before the bell rings. Keep me posted on the brooch, honey. And try to make it to dinner tonight. Bye."

Mom had a dissension team? At least there was safety in numbers.

Lottie came through the curtain and headed toward the kitchen. "Joe's here for a UPS delivery. I'll let him in."

"Wait. I'll do that, Lottie. I want to talk him."

I hurried through the kitchen to the back door and threw my shoulder against it to push it open. Joe, a lanky guy with bushy brown hair, came striding up to the door carrying a huge box.

"Got some flowers for you." He put the box on the landing, then handed me a pen and a clipboard. "Sign here, if you would."

"I've got a question," I said, scribbling my name on the paper. "Is it possible you delivered a package to Tom's Green Thumb on January twenty-eighth that should have come here?"

Joe's cheeks reddened. "Someone had to sign for it, right? Wouldn't they have noticed if someone else's name was on the packing slip?"

"You'd think so." Except that I'd just signed for an order of flowers without checking first. Obviously we needed to pay attention when we accepted deliveries. "Have there been any reports in the last month of anyone posing as a UPS driver?"

"No," he said with a wary glance. "Why?"

I wasn't about to go into the whole long story. "I thought I'd heard something about it."

Joe hesitated, then said, "Look, you didn't hear this from me, but someone at Tom's Green Thumb did complain about a missing order round about that same date. That's not my route, but guys talk, you know? So the driver tells them he doesn't know anything about a missing order and maybe they should check to see if another flower shop got it. That didn't make them very happy. So the driver got canned. You see why I like to keep my mouth shut?"

"I sure do. I don't suppose the driver mentioned Bloomers Flower Shop to the person at Tom's, did he?"

"That, I couldn't tell you. Well, have a nice day."

I pulled the heavy back door shut, thinking about what Marco had suggested—that Mr. Mikala, the supplier, might be involved in the theft. Yet when I last spoke with the man, he sounded as baffled about the brooch being in the shipment as I was. Had he lied to me?

I decided to pick up the phone and ask him.

I explained to Mr. Mikala what the antiques dealer had said about the real brooch, then asked again if he knew how the piece I'd found got into the box. He apologized profusely for my trouble and said he'd read about the theft in the papers. He also said he might have an idea how the brooch could have ended up in that shipment.

In mid-January, he hired a nineteen-year-old man to work in his warehouse, but within a week, other employees complained that the young man was involved with a gang of thieves. They were afraid of him and said they thought the gang was working through him to smuggle stolen goods out of the country.

To play it safe, Mr. Mikala called the police, who then decided to plant an undercover man in the warehouse. Unfortunately, the young man failed to show up for work the next day. The following week, Mr. Mikala read in the newspaper that the young man had been stabbed in the neck while at a bar. No one had seen the murderer; the police had no suspects; and the murder weapon had not been found.

It sounded eerily like Hudge's murder.

"I don't know whether this young man was involved in the brooch theft," Mr. Mikala said, "but that's my only explanation for you. And again, I apologize for your trouble. I hope we don't lose your business."

I assured him it wouldn't affect our relationship. As I was about to sign off, I spotted Grace's note about the salesman and his evening reception. Just out of curiosity I asked Mr. Mikala what he knew about Aloha Florals, Ltd.

"Aloha Florals?" the supplier asked. "They went out of business five years ago."

"Five years ago? Is it possible they started up their business again?"

"I would have heard something. I knew the owner well. His business closed when he passed away."

Something didn't smell right. "A salesman claiming to work for Aloha Florals has been trying to get me to buy flowers from him. He even left a price list." I searched through a stack of papers on my desk, but didn't see it, so I rooted through my purse and found the smooth flashlight. "I can't find the list at this moment, but his business card says, 'Aloha Florals, Limited, Maui,' and the man's name is Keahi Kana."

"Keahi Kana? That's quite an interesting name, and definitely of Hawaiian origin."

"What makes it interesting?"

"Kana is a Maui demigod who is said to have been able to take the form of a rope so he could stretch from one island to the next. Keahi is the Hawaiian word for flame. Loosely translated, his name would mean a god of fire or flame, although a very minor god."

Instantly, my thoughts went back to what the antiques dealer had told Marco. *Some of these middlemen are the actual thieves. They can be notoriously wealthy and are often extremely dangerous. The FBI is working on a case like that in Chicago right now, looking for a man known as the Flame.*

I rotated the flashlight in my hand. "Mr. Mikala, have you ever heard of a man known as the Flame?"

"It's not familiar to me. Why?"

"I'm wondering if the Flame and Keahi Kana are one and the same."

"I couldn't begin to guess. Would you like me to look up Aloha Florals in the phone book to be sure it hasn't re-opened?"

"Thanks, but I can do that on the computer. I've taken enough of your time. You've been very helpful, Mr. Mikala."

I hung up the phone, toying with the flashlight. The man who'd left it had spoken with Grace and Lottie on the phone, and Lottie in person, yet neither had reported anything unusual. Still, because of what Mr. Mikala had said, my gut was telling me to be wary.

In the shop, Lottie was waiting on customers, so I pulled her aside to whisper, "The salesman who left the flashlight, was he Hawaiian?"

"I'm not sure what a Hawaiian is supposed to look like, but if I had to guess, I'd say yes. Nice-looking guy, well dressed and polite, kind of short, though, but with these intense eyes—"

I thanked her and dashed back to the computer to do a search for Aloha Florals. I tried two different search engines, including the one Reilly gave me, yet couldn't find a single listing. In a broader search, I found a link to an obituary in a Maui paper for the longtime owner of Aloha Florals. There were also earlier mentions of the company, but nothing after the man's death.

What was going on?

I took out a sheet of paper and began to make a list, hoping a pattern would emerge. I wrote down everything I could think of, whether it appeared to tie in or not, beginning from the day Lottie unpacked the orchids.

A brooch was found in the bottom of a box of orchids.

A threat letter arrived warning me to stop the protests.

Dwayne Hudge posed as a delivery man to ask about a package delivered by mistake.

A brick was thrown through my door.

I wore the brooch when I appeared on cable TV.

My business was broken into and trashed.

My mom's first copy of the brooch went missing.

Nikki was nearly kidnapped while driving my Vette.

Jillian was kidnapped, her beret was stolen, and then she was released because she wasn't me.

Tara was kidnapped because we were dressed alike.

Charlotte Bebe was run over by her partner, who thought she was about to cut him out in order to include her sister, Honey.

Dwayne Hudge knew who planned the kidnapping plot.

Hudge was stabbed in the neck in front of witnesses while in jail. No suspects.

Twelve copies of the brooch were stolen.

Tom Harding was beaten, left for dead.

Honey Bebe fled the country when someone showed up at her door.

Nils Raand vowed to stop my protests.

Nils Raand thanked Charlotte for filling in for his secretary and paid her.

Anemone petals were found in Charlotte Bebe's shoe treads.

Tom's Green Thumb received an unordered shipment of anemones.

A valuable ivory anthurium brooch was stolen from a Hawaiian museum.

A young man who worked for the supplier was in a gang of smugglers.

The young man was stabbed in the neck while in a public place. No witnesses, no suspects, no weapon.

The FBI has been searching for a man known as the Flame.

A Hawaiian salesman, whose name means god of fire or flame, claimed to work for a supplier that closed five years ago.

I put down the pen and picked up Grace's message again: *Mr. Keahi Kana is giving a reception for clients Friday evening from seven to ten p.m., at the New Chapel Inn and Suites. RSVP required.*

Why didn't a major orchid supplier know that Aloha Florals was back in business? If Mr. Kana was a legitimate salesman, why wasn't his company listed on the Internet? If Mr. Kana was the Flame, was this reception a trap designed to lure me to the hotel? How did he hope to get the brooch from me once I was there?

So many questions—and only one person with answers.

I turned the flashlight over to see the number; then, taking a deep breath, I picked up the phone and dialed. My call was answered with a smooth "Aloha."

"Same to you, Mr. Kana. This is Abby Knight, from Bloomers Flower Shop. I'm RSVPing to your invitation."

"You're a difficult person to reach, Ms. Knight. I hope you're responding in the positive."

My heart began to race. "Yes. I'd love to join you."

"Marvelous. I shall put your name on the list. Suite 212."

"Thanks. And just out of curiosity, may I ask how long your company has been in business?"

"I can guess why you're asking. You are aware that the original Aloha Florals, which started back in 1970, closed after its owner died. It has now reopened under new management as of the first of this year."

He was certainly prepared. "Do you have a Web site, so I can get more information?"

"Unfortunately, our Web site isn't up yet. I'd be happy to provide any information you need this evening."

"Did I understand correctly that you're leaving town tomorrow?"

"Yes, Ms. Knight. Tomorrow my work here will be done. I look forward to meeting you this evening in person."

I hung up the phone and realized my hands were damp from nerves. I wiped them on a paper towel and phoned Marco.

"Hey, Sunshine," he said, "I'm just heading out to Tom's Green Thumb. Did you make that phone call?"

"Yes, and our focus has been wrong, Marco. The kidnappings and thefts aren't connected to Uniworld and Nils Raand. They're connected to the brooch."

"How did you come to that conclusion?"

I filled Marco in on the details of my conversations with Joe the UPS guy, Mr. Mikala, and Keahi Kana, and ended by reading him my list. "What do you think?"

"That you nailed it. Great work, Abby."

"Thanks." I knew I was beaming.

"But you're not meeting this man tonight."

Sayeth Emperor Marco.

"Actually, I was thinking of both of us meeting him."

"No way in hell, Abby. If this Kana is responsible for Hudge's death and Harding's beating, and the FBI is looking for him, it's too dangerous."

"I know that, but how about listening to my idea before you make a ruling, Judge?"

"Not funny."

Wasn't meant to be. "Just listen to my plan, okay? We go to the hotel and ask the hotel manager about Mr. Kana. He'd be able to tell us whether Kana's entertained any clients, or had food sent up for tonight—that kind of thing. I'm sure he'll cooperate if you flash your PI badge. And if there aren't any red flags, we hang around outside Kana's suite to see who else is attending his little soiree. If it seems legit, we go inside and meet the man. If we don't see anyone else, we call Reilly to let him know what we think the man is up to. How does that sound?"

"I'll agree to it on the condition we let Reilly know our plans before we go, so he can have some plainclothes cops on hand."

"Fine. As long as Kana doesn't spot them."

"I'll call Reilly now and set it up."

"Great. I'm going to head over to my parents' house to pick up the brooch."

"Wait for me to get back. I'll take you."

"I'd rather get it into the safe at your bar as soon as possible, Marco. I have this uneasy feeling about the brooch being there. Lottie can drive me over in the minivan. Besides, don't you have to meet your mom at your apartment?"

"It won't take long to get her settled. I should be there by four o'clock."

Was there a word stronger than overly optimistic? Because I knew what would happen. His mom would want to cook something for him and, since he was a good son, well, who knew when he'd get back? In the meantime, I could pick up the brooch and take it down to the bar. But if I kept arguing, we'd end up fighting, and I didn't want that. "Okay, I'll wait."

I hung up the phone and picked up the flashlight to drop it in my purse hanging on the back of my chair. But the silky light slipped out of my hand and fell to the floor. The case split neatly in half and a shiny, dime-sized battery rolled under the desk. I got down on my knees and fished it out, then tried to put the pieces back together, but there was already a battery inside.

I examined the tiny device more closely and saw minute holes in the cover, reminding me of a flattened earbud. I turned it over and saw that it had been glued inside the case.

Then I realized what I was holding. It was a bug. Someone had been listening to me—and was probably listening to me at that moment.

My heart began to thud with sickening intensity as my thoughts raced back over everything I'd said while the flashlight was nearby—my conversation with Mr. Mikala, with Keahi Kana himself, and with Marco—*mentioning that the brooch was at my parents' house.*

Dear God. What had I done? What if Kana went to their house to get it?

But wait. He didn't know where they lived. He didn't even know their names, and he'd have to go through a lot of Knights in the phone book to find them. If he was still listening, I could keep him from getting that brooch.

I dialed Marco's number, but it went to his voice mail so I pretended he had answered. "Hey, Marco, it's me. I'd feel better if you called Sergeant Reilly and asked him to pick up the brooch now. You will? Great. Okay. Love you, too."

I hung up and quietly wrapped the bug in a tissue, then carried it to one of the walk-in coolers and left it beside a bucket of daisies with a sticky note that said, *Bug! Give to cops. Don't talk!* Then I pulled on my coat and ran to find Lottie.

She was helping a woman and her mother select funeral flowers. Grace was serving coffee to a parlor full of people. I couldn't ask either one to go with me. I glanced at the clock. It was two thirty—hours until Marco would show up.

I dashed back to the workroom and grabbed the keys to the minivan.

CHAPTER TWENTY-FOUR

"Dad, it's me," I said into my phone as I headed north through town. "I'm on my way."

"Your mom said you'd be coming. Fill me in on what's going on with this brooch."

Normally, I made it a rule not to have long conversations while I drove, as it tended to distract me, but I needed my dad to know the seriousness of the situation, so I pushed that rule aside and gave him a complete rundown on the status of the brooch and Keahi Kana, aka the Flame, finishing just as I pulled into the driveway.

Dad opened the garage door with a remote device, and I ran inside, hitting a button next to the doorway to lower it again. I hurried through Mom's studio and into the kitchen, where he was waiting.

I kissed him on the cheek. "Have you got the brooch?"

"I put it in the grocery bag in the fridge with some apples from your mom."

"More apples? Do you know how many are still in my refrigerator from the last bunch she sent? We can't eat them that fast."

"Try telling that to her."

I removed the brooch from the sack and tucked it inside the zippered compartment in my purse. "Would you call her and tell her to meet us at Bloomers?"

"I'll leave her a message. She turns off her phone when she's in a meeting."

"Okay. While you're doing that, I'll get your coat."

"I'm staying here, Abby."

"Dad! It isn't safe here. I don't know what this Kana might do. He could be Googling your address at this very moment."

"Let him. He's not going to chase me out of my own home. I know how to protect myself. It wasn't so long ago I was a cop."

A cop who now had almost no use of his legs. "I can't leave you here, Dad."

"Why can't you leave me here? I'm not helpless."

What was I supposed to say? Yes, you are? I knew how much he struggled to do for himself and how hard it was for him to accept his limitations, but he had to face the fact that he wasn't the cop he used to be.

I stewed while Dad called Mom's number and left a message. Clearly, he didn't understand the risk he was in. He hung up the handset, turned his chair, and started toward the living room, calling, "You'd better get going, Ab."

Crap. How could I abandon him? I followed him into the living room, dropped my purse onto the floral print sofa, then tossed my coat on top of it and sat down with a heavy sigh.

Dad parked his wheelchair to face the sofa and studied me for a moment. "If you're staying because you're afraid for me, Abby, you'll hurt me worse than the bullet in my leg did."

I hung my head. "I'm sorry. It's still tough for me to accept what happened to you."

"Sometimes it's tough for me, too, sweetheart, but life goes on. If you keep looking back at the past, you know what'll happen? You'll run into a wall. You can't move forward when you hit a wall, can you?"

"No, you can't."

"Never look back, Abby. Make a decision, go forward, and don't second-guess yourself. You'll be a better person for it."

I kicked off my shoes, sat down, and curled my legs beneath me, resisting the urge to check the time on my watch. "So, Dad, as long as you're in a philosophical mood, maybe you can give me some advice."

"Now? I thought you wanted to get out of here."

I wanted to get both of us out of there, but that wasn't going to happen. "Another fifteen minutes won't hurt. I'll let Marco know what's going on so he won't worry."

I used my cell phone but got Marco's voice mail, so I left him a message telling him where I was and to please call. On the coffee table in front of me sat Mom's decorative glass jar filled with red hearts. After I put my phone in my coat pocket, I picked up the jar and shook it. "You know Mom hates that you saved these."

"That's what she wants you to believe. Actually, it's become a joke between your mom and me. Whenever one of us says something the other disagrees with, the other will say, 'Have a heart and shut up.'" He laughed. "It defuses a lot of tension."

That was actually pretty clever. As I put the jar back on the coffee table, Dad asked, "Speaking of tension, how are you doing with your bodyguard?"

"I'm adjusting to having him around. Marco's mother is coming to town today, though."

"So? She seems like a warm, generous person and she's clearly crazy about you, Ab."

"And I like her, too, but she scares me."

Dad studied me for a moment. "Why is that?"

"What is this, a therapy session?" I joked.

"I'm just curious."

I thought about it for a moment. "I guess she scares me because I'm picturing her as my mother-in-law. Do you remember the Marie Barone character on *Everybody Loves Raymond*? *That* mother-in-law."

"Ah. Now we're getting to the real issue."

"Which is?"

"The marriage."

"We're a long way from that step, Dad."

"As I recall, you said you were going to get engaged."

I began to twist a thread on the sofa. "We are. Some-day."

"Is something holding you back?"

"Want my list?"

Dad laughed. "I'm sure your mother's on it."

"No, I'm serious. I know this sounds idiotic, but to convince myself that I'm making a wise decision, I started keeping track of all of Marco's positive and negative qualities. I call them his pluses and minuses. The only thing is that the minuses are catching up to the pluses."

"Give me an example."

I sighed. "Okay, well, for one thing, I've always admired how forceful and commanding Marco is, but there have been times lately when he's been so bossy, I wanted to cross off his pluses. What I saw as confidence is looking more like arrogance, and his tenaciousness is pure stubbornness. Then there's his strong, silent mode that I used to think was sexy and mysterious. Frankly, that's starting to feel a bit cavemanish."

Dad laughed. "Except for the caveman part, you could be describing your mom." He reached over to take my hands. "Sweetheart, you're viewing two sides of the same coin. Confidence or arrogance? It depends on your mood and the circumstance."

"To a certain extent, sure, but what if I've been wearing those proverbial rose-colored glasses, and I'm just now viewing the real Marco?"

"The real Marco as opposed to the heroic Marco? Yes, Marco has flaws. Who doesn't?"

"I didn't expect him to have so many, Dad."

"Listen to me, Abby. My years as a cop taught me a lot about people. I can size up a man in the blink of an eye and know if he's brave or cowardly, a bully or a phony. Marco is a nice-looking, intelligent, honest, capable man who will stand beside you in good times and bad. The problem is, he's come to your aid so many times, you've put him on a pedestal as some sort of hero. But no one should ever be put on a pedestal, because it's not fair to ask any of us mere mortals to live up to such lofty expectations. He's just a man, warts and all.

"And remember, you're being forced together much more than a normal married couple would be, unless of course you worked together, which presents different problems."

Dad had a good point. I'd been calling Marco my hero for quite a few months, yet whenever he didn't act heroic, I got testy. "So what you're saying is that I accept Marco with his flaws or don't marry him."

"That's it in a nutshell. It's up to you to decide whether

to see Marco's qualities as pluses or minuses, Ab. Look at your mother and me. Maureen could see me as a weak, washed-up ex-cop, but she has never treated me that way. And I see your mom's quirky artistic bent as part of the fun of being with her. I never know what she'll come up with next. It keeps life exciting. And every time I see that jar of candy, I smile. Who would've guessed those silly hearts could bring so much joy?"

I nibbled my lower lip, thinking about Marco's side of our relationship. He rarely complained about me, but when he did, it was usually because I was putting myself or someone else in danger.

"What are you thinking?" Dad asked.

"Just wondering if Marco sees me as quirky and exciting or impetuous and tiresome."

"That might depend on when you ask him."

"Did you ever have doubts before you married Mom?"

"Sure. I worried whether I could be a good provider. I didn't want to disappoint her."

"I don't think you've ever disappointed her, Dad."

"Parents go through a lot their kids never know about, nor should they until they're old enough to handle it. If you want to know the truth, your mom and I went to couples' counseling for nearly a year. We had a rough adjustment after my injury and forced retirement grounded me. I give your mom a lot of credit for sticking with me, Ab. She had every right to leave. I was angry for months. She had to make the decision to see the best in me."

"You both put on a good front, then, because I never suspected that was happening."

"You weren't supposed to. You were in your own world, away at college. Why would we burden you with our problems?"

"But now I feel like I missed out on parts of your lives."

"Would you have felt better knowing what we were going through? Would it have made you get better grades?"

"Nothing short of a brain transplant could have done that."

He smiled, gazing at me with love. "Do you know why I dubbed you Abracadabra?"

"Because I disappeared when it was time for chores."

"That, too. But mostly because when your heart is in danger of being wounded, you construct an invisible shield around it, like that magician who makes buildings disappear. No one can see it, but I've always felt when it went up."

"How come that shield didn't work with Pryce? I was wounded after he dumped me."

"That's easy to explain. He bailed out on you before you realized your mistake and bailed out on him. I had a bet with your mom as to whether you'd ever walk down that aisle with him."

And all along I thought they were devastated by the break-up. My head was starting to ache. I rubbed my temples. "Are you saying Jillian and I are alike?"

"Jillian jilted what, four, five men at the altar? I don't think that's you—at least I hope not. But I do think you're doing your magic trick right now with this list of pluses and minuses, making your case, so to speak, for backing out."

I didn't know what to say to that.

"I've given you a lot to think about, haven't I?"

"Yes, like I'm a coward when it comes to love."

Dad laughed. "The other side of that coin is cautiousness, Abby. What you've got to do is walk a fine line between caution and fear. And I know you can do that. So?"

"So . . . I'll think about what you said."

"And?"

"And . . . discuss it with Marco?"

"That's my girl." Dad held out his arms, and I leaned over the coffee table for a hug.

"How touching," a male voice said.

I straightened with a gasp and Dad wheeled his chair around as a stranger stepped through the kitchen doorway. Short in stature, wearing a three-piece gray business suit, he had caramel-colored skin, black hair, and the hooded eyes of a cobra.

"Ms. Knight," he said softly, hissing the *S*. "We meet at last."

I had to swallow the lump of fear in my throat before I could speak. "Mr. Kana?"

He tipped his head in acknowledgment. "You know why I've come."

"All I know is that you're trespassing," Dad said gruffly. "Get out of my house!"

Kana smiled tightly. "I'd be happy to, as soon as I have the brooch."

"It's not here," Dad said with a defiant lift of his chin.

Kana's eyes narrowed into angry slits. "We all know it is, and I suggest you not get in my way, old man. You don't want to see what happens when I get angry."

"Don't you dare threaten me, you punk!"

I held my breath. What was Dad doing?

"Or what?" Kana sneered. "You'll run me over with your chair?"

Pressing his lips together, Dad started toward him, but Kana immediately flashed a sharp, light-colored blade, causing Dad to pull back. With the knife in his right hand, his gaze locked on my dad, the Hawaiian held out his left toward me. "Give me the brooch, Ms. Knight."

I swallowed hard as I stared at his outstretched palm. I couldn't hand over the brooch. Once Kana had it, there was no reason to keep us alive. But what were my options? Dad wasn't capable of subduing the man, and I knew I couldn't distract Kana long enough to make a call on my cell phone. I could throw something at his head, the candy jar perhaps, in the hopes I could escape in the confusion, but what about Dad? I couldn't leave him trapped with a killer.

"The brooch, Ms. Knight," Kana snapped, making me jump.

Dad wheeled himself backward in one strong motion and reached for the telephone on the table beside the sofa, quickly punching in 911.

In a flash, Kana crossed the room to the table and cut the phone line. "You do not want to attempt anything so foolish, my friend. I do not play games."

"I don't play games, either," Dad said, "especially with a punk like you. And I'm not your friend. I'm a cop."

"A punk like me?" Kana repeated slowly, his nostrils flaring.

"Dad, please don't!" I whispered. But he didn't heed my warning.

"That's right," Dad said, "and if you know what's good for you, you'll get out of my house right now."

In the blink of an eye, Kana was in his face, holding the blade of his knife up to Dad's throat. "And who, exactly, is going to make me?"

I had to stop myself from crying out, fearing my doing so might cause the Hawaiian to make good on his threat. My heart slammed against my ribs as Kana stared straight into Dad's eyes. "You, old man? *You?*"

"Yes, me," Dad said, his voice tight and raspy, as a line of blood appeared on his throat.

I stifled a whimper. Why was Dad goading him?

Suddenly, Kana straightened, looking very smug. "Then come get me." He put his shoe on the footrest of Dad's wheelchair and gave it a hard shove.

I gasped as Dad's head snapped forward, then back. He gripped the wheels to steady his chair, glaring at the Hawaiian, a trickle of blood running down his throat. "If I wasn't in this chair—"

"Come on, then!" Kana cried, waving his knife back and forth, taunting him. "Get up! What's stopping you? Need your running shoes?"

"Abby, get my crutches."

I stared at Dad in shock. Surely he wasn't serious! What did he think he could do?

"Abby."

I eyed the metal crutches propped in the corner, but as soon as I made a move, Kana pointed his knife at me. "Stay where you are." He backed toward the corner, then folded the blade, slipped it in his pocket, and picked up a crutch in each hand. "Are these what you want?"

"Unless you're afraid to give them to me," Dad said.

Kana used the rubber end of one of the crutches to poke Dad's knee. "For a crippled old man, you certainly talk big." He turned and heaved the crutch through the kitchen doorway, where it hit the refrigerator and clattered to the tile floor. "You want your crutch? Go get it."

Dad glared at him. "You son of a—"

"I said go get it!" Kana yelled. But when Dad started toward the kitchen, Kana shoved his wheelchair back again. "Not in your chair. Crawl! Do you hear me? Crawl for it."

My heart constricted. If Kana wanted to humiliate my father, that was how to do it.

As Dad struggled to control his temper, I knew I had to

do something to distract Kana before he humiliated Dad any further—or worse. All I could think of was to get him talking. Maybe that would buy us some time until someone realized we were in trouble.

Suddenly my phone began to play Reilly's ringtone. I froze as Kana glanced toward my coat.

"I know you stole the brooch from a museum in Hawaii," I said, talking over the tune. "Why that brooch? Why the anthurium? Is it the most valuable or was it easier to conceal?"

The music stopped. I breathed a silent sigh of relief.

Kana gave me a coy glance. "Your curiosity seems out of place at such a time, Ms. Knight. You're not stalling, by any chance, are you? Trying to keep me from finding the brooch?"

I could feel my face turning red. I'd never been able to hide my emotions. Still, it seemed to have worked. He wasn't focusing on Dad. "Do you really think I'd keep a valuable brooch at my parents' house?"

He used the other crutch to pull books off the bookshelf against the wall, letting them fall to the floor one by one. "But the brooch *is* here. And you know how I know that."

"You planted a bug," I said. "Too bad I found it."

"You found it too late." He tipped over a ceramic vase, sending it tumbling to the carpet, where it rolled to his feet. He stepped on it, cracking it, then peered inside. "What a shame to ruin these nice things. You could simply give me the brooch, Ms. Knight."

"How about if you answer my questions first, such as why a smart thief would hire bunglers like Bebe and Hudge?"

"I see you prefer to draw this out. Very well. We'll play it your way." His gaze swept the room. How long before he found my purse? "I didn't hire the, as you called them, bunglers." Kana moved around the room, looking under objects, pushing aside drapes. "My error was in trusting someone else to do a job for which he wasn't qualified."

Kana swept a potted orchid and two mirrored picture frames to the floor. "Fortunately, I do learn from my mistakes."

From the corner of my eye, I could see Dad slowly moving his wheelchair backward, in the direction of my mom's antique writing desk in the corner, beyond the sofa. It was a rolltop desk and the top was shut. Inside were tiny cubbyholes where Mom kept bills and miscellaneous items. The desk had a secret compartment. Was that where Dad kept his service revolver?

Trying not to sound as anxious as I felt, I said, "You're referring to Tom Harding?"

Kana was eyeing my coat. "Mr. Harding was a disappointment."

I moved to block his view. "Your plan was that Harding was supposed to receive the brooch and turn it over to you, right? Except that it went to me instead. So Harding hired Hudge and Bebe to get it back. And when they screwed that up for the third time, you killed one of them, then beat up Harding and left him to die."

Kana held out his palms. "Beat him and dirty my hands? No, Ms. Knight, I prefer something cleaner." He reached inside his suit coat and seconds later was holding his knife. His eyes glimmered with excitement as he ran the tip along the padded armrest of the crutch, watching my face as the rubber cushion split in half.

"You know Harding is alive, right?" I asked in a trembling voice.

Kana paused, his gaze registering a tiny flicker of doubt. Then, apparently finished with his demonstration, he folded the knife, slipped it back inside his pocket, and used the crutch to move me aside. Without saying a word, he hooked the crutch under my coat and pulled it toward him, dragging my purse with it. As he lifted the coat into the air, my purse fell to the floor. I flinched, but he didn't seem to notice.

"Did Harding's girlfriend leave the country because she thought you were coming after her next?" I asked, pressing on, as he pulled my cell phone from the coat pocket. "You know she flew to France, right? The authorities are tracking her down right now. She should have an interesting tale to tell them about you."

"Ms. Haven is no longer a threat," Kana said. He tossed the phone through the kitchen doorway, then dropped the crutch and began to pat down my coat, as though it had hidden compartments. My purse would be next.

With a racing heart, I used my shoe to move my purse closer to the sofa, hoping I could slide it underneath. "Just out of curiosity, would you mind telling me how you managed to get a weapon inside the county jail and stab Hudge in a room full of witnesses?"

"There were so many people in uniforms, no one noticed one more, nor do metal detectors register anything *but* metal. But you aren't truly interested in my talents, are you?" He tossed my coat aside. "Just as I am not interested in your pathetic attempts to distract me."

My heart stopped as he leaned over to pick up my purse.

Suddenly, his attention was drawn to Dad. "Stop!" he cried, leaping over the end of the coffee table. He grabbed the handles on the back of the wheelchair and yanked Dad away from the writing desk. He reached inside and withdrew my mom's old cell phone. "Did you think I wouldn't see you?" he cried in a rage.

Dad pressed his mouth into a tight line.

Kana dropped the phone onto the carpet and ground his heel on it. "There! Pick it up if you want it, you old fool." When Dad didn't move, Kana kicked his chair. "I said pick it up!"

My heart was pounding so hard I felt faint, but I forced myself to say, "We don't need a phone. The police know you're here—my boyfriend alerted them. That's why I've been stalling, Mr. Kana, so unless you want to be caught, you'd better forget the brooch and leave immediately."

"Your boyfriend, Ms. Knight, has had a serious accident. I doubt he was able to tell the police anything."

Oh, my God. Marco was in an accident. I stared at Kana in horror. He was watching me now, enjoying the shock that was surely written on my face, so I wasn't about to ask him for details, but not knowing Marco's condition was tearing me to pieces. Was that why Reilly had called? To tell me about the accident?

"He's a liar," Dad murmured. "Don't believe him."

"What did you say?" Kana demanded.

"I said you're a liar," Dad said more forcefully. "A liar and a coward who gets his kicks out of intimidating people he *thinks* are weaker than he is."

"A *coward*?" Enraged, Kana drew out his knife and put the tip beneath Dad's chin, forcing his head back. "You're a crazy old man who knows nothing about me!"

"Please," I cried, "put the knife down, Mr. Kana. He didn't mean it." But Dad kept goading, as though Kana's threat meant nothing to him.

"I've seen too many punks like you, Kana," he said through compressed lips. "I—" Suddenly, Dad's eyes grew huge and he gave a loud gasp. Kana jerked the knife away from his chin as Dad began to struggle for breath.

"Dad, what's wrong?" I cried.

His face turned red, his eyes rolled back, and his head started to fall forward. He caught himself and snapped upright again. Was he having a stroke?

"What is he doing?" Kana asked sharply, stepping back.

"Sugar . . . low." Dad gulped for air, as though he was about to pass out; then his eyelids fluttered and his head fell forward again.

Sugar low? What was he talking about?

Dad's head jerked up, and he struggled to open his eyes. He gasped several times, then said in a raspy voice, "Forgot . . . to take . . . insulin."

"You forgot your insulin?" I repeated in bewilderment. But he wasn't diabetic. He couldn't be thinking clearly. Or had he not told me he had diabetes?

I started toward him only to have Kana jab the knife at me. "Sit down! Over there!"

I watched from the far end of the sofa as Dad made a weak effort to point to the glass jar. "Candy." His eyes closed, his mouth sagged open, and his head dropped forward. Drool leaked from his mouth.

Closing his knife and tucking it in his pocket, Kana lifted the glass jar and held it out in front of Dad. "Is this what you want?"

Dad roused himself and tried to stretch out his hand. "Candy. Hurry."

Kana shook the jar. "Are you sure?"

Dad's jaw was slack, his breathing more labored. "Please," he whispered.

"Then come get them," Kana taunted. He glanced behind him so he wouldn't trip on the books, and in that split second, Dad cast me a look that explained everything. There wasn't anything wrong with him. He had a plan!

"Come on, old man. Here they are," Kana coaxed, shaking the jar.

Dad winced convincingly as he attempted to grip the wheels to move the chair forward.

"Not in your chair," Kana sneered. "Get up! On your feet. What kind of a big man are you that you can't get up and come get them?"

As Dad slumped over, I said, "Please, Mr. Kana. My dad's about to go into diabetic shock. He could die unless he gets sugar into his system. You don't want another murder on your hands, do you?"

"Hey, old man." Kana jostled the wheelchair with his foot until Dad dragged his head up. "Pay attention." Then Kana removed the lid, dug out a handful of hearts, and displayed them in his palm. "Are you willing to beg for these to save your life?"

Dad murmured something, his head sagging. I held my breath as Kana moved up close, until he was inches from Dad's face. "What did you say? I couldn't hear you."

"Please," Dad rasped, "I beg you."

"That's more like it." Kana held out his hand, offering him the candy.

I bit my lip as Dad lifted a trembling hand. What if he were forced to swallow them?

With a smug grin, Kana withdrew the candy. "Perhaps . . . I should eat them instead." He tilted his head back and let the red hearts slide from his cupped palm into his mouth. He moaned as he chewed, as though they were delicious.

At once his eyes widened and his mouth opened like a fish as he dragged in air to cool his burning tongue. But that merely caused him to choke and cough up red goo. He tried to scrape the sticky candy off his tongue. He clawed at his throat, as though to rip out the searing heat.

In a swift, sure motion, Dad grabbed Kana's arm with one strong hand and yanked him forward onto his knees, then gripped Kana's throat with his other hand, practically lifting him in the air. "No one threatens my family," he sneered.

As the Hawaiian fought to free himself, Dad tumbled forward, taking himself and Kana to the floor. "Get my cuffs from the drawer," Dad ordered, keeping up his choke hold.

I ran for the handcuffs in the bottom kitchen drawer, but I yanked the drawer open with so much force that it fell to the floor, spilling the contents. Quickly I scooped up the handcuffs and ran back.

Dad had one of Kana's arms stretched out to the side. His other hand was on Kana's throat. "Snap a cuff on his wrist."

Kana's face was deep red and his eyes watery. Clearly he was in pain, yet even as he gasped for air, he managed a last effort to push my dad away. But Dad held him easily while I followed his commands.

"Loop the cuff around the sofa leg," Dad said.

Quickly, I obeyed, then fastened that cuff on Kana's other wrist.

"Now call the cops," Dad said. He rolled onto the floor, putting distance between himself and the Hawaiian, then pushed himself to a sitting position and leaned against the sofa, breathing hard.

For a second all I could do was stare at my father in awe. I thought I needed to protect him, yet he had saved both of us. He was still the brave police officer I'd always admired. Tears misted my eyes. There was only one cripple in the room, and it wasn't Dad.

At a heavy pounding on the front door, I jumped.

"Police. Open up."

I ran to open the door and there was Reilly and five of

New Chapel's finest. I stepped back and they poured into the living room. Behind them stood my hero—make that Marco—who didn't appear to be injured. I threw myself into his arms and leaned my head against his chest, my arms around his waist. "Marco, thank God you're all right! Kana said you were in an accident."

"It's okay, Sunshine," he said, stroking my hair. "I wasn't hurt."

I lifted my head to gaze at him. "You *were* in an accident?"

"Yes, and lucky for me I had that defensive driver training. But there's an injured limo driver on his way to the hospital and a badly damaged black Cadillac wrapped around a pole at the intersection of Lincoln and Franklin. Are you all right?"

"Thanks to some quick thinking by my dad, we're both all right. Marco, Dad was amazing. He tricked Kana into eating Mom's red-hot candy, then took him down to the floor in a choke hold. He was fearless."

"That's where you get that quality, Abby, in case you hadn't noticed."

"Really? You think I'm fearless?"

"Fiercely."

We went to see how Dad was faring. He was back in his wheelchair, thanks to the cops, with a cloth pressed to the cut on his neck. Kana had been hauled to his feet, re-handcuffed with his hands behind his back, and searched. He was still drooling and begging for water, which Reilly was just now bringing to him.

I filled Reilly and Marco in on our ordeal, how the brooch had ended up at Bloomers instead of Tom's Green Thumb, Harding's role in the theft, and what I'd been able to get Kana to admit.

"So Kana was the mastermind behind the kidnappings," Reilly said, sizing up the Hawaiian.

"Kana planted a listening device in that flashlight he left for me," I told Marco. "That's how he found out the brooch was here. I dropped it and discovered the bug, so I knew he'd heard me call my mom and tell her to have the brooch ready. I dashed over to pick it up, but Kana got here before I left."

"Why didn't you call me?" Reilly asked. "I would've come to pick it up."

"I—" Didn't have a good reason.

"My fault," Dad said. "I asked her to keep me company."

I smiled Dad my thanks, then glanced over at Kana, who was greedily drinking the water. "Reilly, the knife your guys found in his coat is probably the murder weapon used on Hudge. Kana admitted he slipped into the jail and killed Hudge."

"Wait a minute," Reilly said. "No one can just walk into the county jail."

"Then you might want to have Mr. Kana tell you how to fix that security glitch, because he got in. And check with the cops in Maui, too. I'm guessing his knife might have been used to kill the young man who shipped that brooch here."

"You won't be able to prove a thing," Kana said in a hoarse whisper.

"There are people who can help us with that," Marco said. "Like Tom Harding."

"Who, as it happens," Reilly said, "came out of his coma today."

Kana's gaze darted from Marco to Reilly, as though seeking verification, so Reilly added, "Two hours ago. Brain swelling went down. He'll be singing like a bird by tomorrow."

Kana didn't look quite as sure of himself as two officers marched him out to the cruiser.

"Is it true?" I asked Reilly. "Is Harding going to be okay?"

"We still don't know. I just wanted to give the guy something to worry about."

I went to give my dad a big hug. "Diabetic shock. That was an amazing idea."

"Don't sound so surprised," Dad said, but I could tell he was proud of himself.

"You should have seen him in action, Marco." I hugged my father again and whispered in his ear, "I think I have a new hero."

"Abby!" Dad said, giving me a warning look.

"Just kidding."

"So your mom's candy saved the day?" Marco asked, putting the lid on the jar.

I glanced at my dad and we both opened our eyes wide at the enormity of it.

"You can't tell her," I said to Dad.

"Tell her what? That the candy I've been saying nearly wiped out her family ended up saving our lives? Believe me, Ab, she won't hear it from me."

I handed the brooch to Reilly; then we stayed at the house long enough to give statements to the police. Afterward, Marco walked me to the minivan, where I leaned against the side of the van and let him kiss me.

"I'm so glad you're okay," I said. "And I'm very glad you came here with Reilly."

"I had no choice. You gave me an order. 'Pick up the brooch now.'"

I laughed. "You heard only the last part of that message.

I had just figured out that Kana was listening in on my conversations, so I was trying to make him think the cops were on their way to my parents' house. Not that it worked."

"After the Cadillac tried to broadside me, I called Bloomers to let you know what happened, and Lottie said you and the minivan were gone. I phoned Reilly and he met me here."

"As Tara would say, you arrived just in the nick of time, like in the movies. Did you ever find out how those anemone petals got smashed into the treads of Charlotte's shoes? Or why Attorney Knowles fired her?"

"Yes to both. When I went back to Tom's Green Thumb to talk to Robin, she reported finding a mess on the stockroom floor after the anemones were delivered. Most of the flowers were destroyed and petals were all over the place. She said it looked like someone had a tantrum. Anyone walking through the stockroom before they'd been cleaned up would have gotten petals stuck on the bottom of their shoes, and deep treads would've held them there.

"Then Harding must have met with Hudge and Bebe before the flowers were cleaned up. He probably threw a fit when they botched the second kidnapping.

"And as for Knowles, he fired Charlotte for stealing office supplies."

"That's it?"

"That's it." He kissed me. "Satisfied?"

"Yes." I gave Marco a hug. "I'm so relieved you're not hurt."

"How do you think I feel about you and your dad? If you had waited for me to take you to your parents' house, none of this would have happened."

Not true. Kana would have showed up before we got there. But it was over and everything had worked out, so why bring it up? "I'm sorry, Marco. I'll try to make sure it never happens again."

He gave me a skeptical look. "You're not going to list your reasons for not waiting?"

"Nope. I'm done with lists. I'd rather contemplate your positive qualities."

"I'm not even going to ask you to explain."

"Okay, you can kiss me again instead."

His mouth curved up at the corner. "We can do a lot more than that."

"Tonight?"

"Later tonight."

Things were looking up.

"And tomorrow," he said, his lips against my ear, "my place for dinner?"

"Perfect. Just the two of us—" I pushed away from him. "Your mother invited me to dinner, didn't she?"

"Yep."

Things were no longer looking up.

CHAPTER TWENTY-FIVE

"How do I look?" I asked Marco, turning for him. For his mother's Saturday dinner, I'd put on a black pencil skirt and powder blue shawl-neck sweater with black pumps, hoping to impress Mrs. Salvare with my sensible yet stylish outfit.

"You always look beautiful, Abby."

That lie right there was reason enough to tear up my list.

Marco held out my coat so I could slip into it. "We'd better go. Mama will be pulling that pan of lasagna out of the oven in ten minutes. Don't want to keep her waiting."

My stomach tensed at the thought of facing Francesca Salvare. I knew she'd quiz us about our engagement plans, except we still didn't have any. Marco and I had wanted to have our discussion last night, but by the time he'd spent several hours on his PI case, it was so late when he arrived at my apartment, all we could do was tumble into bed. Together. A hot, sweaty, lusty, rousing *tumble*! After which we fell into an exhausted but thoroughly satiated sleep.

We awoke to Marco's cell phone chirping—a call from his mom wondering why he wasn't home. Had he been on surveillance all night? At which point Marco had drawn me against his warm, hard body and assured her he had indeed been undercover.

Because we'd slept in, and it was my Saturday to work, I had to scramble to get to Bloomers before nine o'clock. On the plus side, however, since I no longer had to fear being kidnapped, I got to drive my Vette all by myself. I smiled at Marco as he helped me into my coat. Life was good again.

Except . . .

It was time to face the music. Fish or cut bait. No more waffling. We'd delayed long enough, and I felt certain his mom was going to ask when this engagement was going to happen—she'd certainly hinted enough—and not let us off the hook until we gave her an answer.

"What are we going to say when your mom asks about our engagement?" I asked as Marco opened the car door for me.

"What do you want to say?"

"What do I want to say or what does she want to hear?"

"Whichever."

"Whichever what?"

"Whichever you want to answer."

This was getting us nowhere fast. "What would *you* answer?"

He pursed his lips, thinking. "We should have discussed this last night."

"But we didn't."

He glanced at me. "Are you sorry?"

"About last night? Are you serious?"

He reached over to squeeze my hand. "Happy?"

"Of course, silly, and madly in love with you. How about you?"

He lifted an eyebrow. That little gesture was enough to

make my pulse race, especially after last night. "Same here, Fireball."

So why were we both dancing around the idea of commitment?

When we pulled up in front of the white two-story that housed Marco's apartment, I noticed my parents' specially equipped van parked at the curb. "Marco, what are my parents doing here? I talked to my mom on the phone this morning. She didn't mention anything about coming over."

"They must be planning another ambush."

"Maybe we shouldn't show up."

Marco gave me a look that said, *You have to be kidding.*

"My Prius is gone," Marco noted as he walked me to the front porch. "That means Rafe isn't back yet. He said he had to drop something off at his girlfriend's place, but he promised to be here in time for dinner."

"Is this the girl from Hooters? The one he wanted to impress with my Vette last night?"

"That's the one."

"He's not going to leave her to come back here for dinner, you know."

"I agree."

Great. No Rafe to distract Marco's mom. It was just us and the parents. I nibbled my lower lip as we climbed the steps to the second floor and stepped into his living room. It was a decidedly masculine space with lots of big furniture and a huge, flat-panel TV. My mom was seated on the sofa, my dad was in his wheelchair, and both had glasses of wine. Dad's crutches, I noticed, were near the staircase. He'd had to use them to get up the stairs.

"You didn't tell me you were coming tonight," I said to them, as Marco took my coat.

"Your mom just informed me two hours ago," Dad said.

Mom merely smiled.

At that moment, Marco's mother bustled into the room, a younger but not quite as pretty version of Sophia Loren, luxurious dark hair, wide smile, gorgeous curves and all. She wore a black dress with a colorful apron tied around her waist and had a wooden spoon in her hand.

"Bella Abby!" she cried, enveloping me in a warm hug. "I'm so happy to see you." She turned to Marco. "Why are you standing there? Get her a glass of wine and one for yourself. Dinner is ready and where is your brother? Well, no matter. He'll be here soon. Everyone, come eat!"

We arranged ourselves around Marco's table, where Mrs. Salvare lifted her wineglass and waited for us to follow suit. "Now, then, I believe we have someone who wants to make an announcement."

I gripped Marco's fingers under the table. Yikes!

My mom cleared her throat. "I am happy to announce that my dissension group is going to meet with Mr. Raand and members of the local media at Uniworld next Wednesday evening to discuss the new dairy operation."

Whew! That was close. "Raand agreed to that?" I asked.

Dad sent me a look that said, *Let your mom finish.*

"We are going to demand that no bovine hormones, or any other kind of hormones, be used on their cows," Mom continued. "Instead, we are going to ask them to implement a method that dairy farmers around the world have been using for centuries, namely, that they will talk to their cows, provide calming music for them, and name them."

"Brava, Maureen," Mrs. Salvare said, applauding.

I clapped, too, although I kept picturing Nils Raand's stupefied expression when he heard their demands. "That's a great plan, Mom, but do you think you have a chance of getting Uniworld to cooperate?"

"I certainly do, and here's what I intend to read aloud," Mom said, pulling a sheet of paper from her purse. "According to an article in *USA Today*, in a study conducted by scientists at Newcastle University in Newcastle upon Tyne, it was discovered that more affectionate treatment of cattle, including giving cows names, can increase milk production by more than sixty-eight gallons annually."

Mom looked up at us. "The reason for that is chemical. When a cow is treated cruelly, the stress causes the release of cortisol, a hormone that inhibits milk production. By using bovine hormones and creating oversized, painful udders, Uniworld would actually decrease milk production. And anyone drinking that milk would not only get a dose of bovine hormones, but cortisol as well.

"We'll hold a press conference immediately after the meeting. And if that doesn't get Uniworld's attention, the threat of having a teachers' union after them should."

Who knew my mom was so wily?

"The local newspaper promised to print a series of articles about the dangers of bovine hormones," Dad said. "They're already calling your mom the Cow Whisperer."

Dear God.

"Maureen, you are brilliant," Mrs. Salvare said.

"Congratulations, Mrs. Knight," Marco said, and lifted his glass to her. We toasted her and drank the wine.

"Now," Mrs. Salvare said, "how about a toast to our young couple, eh? Such a bright future before them. Am I right, Marco?"

I glanced nervously at Marco. Here it came.

Suddenly, a door opened somewhere and we heard footsteps pounding up the stairs.

Marco said in relief, "Rafe is here."

"Then we'll wait," Mrs. Salvare said, glancing at my parents with a shrug. "The bambinos, they give us gray hair, eh?"

"Hear, hear," Mom said.

I could've said the same about parents.

Rafe strode into the kitchen wearing his parka, his cheeks red from the cold. He was out of breath and a bit giddy. "Sorry I'm late. I brought someone for you to meet." He waved the unseen person toward him.

A young woman came around the corner, smiling shyly. I guessed her age at maybe twenty years old. She had neon orange-red hair that touched her shoulders on the sides, then angled up sharply to the nape of her neck in back. "Hi," she said, giving us a little wave.

I smiled at her.

"Raphael, are you going to introduce your guest?" Mrs. Salvare said, rising from her chair.

"Sure," he said, helping her remove her long, black coat. "Everyone, this is Cinnamon."

Everyone stared. Everyone couldn't speak because everyone couldn't stop gaping at Cinnamon's chest, which was mostly bared to everyone's gaze. In fact, her wraparound dress was pulled so tight and cut so low, it was clear she had nothing on underneath.

Everyone was appalled.

"Okay," Rafe said to Cinnamon, and began pointing. "That's my brother Marco, his girlfriend, Abby, my mom, and Abby's parents, Mr. and Mrs. Knight."

Mrs. Salvare pulled herself together to say kindly, "Cinnamon, you'll join us, won't you? We have delicious lasagna and crusty bread and—are you old enough to drink wine?"

Cinnamon giggled. "Why not?"

Marco pulled up an extra chair and Cinnamon settled

into it. Everyone tried not to watch as she bent to lay her purse on the floor.

Setting an extra plate on the table, Mrs. Salvare said to Rafe, "Tell me how you met your, er, Cinnamon."

"We work together," Cinnamon volunteered.

Uh-oh. Time for the big reveal.

"Would this be at your bar, Marco?" his mom asked.

"Oh, no," Cinnamon said happily. "At Hooters. I'm a waitress there."

I could tell by Rafe's expression that he hadn't clued Cinnamon in on the need for secrecy. My dad put his hand to his mouth and coughed. I knew he was hiding a smile. My mom smoothed her napkin on her lap. Marco rolled the wineglass in his hand.

"Hooters bar," Mrs. Salvare said, trying to hold her smile in place, "is where you work now, Raphael?"

Cinnamon rubbed Rafe's shoulder. "He's the cutest, smartest guy there."

Rafe gazed at her like a besotted puppy. Marco studied the wine in his glass. Everyone else watched Francesca's face.

"Well, then," Marco's mom said, raising her glass once again. "To new . . . jobs . . . and new relationships." She smiled at me. "To our happy couple, who I hope will share their plans now."

I squeezed Marco's hand again and he squeezed back. My stomach knotted. Now or never, Abby!

Rafe jumped to his feet. "Okay. Why not?" He smiled at Cinnamon, then glanced around at the rest of us. "We're engaged!"

Everyone was too stunned to react. Except me. After all, I *had* told him to surprise his family. I raised my glass and said a hearty "Congratulations."

*   *   *

"Can you believe Rafe is engaged?" I said to Marco, as he walked me out to my car later that evening. "Cinnamon can't be twenty-one yet, if that's her real name."

I couldn't help chortling a little. "I thought your mother was going to faint when Cinnamon took off her coat. But I give your mom a lot of credit. She was very gracious, even after Rafe dropped the bomb."

"Wait until Mama has Rafe alone, Abby. Then there'll be fireworks."

"Seriously, who could blame her for being upset? Rafe dated that girl exactly once. He met her only a week ago. And you call me impetuous?"

"I don't know what Rafe is thinking. He can't support himself, let alone a wife."

"At least his announcement took the heat off us."

"It did that."

"So we're off the hook?"

"Yep."

"Good." I took a deep breath. "Then I have to confess something."

Marco cast me a dubious glance. "Okay."

"I was keeping a list of your good and bad qualities."

"You were?" His dark eyes searched mine. "Why?"

"I know it sounds silly, but I thought it would make the decision to get engaged easier. You know, like weighing the pluses and minuses of a situation? Anyway, what I realized is that listing things like confidence and reliability is all well and good, but what truly matters is that we love and trust each other, enjoy being together, and agree on the important things in life. We do agree on the important things in life, right?"

Marco pulled me close and wrapped his arms around me. "I think we do."

"I do, too. I mean, we both believe in justice, honesty, and solid values. We both have strong morals and close family ties. We're hard workers, know how to save money—"

"And want to have a family of our own," Marco supplied.

"Not a big family, though."

"Two?"

"Two. Someday."

"In the not-too-distant future."

"We'll need to discuss that further . . . along with the long hours you put in on your various jobs. But that's what's great about our relationship. We can discuss these things."

Marco eyed me warily. "Are you going to start another list?"

"Maybe I should."

"You actually wrote down my pluses and minuses?"

I shrugged. "Like I said, I thought it would help me decide."

"Did it?"

"Well, yes."

"And?"

"And what was my decision?"

"Yep."

"My decision was yes."

"So that's your answer, then?"

"To what?"

We were standing alongside my yellow Corvette in the cold, in the dark, in the snow. Marco reached inside his coat pocket and pulled out a tiny black velvet box.

"To this." He opened the box, displaying a diamond ring inside.

I stopped breathing.

He took the ring out of the box. "Will you marry me, Abby?"

Oh, the thoughts that raced through my mind as I stared at the sparkling token of commitment: children, my family, Marco's family, our careers, money, wedding plans, change!

Okay, Abracadabra. What will it be? Say yes or pull up that protective shield?

My eyes filled with tears as my gaze shifted from the glittering diamond to the face of the man I loved. Was there even a doubt?

I nodded, smiling through my tears. "Yes, Salvare. I will."

ABBY

PLUSES	MINUSES
~~Protective~~	~~Bossy~~
~~Confident~~	~~Arrogant~~
~~Open-minded~~	~~Stubborn~~
~~Sexy~~	~~Pontifical~~
~~To the point~~	~~Blunt~~
~~Fearless~~	~~Feckless~~
~~Optimistic~~	~~Naive~~
~~Generous~~	~~Uncompromising~~
~~Positive~~	~~Strong-willed~~
~~Tenacious~~	~~Unyielding~~
~~Introspective~~	~~Inattentive~~
~~Peppy~~	~~Hyper~~
~~Great kisser~~	~~Workaholic~~
~~Great body~~	
SHE LOVES ME	

Don't miss the next delightful
Flower Shop Mystery,

Dirty Rotten Tendrils

Available in October 2010 from Obsidian

Monday

My destination that morning was Bloomers, my cozy flower shop located across the street from New Chapel, Indiana's, stately limestone courthouse. I was taking a circuitous route to get there, however, because, strangely enough, the public lot where I usually parked was full. So I'd left my refurbished and much-beloved 1960 yellow Corvette under a shady maple tree across from the YMCA and started off for a leisurely stroll around the square, soaking in the sunshine of the brilliant early-spring day.

I love my small town. In New Chapel, unlike big cities, you won't experience heavy traffic snarls, clouds of toxic exhaust fumes, or frustrated drivers honking horns at every tiny irritation. What's more, you can park in a public lot for about two dollars a day or, as in my case today, along any side street for free. Try to do that in downtown Chicago.

I sniffed the air to catch a whiff of the crocuses blooming in the old cement planters that rimmed the courthouse lawn. They'd be followed by daffodils and tulips, and then by Knock Out roses, all of which would suffer benign neglect by the parks department employees until the winter snows blanketed them once again.

Up ahead I saw Jingles, the ancient window washer, wielding his squeegee with extreme precision against a boutique's display glass. "How's it going, Jingles?" I called.

"It's a different kind of morning, Miss Abby," he said solemnly, then pulled the wet squeegee from the top of the pane to the bottom and dried it with his yellow rag.

Jingles wasn't normally given to deep thought, and for him, that comment qualified as one. "It'll be fine, Jingles," I called. "We've got solid citizens in New Chapel. They're not going to go crazy because a local boy who took first place on a reality show is coming back to town."

Jingles just kept wiping the glass. On the other side of the window, the shop's owner was setting out an array of tropic-bright purses and stylish spring jackets. She waved and smiled.

Another benefit of small-town life was the friendliness of the townsfolk. Also, the easy pace. You could amble down any sidewalk and not be bothered by rushing commuters, jostling crowds, jackhammer drilling, or vendors shouting—

"Hey! Look out!"

A man in a cherry picker gestured frantically toward an old wooden sign dangling by one nail over the gift shop's doorway. With a gasp, I jumped back seconds before the sign broke from its tether and crashed onto the sidewalk in front of me, kicking up a cloud of dust and debris.

The shop owner, Mr. Hanley, who was about one hundred forty years old, called from the recessed doorway, "Sorry, Abby. Gotta get my new signage up today, you know."

His *signage*? He pointed to a shiny new sign leaning against the side of the store. Instead of HANLEY'S GIFTS, it now said YE OLDE GIFT SHOPPE.

"No harm done, Mr. Hanley." I shook detritus from my hair, brushed off my navy peacoat, took a deep breath, and continued up Lincoln Avenue toward Franklin Street.

At that moment, a white pickup truck sporting the town logo pulled up alongside me with a shriek of dry brakes and a backfire of thick gray smoke. A man in tan overalls jumped out to place orange cones around a cracked square of the cement sidewalk. Another man followed with a jackhammer, which he immediately fired up.

Plugging my ears with my fingertips and trying not to inhale the fumes, I scurried toward the corner. As I waited for the light to change, I was joined by at least ten people, with a dozen more on the sidewalk across the street. On the green light, we surged forward en masse and narrowly missed being run down by a white stretch limousine. The driver laid on his horn, glaring at us as he sped past. Two black limousines followed. They honked, too, just for the practice, I suspected.

Behind them came a line of vans with satellite dishes on top and markings on the side for the four national television stations, ABC, CBS, NBC, and Fox, and our local cable channel, WNCN. They were followed by several more vehicles with men hanging out the windows armed with huge cameras with telescopic lenses. Three police cars trailed the parade, their sirens and lights fully engaged as they approached the courthouse, as though to impress upon the citizens the importance of the limousines' occupants.

"That was him in the white car!" someone behind me screamed, and at once I was swept along in a tide of people in their stampede to follow the convoy, now creating a snarl of horn-honking traffic on the far side of the square. I managed to break free at the curb and make a frantic dash to safer shores.

As I stood with my back pressed against the door of the Down the Hatch Bar and Grill, people began to descend onto the courthouse lawn in droves, some carrying signs that said, WE LOVE YOU, CODY!, others waving banners, caught up in the kind of frenzy that only a celebrity could create.

And then, as though someone had cried "Action!", all along the streets surrounding the courthouse, workers emerged, some carrying paint cans and ladders, others erecting scaffolding, pushing wheelbarrows stacked with bricks, and toting brightly colored awnings. The parks department even sent men to spruce up the cement planters.

I stared around the square in astonishment. Then I noticed Jingles watching me with a look that said, *I told you so.*

The door behind me opened suddenly, and I had to grab on to the frame to keep from falling in. "Morning, Buttercup," my boyfriend, bar owner/ex–Army Ranger Marco Salvare, said, kissing the top of my head. "Lots of excitement in town today."

I turned to face him, trying to form my distress into a coherent remark. Marco's forehead wrinkled as he studied me. "Are you okay?"

"I want my small town back!" I wailed, and flung myself into his arms.

Seated across from Marco in the first booth at Down the Hatch, which wouldn't open until eleven o'clock, I propped my chin on my hand and sighed grumpily. "If this is a sign of what's to come, I'm leaving until it's over."

"Come on, Abby. It's not that bad. Besides, when was the last time a celebrity came to New Chapel?"

"Cody Verse is hardly a celebrity. Two months ago, only

a handful of people had even heard of him. All he did was win a contest."

"You say that like it was the local spelling bee," Marco said. "*America's Next Hit Single* is a national television event. Cody had to outperform thousands of people just to get on the show."

"I get that, Marco, but come on! He didn't win the Nobel Prize. He sang a song that he cowrote with his friend and then took all the credit for."

"Or so his friend claims," Marco reminded me. "A friend who stands to gain a lot of money if he wins his lawsuit. Don't scowl at me. I hear what you're saying. Cody Verse's sudden fame has been blown all out of proportion."

"It doesn't hurt that he's dating Lila Redmond, either." Lila was the new It Girl, the hottest starlet since, well, whoever the last It Girl was.

Marco leaned back to stretch, lacing his fingers behind his dark, wavy hair, putting his hard-muscled torso on display. Today he was wearing jeans and a formfitting navy T-shirt with the white lettering *Down the Hatch* running the length of one sleeve. He was a yummy-hot male and all mine.

"I need coffee," he said, and got up to go to the coffee machine behind the bar. "I didn't get home last night until two in the morning." He held up the pot. "Want some?"

I shook my head. Not to hurt Marco's feelings or anything, but his bar was not known for its coffee. Or its decor, for that matter. The last time Down the Hatch had been decorated must have been in the seventies, when burnt orange, avocado green, and dark walnut paneling were all the rage, and a blue plastic carp passed for wall sculpture.

I heard cheering in the distance and got up to look out

the big plate-glass window at the front of the bar. "You should see the crowds now. Little kids, too. Did they call off school today? Maybe the mayor declared a holiday . . . Cody Verse Day."

"The lawsuit should be settled in a day or two," Marco said, coming to stand beside me with a coffee mug in his hand. "Then everything will return to normal."

"With Ken 'the Lip' Lipinski as his attorney? No way. When I clerked for Dave Hammond, I sat in on a few trials and saw Lipinski in action. The Lip is the kind of lawyer all those nasty jokes are about. He lies, stalls, grandstands, and cheats, and somehow manages to get away with it because he wins huge settlements for his clients. Trust me, Marco, Lipinski will do everything in his power to turn this lawsuit into a major media event."

"And Dave will do everything in his power to keep that from happening," Marco countered.

"I'm afraid he'll be fighting a losing battle. Dave usually refuses to take a case when Lipinski is on the other side, but this time he was hired before he knew who the opposing counsel was. Now he's stuck."

Marco took a drink of coffee. "Why doesn't he withdraw his appearance?"

"Because the Chappers have been with him for a long time, and he wouldn't do that to loyal clients. Have you noticed that Dave hasn't been himself lately, like something's weighing on his mind? Maybe it's his caseload. Being a public defender is never an easy job, and with the crime rate rising, he's busier than ever. Or maybe he's having some kind of midlife crisis. Whatever it is, having to deal with the Lip in a big, splashy civil case isn't going to help him any."

"I thought Dave's client was a young guy—Cody Verse's

high school buddy," Marco said, heading for the bar. "Sure I can't get you some coffee?"

"No coffee, thanks. And technically, yes, Dave's client is Andrew Chapper, one half of the former Chapper and Verse duo. Andrew's grandparents have been with Dave since he first hung out his shingle. They're the ones who brought Andrew to see Dave. Apparently, they raised Andrew after his parents died in a car accident."

Marco came back to the window carrying a full coffee mug. He put his arm around me, and I leaned my head on his shoulder.

"I wish I could help Dave somehow," I said with a sigh. "Proving that Andrew cowrote the winning song is going to be tough. And who knows? It might not even get that far. If the judge rules in Lipinski's favor on his motion to dismiss, it's all over. Case closed. Andrew loses."

Marco nuzzled my ear. "It's not all bad news today, Sunshine. We've got something to celebrate, remember? Your engagement ring should be resized and ready to wear."

Oh, right. About that . . .

With the corners of his mouth curving in that sexy way of his, he lifted my left hand to his lips to kiss my fingers. "What do you say I pick it up and give it to you at dinner tonight?"

"Marco, we need to talk."

Kate Collins

The Flower Shop Mystery Series

Abby Knight is the proud owner of her
hometown flower shop. She has a gift for
arranging flowers—and for solving crimes.

Mum's the Word
Slay It with Flowers
Dearly Depotted
Snipped in the Bud
Acts of Violets
A Rose from the Dead
Shoots to Kill
Evil in Carnations

"A sharp and funny heroine."
—Maggie Sefton

**Available wherever books are sold or at
penguin.com**

The Bestselling
Blackbird Sisters Mystery Series
by
Nancy Martin

Don't miss a single adventure of the
Blackbird sisters, a trio of Philadelphia-born,
hot-blooded bluebloods with a flair for
fashion—and for solving crimes.

How to Murder a Millionaire
Dead Girls Don't Wear Diamonds
Some Like It Lethal
Cross Your Heart and Hope to Die
Have Your Cake and Kill Him Too
A Crazy Little Thing Called Death
Murder Melts in Your Mouth

**Available wherever books are sold or at
penguin.com**

GET CLUED IN

Ever wonder how to find out about all the
latest Berkley Prime Crime and
Obsidian mysteries?

berkleyobsidianmysteries.com

- See what's new
- Find author appearances
- Win fantastic prizes
- Get reading recommendations
- Sign up for the mystery newsletter
- Chat with authors and other fans
- Read interviews with authors you love

Mystery Solved.